# OCCUPY
# ME

TRICIA SULLIVAN

# OCCUPY ME

GOLLANCZ
LONDON

First published in Great Britain in 2016 by Gollancz
An imprint of the Orion Publishing Group
Carmelite House, 50 Victoria Embankment, London EC4Y 0DZ
An Hachette UK Company

A CIP catalogue record for this book is available
from the British Library

ISBN 978 1 473 21296 1

1 3 5 7 9 10 8 6 4 2

Typeset at The Spartan Press Ltd,
Lymington, Hants

Printed and bound by CPI Group (UK) Ltd,
Croydon, CR0 4YY

The Orion Publishing Group's policy is to use papers that are
natural, renewable and recyclable products and made from wood grown in
sustainable forests. The logging and manufacturing
processes are expected to conform to the environmental
regulations of the country of origin.

www.triciasullivan.com
www.orionbooks.co.uk
www.gollancz.co.uk

For the care-givers
with their eleventy-billion kinds of strength
and for anyone
who is a long way from
Home

# HD waveform launcher instructions

**Appendix F**

**Warning**: Internal gravity subject to change. If device is to be moved we recommend engaging an optional anti-slip app available as freeware.

Switching from scan to launch mode:

1) Engage HD mode bio template
2) Ensure docking port has been cleared to prevent **leakage** from host system (see section 3.8)
3) Reset clock and localization parameters
4) Remove launcher from host
5) Reconfigure according to expected local conditions

Notes on configuration:

If rendering backward-compatible choose a configuration with a temporal range of 1–2% centred on the desired locale to avoid achronality errors. Commonplace personal items with practical application are usually the most effective. Eyeglasses, hand luggage, writing implements, and simple garments are easiest to make backward-compatible.

Forward compatibility is not advised.

# The briefcase

Out of the blue. That's how the briefcase turned up in your life. The Audi's security camera shows images of a man very much like you approaching the car. GPS records put the time at 4:37 this very morning in the parking lot of Short Hills Mall. The man opened the door using your own biometric signature. A hand very much like your hand placed the briefcase on the passenger seat gently enough to suggest that its contents were fragile.

Or explosive.

But you weren't there.

The Audi is now in the VIP parking area at IIF headquarters near Amagansett. Its records claim that you drove it to the mall at 3:53 – you have no memory of that, either – and then you drove here. Now you sit in the driver's seat, yawning, trying to piece it together. You remember bringing a bottle of Kathryn Hall Cabernet home to Ayeisha in tacit apology for the long hours you've been putting in by Austen Stevens' bedside; that's all gone on far too long. But Ayeisha was on her way out to kendo class. She paused only long enough to remind you to check the kids' spelling homework before you put them to bed.

You accepted the snub the same way you accept the condescension of Stevens himself – with equanimity. Long ago you renounced the way of violence. You do not allow your will to collide head-on with others. Not anymore. There are better ways to live.

Equanimity does not come easily at this moment. Why did you leave the house in the middle of the night? Whom did you meet at the mall? There are no records in your phone. You haven't a clear memory of coming back to your senses after the fadeout – for that's how the episodes feel. They aren't blackouts, as such, because their edges are always indistinct. Usually you can feel yourself *going* for some time before the event; coming back is gradual.

Evidently this person appearing to be you was driving east on the Long Island Expressway in a semi-conscious state when a pickup cut him off and activated the car's emergency evasive routine. The jerk of the chassis roused you from microsleep. You took control of the vehicle, blinked a few times, and flailed for memories that would not give themselves up.

This isn't the first time you have gone away from yourself, but it is the first time you have returned in possession of an object that you aren't supposed to have.

You noticed the briefcase when you pulled into your usual space at the IIF compound and opened the door. The interior light illuminated the thing on the passenger seat, big and awkward and too cheap-looking to be anything you would have purchased for yourself. The corners are brass, battered and scratched, and the faux-leather outer covering has begun to crack. It's heavy enough not to have slid forward onto the floor when you braked suddenly on the expressway.

You can't bring yourself to open it.


You message Mort. He has a snot-laden bass voice that makes him sound old and fat; he is twenty-nine and willowy. There's white noise in the background and he is panting through his morning workout.

'Hey, Kisi! You in?'

Still fuddled, you murmur, 'I'm sorry? In?'

'Climbing weekend? Vermont? It's all I'm living for right now. Tell me you're in.'

'Oh . . . Well, OK, maybe. Depending on my patient.'

'Your patient is tough as shit, I'll give him that.'

'Mort, I have a question for you. It's quite sensitive. Are you alone?'

'Yep.'

3

'I suspect I've got a neurological condition. I've been having memory lapses.'

The white noise stops.

'Just turning off the treadmill. Tell me more.'

You tell him about the episodes. How they started several months ago, seemed to stop, and now have returned with a vengeance. Sometimes you lose five minutes. Sometimes hours. Mort asks questions and you omit nothing – except for the briefcase. Mort is a neurosurgeon, not a detective, so?

'I can give you a referral,' Mort rumbles. 'You'll need scans. But if you want to know what I think as your friend, I gotta tell you there's every chance it's stress.'

'Stress?' Your laugh sounds alien. You glance around the interior of the Audi in a haze of disassociation. You stare at the top-end phone in your hand. You think: stress is growing up with people around you dying of mysterious illnesses. Stress is being shot at. Stress is being twelve years old and bleeding out in the forest, alone. You laugh.

'What stress?'

'I mean, come on – when is the guy going to die, already?'

'Soon,' you say softly. 'It will be soon.'

'And you don't see any conflict of interest between you taking care of Austen Stevens in his last days and your history with the company? No problem, huh?'

A whiteness passes before your eyes. You hate talking about these matters. Everyone knows that. Mort is using the conversation as an excuse to wedge open a door, to air all his opinions about the choices you have made, professionally and morally. Choices that Mort, privileged scion of a New York City medical dynasty, could never begin to understand.

'I am not stressed. I am not neurotic. Something else is going on. Could I . . . You don't think this is part of a disease pathology?'

'I can't diagnose you over the phone, Kisi. Remember, my job is to cut people and fix their brains. I'm sending you the name of a friend at Mount Sinai.'

'Not a psychiatrist.'

'You say that like it's a dirty word. No, not a psychiatrist. A clinical neurophysiologist. OK? And take a vacation. Not with the kids! Take Ayeisha to Barbados or something.'

Ayeisha. You put your hand over your eyes.

'I have to go,' you say.

'Cheer up, dude,' Mort says, turning on the treadmill again. 'Maybe your guy will kick it today.'

That is what you hope every day. Every single day.

You almost don't bring the briefcase in with you. It is insanely heavy. Just as you are about to give up on dragging it out of the car it makes like a punch line and lightens. Its contents shift and it actually jerks in your clenched hand. As you stagger across the damp lawn of Austen Stevens' estate you ask yourself what you will do if its contents turn out to be *alive*.

# Invest in futures

When you get into the patient's suite you set the briefcase beside the bed.

'His hands and feet are cold,' Maja says. 'Mucus is building up in his throat. But he's responsive. I can call the family if you think it's appropriate.'

'Go home. Ask Eloise to call them when she gets here.'

Instead of reading the patient's notes you find yourself studying the scar that stretches across your left palm from the finger webbing to the wrist. It looks like the outline of a flame.

You have cheated death more than once. So has Austen Stevens. But today, surely, it will be over.

Today. Today. Today.

Your heart beats a demand for the death. If you had known what this job would be like, maybe you would have thought again. When he first asked you, the bonus on the table was a godsend. The chance to get funding to set up a teaching hospital back home. So what if this is the man who crippled your country in its infancy? Time has moved on. You have grown strong. You derive strength from overcoming the desires of your ego. Every day for weeks, as you have cared tenderly for the one who would have seen you dead, as you calibrated medications and discussed the finer points of treatment with the hospice team, every day you said to yourself: today. Today he will die.

Austen Stevens should have been finished weeks ago. The family credit your assiduous work for this extended period of survival – a twisted, rusted-nail irony.

The death must come soon now, and then you will be free.

The thought tastes like wine.

\*

In his sea-blue bed by a window within sight of the shimmer of the Atlantic, the husk of your employer's body reclines with burning eyes. For weeks those eyes have watched the news feeds, tracking the markets while Stevens' fingers continue to administer more of Invest In Futures than the Board cares to admit. Official word is that Stevens has handed over the reins to the new CEO, but this is not entirely so. He is still making plans, dealing. He'll never stop.

When Eloise, the day nurse, gently rearranges pillows, the old man displaces his breathing mask and says, 'Do it now, Doc. Wait any longer and you'll lose me.'

'Do what, Mr Stevens?'

The patient's fingernail is dark blue as he points to the brief-case like he knows all about it.

'Put me on the ship.'

You jolt, physically. Eloise touches your arm.

'Sometimes the dying see things differently,' she murmurs. Eloise has been kind to you, even though they all must wonder why Austen Stevens has summoned an orthopaedic surgeon to watch over his final days. You nod and move away; her proximity has made you aware of the sweat breaking out on your forehead. A singing in the bones behind your ears makes you shake your head. You have never had a panic attack, not in all the bad years since the forest. Now of all times? No.

You point.

'It's a briefcase. Not a ship. See?'

Eloise says, 'I'm going to check if the family are here yet.'

The squeak of her rubber soles on the parquet makes your teeth scream. What is wrong with you?

'Remember, I saved you.' The old man's voice sounds like distant gulls. 'I didn't have to. It was on my own conscience.'

'Your conscience,' you say, forcing a smile. 'Where would your conscience have been if not for the eyes of the world?'

Austen Stevens' eyelids droop. You don't often argue. The old man likes it too much.

'I upheld my obligations. We paid compensation.'

'A fraction of what you owed. My country is still waiting for most of the money, so many years later.'

He tries to bark a laugh at your audacity but ends up making a series of damp, wheezing sounds instead. His marbled blue eyes fall closed and he sucks a deep breath on the oxygen mask, his slippers jostling one another with the effort.

'That's business, kid.' The Brooklyn accent comes on strong. 'Blame your government. I did more for you than compensation ever could. There was nothing for you in that village.'

*Because you took our way of life away.*

You do not say this. It's a tired exchange.

'You could have been a big man, rich and influential in your country. But you are a healer, a man of honour. You will build great things. I thought we respected each other. If I were such a terrible person I wouldn't let you near me. I wouldn't let you speak to me the way you do. But I know you are going to save me now. This deal is good for us both.'

He's living in a fantasy world now; it won't be long. Speaking so many words has taken it out of Stevens. He lays there for a time, drawing on the oxygen mask, his breath rattling.

'The ship,' he gasps. 'I want to see the thing you promised me.'

It's strange. Even when Stevens is making up lies from whole cloth, glossing over the horrors he was party to in the oil fields, still there is something compelling about this yellow-grey collection of sinew and hair and neck-wattle persistence. There is power. Invisible in a failing body, it is a power such that lands and peoples should fall before him and gods should be thrown from their homes and time should tear open on his command and Austen Stevens should lie there, like milk.

'I can't open it. There's no key.'

Stevens sighs. 'Stop fighting me. It's over.'

Beneath his eyes there are lizard wrinkles like obscene smiles, purpling with pooled blood. You can't help recalling the reflections in the pools of crude oil that lay open in the forest. You remember what you saw there: ancestors risen from the smoke of the burning oil, and sometimes other creatures, too. Spirits. The warnings they spoke to you.

In summers during medical school, you worked security on the ships. As a trusted employee, you were assigned by Pace Industries to block weapons from reaching militia supporters, and you did your job – on paper. The reality was something else. The official security forces were such a joke that you used to amuse yourself by tricking them. Ships that were supposed to be empty came in full of guns. Ships that were supposed to carry skimmed barrels of crude oil away for the private use of Austen Stevens, these went light. You obtained some gratification from skimming a skimmer; much of the old man's personal fortune came through gains that were illegal even by the shady standards of the industry.

It was a biting sort of gratification. For more than a generation Pace Industries cornered your people and attacked your land, and a succession of militias fought back, and the government men stole everything they could. Every year brought violence. As a boy you were 'rescued' from the local militia at the age of twelve when company engineers found you dying in the forest after you stepped on a land mine. Because you were a child and the company were keen to improve their public image, they rehabilitated you, educated you, made you a poster boy for their beneficence. But the word for how you feel about this is not 'grateful'. There is no word for your feeling. You remember your friends who died. You remember the fires.

You say: 'Do you believe in ghosts?'

Stevens produces a weak smile. 'Do you believe in the future?'

You feel your heart moving inside your ribcage like a disturbed animal.

There is a moment, a beat of nothingness when it feels like anything at all might happen. Time hangs there, densely packed with possibilities.

And then it begins.

There is a sudden heat in your nose; blood is trickling on to

9

your upper lip. Annoyed at the sign of weakness, you throw your head back, grabbing a linen napkin left over from the patient's untouched breakfast to blot away the blood. This is no panic attack. Next comes a seismic cracking sensation at the base of your skull, as if you've been struck from the inside. Your teeth loosen, or maybe it's your knees, and you go slack as a plastic bag.

Someone steps into you from deep within. It is as if you are nothing more than an extra set of clothes. For a moment you and the other person are superpositioned, neural patterns rearranging themselves and ligaments jockeying for control. You reel sideways and have to catch yourself on the frame of the window. Outside, the sea tilts.

The intercom announces the arrival of the family.

You try to say, 'Give us a moment, Eloise,' but you no longer have control. Your marrow reconfigures its molecules. That illicit cheeseburger fat melts to oblivion, and your gimpy left leg straightens. The pale scar tissue on your left hand dissolves as if you've never been hurt. And oh, you feel brightly alive, a wild being from a place of saturated colour and loud music.

The braying voice of Rachel Stevens ripples through the wall.

You want to put the cloth to your face again. It's an automatic gesture, born of embarrassment at the family walking in when you are in this condition. You compute medical possibilities. Not a stroke. Not a seizure. Not a panic attack – surely, dear god, Mort could not be right about this one—

The thing in your hand is not a linen napkin. It's a pistol, icy cold.

You can hear yourself breathing fast, shallow.

There is a soft knock and Eloise is holding the door open for Mr Stevens' middle-aged daughter Rachel and her bald husband. His third wife comes in, too; she's younger than Rachel. They bring a chilly breeze from the air-conditioned hallway. The wife is holding an eco-friendly thermal coffee cup in her manicured hand. Rachel is talking in Mandarin through a discreet headset; she doesn't even look at her father, just stands by the piano, conversing nasally. She would be the one who insisted on barging through without waiting to be invited.

Your hand slides the gun into your jacket pocket. You have nothing to do with this. The jacket feels tight across your chest and back; you have more muscle tissue now.

'Thank you, Eloise,' your voice says. It sounds soft and furry like a late-night radio DJ. Breathing under control now. Someone else's control.

Eloise shuts the door and stations herself near Rachel, hands behind her back.

'You may go, Eloise,' your voice says. She gives you a strange look.

'That's OK, Dr Sorle,' she says.

'You should go now.'

'Can he hear us?' It is the young wife. She looks down on her husband, who has subsided into silence, eyes shut, the breathing mask lying unused on his chest.

'Dad, can you hear me?' Rachel shouts. 'The gold mine is a lock. We sign tomorrow.'

Rachel's bald husband shifts his weight and looks at the ceiling as though wishing himself somewhere else. Not getting a response from her dying father, Rachel turns to you.

'It's a good deal for your country,' she informs you brightly. 'Wei Xha will do wonders for your revenue.'

Your voice says, 'In fact, it will be the children of my country down the mines and your children putting our wealth up their nose at parties.'

Then the gun shoots her.

The gun has a silencer. The greater noise comes from Rachel herself, collapsing on the exposed keyboard of the Bösendorfer. Eloise drops to a crouch; Rachel's husband makes a dive for the hall door and is caught with three bullets. But it's the wife who attacks you, charges at you like a weedy Vivienne-Westwood-clad linebacker.

You feel the muscles in your legs loading, your back stiffening

11

as your left hand shoots out and seizes her by the throat before she can get close. Your right hand, holding the gun, hits her across the face and then flings her off. She hits the floor under the piano, which is still resounding; then she goes still. Eloise is sobbing and calling you crazy as she begins performing first aid. The bullet has lodged in Rachel's right femur. It's serious, but not fatal.

'Keep quiet,' your voice commands. 'I have no quarrel with you.'

*I have no quarrel* ... It's an antiquated turn of phrase. You are trying to divine who or what has taken control. It feels like being on the brink of drowning. You can just about snatch enough consciousness to build an inner narrative, but you are beginning to doubt sequences. Matters are getting scrambled.

You find yourself standing over Stevens. He is in a wild rage, struggling to get out of bed, flailing at you with his wretched little arms and legs.

'My daughter,' he gurgles. 'I'll kill you.'

'I think not,' says your voice in the same old-fashioned way. 'If you had been satisfied with my earlier proofs, none of this would have been necessary. I told you I didn't want to come here again myself. It's a difficult, costly journey.'

The old man subsides on the bed, but only from exhaustion. He sucks on the mask.

'I saw the angel.'

'So you did. The money was to have been transferred after that sighting. It was not.' An undercurrent of menace. 'Stop dicking the good doctor around.'

'I had to make sure. I put in safeguards. For all I know someone drugged me and I was hallucinating. You want to do business? I'm running out of time. Dear god, my daughter.'

'She may yet be saved. I expect the money to be shifted *now*.'

Stevens gestures for his stylus and pad. His hands tremble. 'It's done. I sent the details to your phone. Get them to my guy in the UK before the deadline and the funds will move.'

You check your phone. An address in Edinburgh. A couple of apps and a series of what must be passwords.

'Not good enough,' your voice tells him. 'This is another delaying tactic.'

'Rachel needs an ambulance, Dr Sorle,' Eloise says in a ghost voice. 'Are you going to shoot me, too?'

So many seasons of spiritual effort that you stockpiled, they are ruined in a moment.

The blue nails are clawing at your arm. The voice comes after a series of gargling coughs.

'It's how we set it up. Liam holds the purse strings. Doc, I'm afraid. Put me on the ship.'

The being inside you puts your hand on the briefcase. 'The ship is right here. As we discussed.' You are fighting the thing that has possessed you, and it grinds your teeth. Surprising that they make no sparks in your mouth. 'It is a receptacle for your waveform. It will carry you where you need to go.'

When your hands settle on the briefcase this time, the latch responds. The case falls open and where its insides should be there is an absence.

It is in such an absence that time snaps apart, clean and sweet. Time itself.

Austen Stevens leans forward a little, pausing for oxygen. He waves a ropey, palsied hand at the briefcase. It's as though he has forgotten how to speak.

'What now?' he says at last, and turns supplicant eyes up to the man who shot his daughter.

'Get in.'

Stevens licks his lips. 'Help me.'

You wonder what would your mother say, to see you now? She drives a water taxi and gives away the money you send because she says she doesn't need it. Would she berate you or would she say, 'Yes, my son, do this thing to clean up the world of this evil'?

It is unwise to think of the judgements of mothers at times like these.

A curious sound begins. It seems to originate in your bones. You feel your heart going dubstep. Your awareness divides like an embryo increasing its own provenance from within. The sound skirls over your skin and raises your hairs. Artwork rattles on the walls.

Your voice says, 'Eloise, help Mr Stevens out of bed.'

Eloise gets up and walks unsteadily towards you. She steps across the body of the dead husband and comes to the bedside. She smells of urine. You throw the blankets back from your patient's emaciated legs, scattering pillows. Austen Stevens with his pot belly and stick limbs weighs no more than a large dog. Your gun points toward the briefcase.

'Put him in there. Carefully.'

The briefcase emits the noise of a thousand traffic jams, the wailing of birds, a bass drone worthy of a cruise ship's horn as if somewhere deep in the tacky naugahide the Love Boat is about to sail. There's a smell of oil burning. But the inside cannot be seen. It's a void. Not black, not even white. Eyes just can't process whatever is there.

Eloise lifts the old man and sets him upright on the rug beside the briefcase, holding the oxygen tank for Stevens while he takes one last hit. He wavers like a reflection on ruffled water.

'You must step in, Mr Stevens,' your voice says. Pent anxiety ripples through you. Stevens stands upright, gasping, and pushes Eloise away.

'Don't let him fall.'

'I got this.' Panting with effort, the old man lifts one Abercrombie & Fitch clad leg by six inches and, with shaky control, lets it down it into the open space of the briefcase. The foot and then the leg disappear, and then he seems to fold like a paper airplane until he is holding the top edge of the briefcase and lowering himself in entire. It's like a magic act where the girl disappears. The oxygen tank comes last; there is a burst of noise, a gout of smoke – and the case falls closed.

Your fingers snap the locks shut and seize the handle of the briefcase. You try to lift it, but it weighs as though filled with rocks inside rocks, exponentially increasing functions of rocks all pressed inside like gravity trying to hide up its own back end. You can feel the radiation of its efforts as a kind of pulse in your clenched fist.

Eloise is panting. Furious.

'I'm going to help Rachel,' she says. 'If you want to shoot me, do it now.'

The pistol comes up, cocked. You step around her. You are fighting a strong, strong impulse to pull the trigger on Rachel again. Your hand has aimed the gun at her head but you won't let your finger pull back on the trigger. You *won't*.

You go out the door and the gun discharges into the azaleas, harmlessly. Silently you give thanks for this.

You hear Eloise calling 911 as your legs take you through the sliding glass door and out across the lawn. Then the sound of the lawn sprinklers overpowers her faint voice.

The Audi comes to meet you in the private parking lot. The door slides open and you lower yourself, depositing the briefcase in the passenger seat as smoothly as if you rehearsed. The car accelerates through the automated barrier. You are away.

While the car drives, you book a flight on the false passport you never knew you had. You call Ayeisha, but you don't sound anything like yourself.

'I have to take him to London.'

There is an unhappy pause. Then she says, 'This is wrong. It should have been over by now. How can he go to London? What are you doing for him to make him hang on like this?'

Her voice calls you back to yourself. The scar on your hand bubbles into existence and the six-pack melts to lard under your seat belt. You swallow against the lump in your throat.

In your own voice you say, 'I'll call you when I get there. Kiss the girls for me.'

'You can kiss my ass,' she says, and hangs up.

# Help wanted

resistance.web/deployment

## VACANCY – TEMPORARY

Transatlantic flight attendant

In addition to usual duties we require handling of sensitive information and classified passengers. There will be very occasional opportunity for physical and mental intervention, and the successful candidate will be required to respond instantly to transmitted cues. We require a high level of empathy coupled with mature judgement and absolute discretion.

Applications welcome from experienced angels with minimum Level 3 clearance. You will hold flight attendant qualifications as well as advanced life-saving training. Patience and physical endurance essential. Reply code RKL39J.

# Good old hindsight

In the very moment when I was throwing the hijacker off the plane I found myself remembering what the other angels had said when Marquita lined me up for this job.

They said, 'It will be perfect for you.'

They said, 'It has a great dental plan.'

They said, 'You'd be surprised how many angels work as cabin crew for commercial airlines.'

And then they quoted me a lot of statistics.

I'm sure they were partly right. It's no coincidence that most airlines have an angel somewhere on staff. People need us up here. Folks on planes are scared, for all kinds of reasons. Scared of flying, scared of crashing, scared of terrorists. Some of them are leaving home and moving to new countries. Some are running away from oppressive governments, from bad love affairs, from angry creditors. Or just escaping the daily grind, moving towards hope of a reprieve. An airline flight is a conditional space, a great equaliser. Everybody's up here together, strangers. In between destinations. All vulnerable. Sure, you have your jaded business travellers who never look up from their tablets long enough to notice the sun rise, or the unfolding of clouds, or the white-speckled waves below where the whole mystery of the ocean is spread out like a magic carpet. But those people are usually in business class. I never work there if I can help it.

Most of the cabin-class passengers are aware that they're doing something extraordinary by flying. Even if they only let out a fleeting smile when looking out the window, or utter a silent prayer on landing, most of them sense that they are close to heaven. And heaven isn't what you think it is. Heaven, even glimpsed side-on, is awesome. While folks are hurtling along at angel-altitude, their souls are open. Their hearts are accessible.

Their minds can be touched. I'd like to think that a little nudge from me at the right moment on a flight can bring about long-term changes on Earth.

So I was on a flight from New York to London. It's not my usual run, but I was asked to fill in at the last minute. Sometimes this means the Resistance is involved, sometimes not. I'm the kind of person who is ready for anything, even when I'm going down the aisle on the starboard side of cabin class with my coffee pot.

'Coffee? More coffee for you, madam? Coffee?'

On the port side, Rory was moving the opposite way with his teapot. The two of us sounded like a little musical number, my deep contralto and his reedy tenor calling and answering. *Coffee, tea. Tea, coffee, coffee?*

As I moved, I spread higher dimensional wings over them all. I touched them with invisible feathers. I soothed an insomniac grandmother with liver trouble and her Xanax-popping granddaughter. The baby on the Xanax-popper's lap stopped crying when my unseen feather brushed the top of her head. I gave the respite of sleep to the university student returning to school after a funeral, who stared at the blurry photograph in his hands with bloodshot eyes. I shone compassion on the shuttered windows of a London cabbie's angry mind, softening the edges of his vision. Nudging open a little space in the wall of his anger so he could maybe see things differently. Feel something. Realise how close he was to home, just that moment.

And then I clocked 72B. And there he was. After all this time. My hijacker. He was hot. Hot like eye candy, hot like stolen goods, hot like radioactive. Hot. Like fucking fire, fly too close to the sun, melt your wax, *hot* goddamn it.

Hot because I hated him. Because I needed him. Because I didn't know who he really was. Because after jerking me around two times, he now had the nerve to sit on my flight like nothing ever happened? Really? Because I'm twice his size and I bend iron bars for breakfast.

Over a year had passed since he had hijacked my waveform

launcher from within. He'd used my own hardware to launch me into this odd corner of spacetime before stealing the launcher and leaving me stranded here. I'd only seen him once before in the flesh, but I never forget a waveform – especially one that's been messing with my business.

He used me. He lied to me. He stole my insides, then offered to sell them back to me in exchange for my help – and then he abandoned me. Here I was, working as a soldier of the Resistance, serving coffee and soothing babies. Me.

Pissed off doesn't begin to cover my feelings about this.

He was a small man, and what there was of him was immaculate and contained. He was the kind of person artists would fight over – not exactly beautiful, but surprising: *interesting* to look at. He was wearing a leather jacket and had his iPod in his ears as he gripped a news magazine in lovely, long-fingered hands. His hair was immaculately braided. He had sculpted cheekbones and a wide, flat nose with the kind of nostrils that would flare and flicker during sexual exertion. Don't even get me started on his lips.

But all that physicality was just a cover. He had stolen me from my nest, taken me for a joyride somewhere, and dumped me. What kind of person does that? What might he do next?

I experienced a falling sensation. I don't like to admit it, but maybe it was fear. It was the kind of feeling that puts a sharp edge on everything in the world. My wings began to swell instinctively. My thighs bulged and my back started to broaden – all the strength training I do becomes obvious when I'm under pressure. I had to stop pouring coffee and focus all my efforts on maintaining my Earthly appearance, or the wings would burst into visibility.

The passenger I was serving cleared her throat. I held up an index finger without looking at her. *Wait.* She let out a peeved sigh. With great control, I faded the wings and shrunk my body, literally pulling myself together. I would not let my hijacker freak me. I would not. I would have control.

Then I turned to her, apologised, and took her cup.

'Enjoy the rest of your flight,' I said in my smoothest voice, and gave her an extra surge of loving kindness just to prove to myself that I could. She smiled like a kid cuddling her security blanket and took a sip.

I walked back up the aisle and set the coffee pot on the cart. Then I headed for 72B, ignoring the passengers trying to get my attention for coffee. I moved with careful deliberation, but even so I could hear the thunder of my own footsteps. I am much larger than I appear.

I stood over him. He glanced up from his magazine and as his gaze passed over my chest he did a double-take. I glanced down and saw that the top button of my blouse had popped off in the sudden Bill Bixby-to-Hulk surge just now. I'd been so worried about my wings breaking into visibility that I'd forgotten about the other effects of my body beginning to assume its true size.

I have muscle, you know.

I bent down beside him so that 72A wouldn't hear me. 72B wriggled a little in his seat, making it obvious how uncomfortable he was. Of course, he didn't fool me. I could sense his instability like a fault line in the fabric of reality.

'Did you forget you made me a promise?' I murmured. 'Get up. Come with me.'

I don't lay on the Jedi mind tricks often, but I know how. He was walking ahead of me up the aisle before he even realised what was happening. We stood by the seats reserved for cabin crew, alongside the emergency exit.

This wasn't an American flight, so I didn't have the problem of an air marshal getting in my way. But I also had no backup. I mean, Rory? Your grandmother could snap him like a toothpick.

'Give back what you took from me,' I told 72B quietly.

He blinked charmingly. 'Pardon?'

'Where is it? You said it was safe.'

'I'm sorry, uh...' He checked out my badge. '*Pearl*, there's been some mistake.' His glance tripped to the locker over his seat, then returned to me. He was worried about something up there. Oh, great. Had somebody sneaked a detonator past airport security *again*?

'You've wasted my time for a year. I've had enough of this. You said if I did the helicopter thing I'd get it back. Then you blew me off. So give it back now, or I'll crush you back into HD where you come from.'

'HD, where's that? I live on Long Island.'

There was an uneasy coupling of annoyance and nervous laughter in his voice. His accent was indeterminate: a little New York City, a little London, a little... Cameroon? Congo? I couldn't place him, and I took this as another sign of his metaphysical transience.

'Higher dimensional space,' I seethed. 'It's not in Nassau County.'

'I really don't know what you're talking about, Pearl. I'm going back to my seat now and I want to be left alone.'

I stepped to block his way.

'What's in the overhead compartment?' I whispered.

He swallowed. If ever I saw a guilty face, his was it.

'It's my launcher, isn't it? You're carrying it around? Get it down and give it to me. If you've endangered these passengers in any way...'

I was swelling again. Shit. In my disguised form I'm required to maintain the dimensions of female cabin crew; i.e, undernourished. But my real body is considerably larger and stronger. My wings were screaming to get out. I'm not supposed to show my wings. Small but targeted acts of human kindness, that's what the Resistance permits. Problem is I don't do 'small' very well.

'You stole from me,' I said softly. 'And then you used my better nature against me. Do you even know what I am?'

'A lunatic?' he guessed, and tried to move around me the other way. He was agitated; frightened, even. Out of his depth, like a two-bit gangster in a monster movie. 'I want to speak to your supervisor.'

21

I used my wings to make nearby passengers feel sleepy. Multi-tasking is a big part of cabin work anyway.

'I've had enough of your games. Get whatever's in that compartment down. Now. I'll give you ten seconds before I crush you back to the dimension you came from.' I flexed my fist. 'You'll be like a piece of spaghetti stretching from here to Charybdis.'

'OK, that's enough,' he yelped, wild-eyed, as if he really were scared of me.

'Three . . . four . . .'

'Look, you've made a mistake. I'm a doctor! I can prove it!'

He was climbing on the seat to try to get around me, but I threw out an arm and grabbed him.

I said, 'Six!' There was an electric shock as we made contact. And I'm not talking about the frisson of meeting a sexy stranger. I'm not talking about two people walking across a carpet in their socks and then a spark flies. I'm talking a *jolt* that physically throws you back.

Well, it threw *him* back. He got his feet under him halfway down the aisle, and he fumbled at the overhead locker, never taking his eyes off me.

By now I was up to nine.

The look on his face was so convincingly freaked that I might have been tempted to hesitate, to question whether I'd made a mistake and whether he was just a regular guy – if it hadn't been for the feeling of him on contact. I knew him all right. If he'd launched me from HD then there was nothing he wasn't capable of. He had to be stopped.

I said, 'Ten.'

He said, 'Help!'

'Fasten your seatbelts, everybody!' I shouted. I thought about my spiritual commitment to this job. I thought about the dental plan. There was no choice. I had to take care of this.

He had his luggage down and was holding it in front of him

as a shield. It was a black 1970s style briefcase. Like something out of the *Rockford Files*. Oh, please.

I strode down the aisle and grabbed 72B with both hands. We wrestled; I was a lot stronger. He screamed and kicked, scrambling against me and swinging the briefcase around. In a second he'd give one of my passengers a concussion.

I unleashed.

In hindsight, it was stupid of me. Good old hindsight.

I began to grow. My muscles popped out. I braced my legs against the seats and with a surge, black-feathered wings burst into this world, jamming between the overhead lockers and the seats. Passengers were shouting. Even Rory was lady gaga, his mouth hanging open.

The hijacker shoved the briefcase at me.

'Take it!' he screamed. 'I don't fucking care anymore! Just take it!'

'What are you talking about?' I said. 'That's not my launcher, it's a briefcase.'

'Be careful, the gravity—'

The briefcase hit me in the chest and I grasped it with both hands. It *was* my launcher. It was my stolen launcher and it weighed about 1/117th of a neutron star but whatever gravity it was operating under, the force vector didn't point down. It pointed up. I managed to grab the handle as it swung into the air. My arm windmilled like the tail wagging the dog. The briefcase pulled me into the ceiling of the plane.

What happened next was completely outside my experience. The briefcase hit the ceiling and tore through it like a hot knife through butter. It ripped the ceiling panel off and tore a hole in the fuselage. Just like that. Only my wings braced against the cabin ceiling stopped me from shooting out into the sky.

And then, just as suddenly as it began, the force on the brief-case stopped. I was still holding it, but it was outside the plane in the freezing wind. I found myself trying to establish a position with my feet on the tops of seat rests, looking for leverage to pull the briefcase back in. I think I stepped on someone's head. Rory screamed and ran for the intercom. Air rushed out of the cabin. Oxygen masks deployed. Empty plastic dinner trays flew off the food cart and into the blue.

And then came 72B. There was something almost poetic about the way he shot past me. He looked like a doll as his slim body was sucked into the sky. He tried and failed to get purchase on the plane's hull; then he grabbed on to my arm, then the briefcase itself as the drag of the plane's passage tore at him. His face was a mask of human terror, but I knew better. No human could have done the things he'd done to me.

His mouth was moving. It was like a cartoon.

'You've got the wrong man. I'm not that guy.'

Together we tumbled over the roof of the plane. We slid a little on the freezing surface, lifted and bumped by an impossibly strong wind. Then we went over the side. I glimpsed a passenger's face through a little window as 72B and I pitched into the sky.

The plane sailed on its way above us, and he still had the briefcase in a frantic grip. In the roots of my teeth I felt his despair, his fear, his incalculable hate. I had to get him off me before he climbed into my insides and took control of me. Like before.

I flapped my arm violently as if shaking sand out of a towel, but instead of shaking him off I lost my own grip on the briefcase.

*No.*

He was still clutching it like a child holds a teddy bear as he fell away from me. I watched him go. Smaller and smaller, a tiny dot with arms and legs flailing, he fell.

Just like a human.

*Never revealing his true nature. Falling to certain death.*

Oh, shit. Oh shit ohshit oh*shit*. I must have made some kind of terrible mistake.

I thought: Why did I ever let Marquita talk me into this stupid job?

# Quetzlcoatlus with the very big teeth

*Another perfect day at your perfect job, Pearl. Pour them coffee, soothe their troubles, and punch a hole in the fuselage at 32,000 feet.*

I don't fly much. I mean, fly-fly, with my actual wings. (The Resistance discourages it; in fact, my wings seem to be an embarrassment to my employers. The title 'angel' isn't supposed to be taken literally.) But I knew enough about flying to understand that even with my wings folded, there was no way I could catch up with my hijacker. It was physically impossible. He had a head start. Gravity acted on us both equally, and with my greater size I offered more air resistance. No matter what I did, he would smash into the waves of the north Atlantic and be destroyed before I could swoop beneath him to break his fall.

It was a terrible realisation.

Self-recriminating thoughts were banging around inside my head like a swarm of stinging bees. I had no time for them. My heart was swelling with the determination to make things right. And my wings, after all, hail from higher dimensions.

I had to save him.

I was spiralling downward, my skin battered by the brute force of the air, opening my wings slightly and turning my body in the air so that I could track him visually. Below and to the south I could see a dark speck somewhere between me and the bright sea. I fixed my eyes on him, willing away all human limitations. Living among humans, I'd picked up baggage; I had to drop all of it as one. No pain, no sorrow, no fear, no limits. I was a messenger. Pure intention, expressed physically. I *would* save him.

I leaned into HD. My body folded like a paper airplane and I went down as a shaft, shedding importune photons like confetti. He got closer and closer. Every beat of my heart was dedicated to this one thing. Fly like an arrow. *Fly*. Every breath. Every impulse to muscle and every thought. My teeth sang in the wind.

I passed him in a flash. The sea was getting near. I curved beneath him and began to rise, like a needle sewing the air. He grew larger now as he came down, holding on to the handle of the briefcase as it seemed to drag him down. His legs were flailing horribly – he hadn't lost consciousness. I moved up towards him, to slow his descent, to catch him gently and then battle gravity. Reverse what I had done. Undo my mistake. I would be so gentle. I would make sure he was not harmed.

As I rose toward him, the sun was above him and his body lay in silhouette, a black star-shaped mass, falling. I opened my arms, spreading my wings, preparing to absorb the shuddering momentum of contact—

—and the briefcase flapped open.

A fireball burst out of its open mouth. The fireball engulfed the briefcase. It engulfed the man. It hit me like a star.

At first I didn't feel pain. There was a physical jolt as the heat struck me, and I veered away from the light of it, folding my wings back and diving for the sea through a roiling cloud of black smoke. I smelled oil. I looked behind me and saw tiny flames racing along my feathers. Above me: what had come out of the fireball.

What had been a man and his briefcase was now an animal of epic proportions. It was flying. I formed the hasty impression of a giant bat. Claws extended from its outstretched limbs. Its smoking translucent wings fanned out as wide as a house, and its long, narrow head on a sinewy neck craned back to take in the sight of me. It looked like a giant pterosaur displaced by sixty million years, give or take. It was coming after me now.

The teeth were bigger than you'd think possible.

I indulged in a split second of self-congratulation: 72B hadn't been innocent.

Then my hair caught fire.

26

I folded my wings and dived like a cormorant, corkscrewing in the air. I smacked at my head to put the fire out. The water spun towards me, bringing with it the shadow of the pterosaur flying between me and the sun. I saw a whale spout not far away, and light dazzled on the waves with a hypnotic intensity. The light made me feel detached. I would soon be with it, pure and empty. The whale would be the whale, and I would be the light, and I hoped the oxygen would last long enough for the pilot to get the plane down from the upper atmosphere. They would have to make an emergency landing. All my fault. And I am but here to serve.

I could see the individual waves now, and smell the decay and salt and the rising cold. The shadow on the water grew bigger as the great wings followed me down. I approached my own reflection, hurtling from on high, burning. The fire had spread to my uniform.

The pain was like nothing I'd ever felt. I tried to retract my wings into HD, but they wouldn't go. I glanced back, straight into the open mouth of the animal. Its teeth were long, slanted spikes, gates to a purple-grey throat veined with white. Deep inside was a darkness that looked like more than darkness. It looked like the end. I turned my face away.

Water hit me, aggressive, pulling me in. Stunned by its icy weight, the absence of noise, the sudden otherworldly stillness, I sank. The fire ceased, but everything was pain as freezing cold curled around me. I could sense the organic matter suspended in the water as it shifted, adjusting to my presence. Everything in my orbit cleared as if all life were giving me space, getting out of my way. I turned over and looked back up toward the surface, still sinking. I could see the pterosaur's head and its blurred eyes, staring down at me.

It glided over me, circled, eyed me first with the left eye, then the right. I swear there were lasers in those eyes.

But it didn't come for me. It flapped ponderously away across the surface of the water, leaving me in the cold.

Airless, numbed by cold and heart slowing, I dragged myself to the surface by the power of my arms and legs. Back, abdomen. Neck. Straining against the depths and working without oxygen, I swam up until finally I got my head out of the water. Wind battered my ears so hard I couldn't hear myself gasping.

I spread my wings on the water to stop myself sinking. I couldn't see the plane anymore. Or the pterosaur. I was alone.

What. The fuck. Just happened.

My wings sang with pain, but they were not as badly damaged as I'd expected. A residue of black oil oozed from the feathers. It left swirling rainbows on the surface of the sea. I could find no logic for the oil. The protective mechanisms in my skin would repair the burn damage faster than human skin could fix itself, but I couldn't imagine what had happened in my wings to produce oil. If anything, oil should have made my feathers burn faster.

There were archives written in my skin, in my bones – but most of all in the higher dimensions of my wings. Imagine living in a library, surrounded by all the wisdom of the ages. Now imagine that you *are* the library, but you don't know how to read yourself. It's a weird, pregnant sensation. Knowing and not knowing.

Now archives were unresponsive. Probably waterlogged. I wasn't thinking so good. It seemed I had no choice but to drag myself through the sea. Towards land, however far away.

I began to swim. The sea was frigid, but I was getting used to it. Little by little, my body returned to its smaller, more disciplined shape. The wings folded up. My head cleared a little.

After a couple of hours I saw a fishing boat. I wasn't really surprised. When you work for the Resistance, you expect funny coincidences to govern your life. This coincidence came in the form of a Portuguese fisherman going on deck for a cigarette and spotting me, against all odds, among the whitecaps. They picked me up. I pretended not to understand Portuguese so I wouldn't have to explain how the remnants of my clothes were blackened or why I had no hair. It was awkward, but I had no qualms about mentally smoothing the sailors down so they wouldn't ask too many questions. The man who had first spotted me rhapsodised about the beautiful light in the water around me, but his crew mates thought he was drunk.

They wrapped me in blankets and fed me. When we got closer to land I borrowed a phone and called Marquita.

'You're in trouble now,' Marquita said cheerfully.

'What happened to the plane?'

'Emergency landing. Reykjavik. Pilot's a hero.'

A weight lifted off my heart. Then Marquita said:

'Boss wants to see you.'

'You put me on that plane on purpose,' I said.

'I did,' she acknowledged. 'But I never know outcomes. That's the acausal nature of the system.'

That night I slept on the sand by Viana do Castelo in northern Portugal, thinking of Marquita and queztlcoatlus and the man falling helplessly – *why hadn't he folded up to HD to escape?* I shuddered and curled my crispy wings around me for comfort. Little stars fell down and twinkled against my skin, fading in and out like fireflies. All night.

# Fridged

I arrived on this Earth because I was hijacked.

First thing I remember is being trapped in a refrigerator. Light was coming through bullet holes in the side of the fridge, five of them arranged in a haphazard domino pattern. The fridge was empty except for me and a residual smell of mustard.

I pushed from within until the door gave. My fingers grasped the rubbery lip that had sealed it shut and I began dragging myself out of the cold and into a more general darkness. My self: whatever I had become. I wasn't quite sure yet. The wings were tightly folded. At first I didn't even know they were there because I was all folded mentally, too, like an origami giraffe.

The fridge was an emperor-sized Mayfield 4910. It lay askew on the side of a messy hill of metal and plastic cuboids: dishwashers, ovens, toasters, microwaves. It wasn't plugged in; the cold must've come from a small energy deficit in the process that had launched me. I was still catching up with myself; I percolated into my own skin shivering.

I was already forgetting the details of the hijacking.

I grabbed the edge of a nearby cappuccino machine to pull myself to my feet; the steel surface was so cold that my fingertips got stuck to it. I shook it off. Icy fog roiled around my feet and in the dim yellow light of industrial lamps I could make out the silhouettes of heavy equipment: a JCB, a couple of quad bikes, a car crusher. Just below me was a trailer with its curtains drawn. There were red geraniums on the steps.

I picked my way down the junk mountain, dislodging a washing machine that tumbled loudly to the bottom of the pile. This brought a pit bull running from around the back of the trailer. She saw me and swallowed her own bark, whining and licking with ecstatic doggy greeting. As I bent to stroke her the door to the trailer swung open. In silhouette stood a slender man. He hugged himself, shivering, and I saw the whites of his eyes flash as he felt the waves of cold roiling down the appliance mountain.

'What is it?' he said in Arabic. 'Who do you see?'

She didn't go to him at first. She liked me too much.

'Nasra? Nasra!'

From inside the trailer I could hear an American ad for air freshener on TV. Silently, I sent Nasra back to the man and slipped behind a commercial oven. My body was not young, but it was substantial, dense with muscle, and it moved well. The man came out with a flashlight. He wasn't in any particular hurry, and when I saw his beam point away from me I took the chance to run across open ground and hide again, this time behind the JCB. Nasra didn't give me away. She pranced around the man as if all this were a game.

*Good dog*, I thought, and she whined, hearing me.

After a half-hearted tour that failed to disclose me, the man returned to his television and the dog to her rawhide chew. I took a better look around. I was inside a fenced compound with a lot of big machinery intended to crush and rend. There were offices, two warehouses, and stacks and stacks of junk. A sign over the locked entrance read: **Dubowski's Environmental Reclamation**. Beyond the fence was a two-lane highway. Cars swooshed by.

All this while, imagine me fumbling to get up to speed.

My body: not much shy of two metres tall, wide-hipped, umber in colour and packed with lively muscle and enough fat to last a long winter. My grey-streaked twists bounced around my shoulders when I moved. I was fond of myself already.

The place: Long Island, New York, North America. Second quarter of the twenty-first century.

Banners of stories unfurled in my memory; narrative salad. Event snippets, language units, satellite maps, all colliding in me. By the time I was twenty-two minutes old I knew everything

I needed to know to orient myself. But I didn't know where I had come from, before the hijacking. And I didn't know why I was here. The waveform that had invaded my simulation and launched me had been human or closely associated to humanity; I was sure of this because when something comes inside you it reveals its nodes and frequencies, its pecularities. Like a stupid criminal, the hijacker had left fingerprints of its humanity on me. But what had it wanted with me? I could no longer remember the details of what I had been doing when it took me over. I been training for something, learning...? No, the memories of that belonged in some other form, some other world. This newly-assembled body didn't know anything about that.

All night I hid.

At dawn the man came out of the trailer and scaled the junk heap. He peered at the half-open fridge. It was in good shape apart from the bullet holes. He roughhoused it down the pile and managed to roll it until it lay at the end of his trailer. There, he threw a tarp over it and left it. Workers started to arrive.

During the day, the plant was busy. Seventeen old cars and one school bus were crushed in a noisy machine. Shards of scrap metal spewed out of another machine to form a mound of aluminium curls that roasted in the mid-afternoon sun. Trucks rolled in and out. People walked around talking on phones and drinking out of cans.

I identified where the security cameras were; they gave perfect coverage of the perimeter, but there were blind spots in the interior of the plant, mostly due to machinery and piles of wreckage obscuring the view. I amused myself by plotting pathways around the complex using the cycling of the cameras to conceal my movements.

The trailer man had his curtains closed all day. He emerged in the evening and locked up the plant, fed the dogs, put a lawn chair out in front of his trailer and drank a glass of tea. Then he flipped the tarp off of the fridge and checked it out with a magnifying glass. He poked around inside, knocking on it and listening. Then he took a screwdriver and started to take it apart. He was going to strip it for parts.

I panicked a little. More than a little. My hijacker had sent me on a one-way trip through the launcher, which must still be embedded in the frame of my origin. If the refrigerator still held HD components of whatever mechanism it was that had sent me here, the night watchman could destroy or decalibrate them unknowingly. Without the refrigerator I had no hope at all. I'd be stranded here forever.

The whole thing was like one of those dreams where you are taking a test and you haven't studied and you aren't wearing underwear. I know you have them.

I picked up an empty bottle of Snapple and pitched it at the top of the car-crusher, some hundred feet away. It shattered musically and rained down. The dogs went running. While the man was investigating, I went to the refrigerator and rapidly put it back together in the reverse sequence that I'd seen him use. I heard him walking the perimeter; then he went to the office to check the video. While he was in the office I picked up the fridge and carried it behind a dumpster full of reclaimed plastics. I hid it under some sheeting.

It felt really good to lift that fridge. My body craved the sensation of muscles contracting. I wanted to lift *everything*. But I stayed hidden, even when the man came back and saw the empty place where the fridge had been.

He walked three times counterclockwise around the junk heap, muttering and giving little paranoid glances around himself. Then he went inside again. I crept after him and saw him studying the video.

While he was doing this I took a toaster oven, a games console and two bread machines. I carried them to the blind spot between the crane and the pile of metal shavings and hid them under the metal. I waited for him to go back to his video screen, and then I took out the games console and diagnosed its problem: there was a Lego laser pistol jammed inside the casing so that it interfered with the power supply. Easy.

In the morning, while the night watchman was handing off to the day manager, I put the console on the steps of the trailer. In return I took a few tools, things I'd need for the other repair work. I overheard the watchman's name: Akele.

The yard was a loud place, always moving. This was to my advantage. I like to eat but don't need to; I can pull energy in other ways. I don't need to sleep the way humans do – my system can work in parallel, cleansing different regions of my anatomy on a cycle, like dolphins sleeping one side of the brain at a time.

My only real need is weight. Moving it. Metal, or stone, whatever. My body cries out for it. Anything really heavy will do. So I lifted the bucket of the bulldozer and set it down. And lifted it again. And set it down again. Boring, but effective for the moment; it satisfied my system, kept me functioning. I stayed out of shot of the security cameras, and whenever someone came, I got out of the way. Fast.

On the second night I took the fridge and buried it under the pile of metal shavings where I kept my other appliances. Then, to distract the night watchman, I left him more 'gifts' in the form of repaired things. I knew I had to figure out how to get back through the fridge soon, because the pile it was hidden in was scheduled to be taken for melting at the end of the week.

On the third night, when Akele was temporarily distracted watching the Knicks game, I went to the place where damaged cars were waiting to be crushed. Stripped of anything useful, they were still substantial. Heavy.

I was famished.

Nasra came to keep me company, sniffing among the cars as though trying to help me find what I needed. I started to pick up a Saturn, but it wasn't heavy enough. Dodge pickup; that's what I needed. I got under the rear end and lifted the bumper to my chest, at which point I stuck. I needed almost everything I had to keep the bumper at that height, and I had run out of biomechanical advantage to get it any higher. I had to shift my grip, and I dropped into a lower stance to compensate for the fall of the car when I momentarily let go of it. With my hands palm-away I could power the thing up over my head like an Olympic clean-and-jerk. I held it there, braced, thrilling to the sensation of strain, of torment, of utter exertion against the force of gravity.

I shifted my grip again. I got underneath it. I grabbed the undercarriage and walked a few steps, and then, because it felt so good, and because I couldn't stop myself – and because I am an idiot – I threw it.

That's when my wings unfolded.

It was a spontaneous thing, like when you break out in a sweat.

The smoke-stained underbelly of the car sailed over me with its greasy pipes and rivets, and I saw stars, clouds, fleets of sub-space amoeba transports, lightshot with the hotsauce of pulsars. I saw right through the world to what must have been my home. So much pleasure through every corpuscle of this fragile watery body, all released with the appearance of the wings that were hooking me into HD like your finger in a wall socket.

The car sailed several feet in a semi-parabola and hit a ruined ice-cream van with a bang. Nasra jumped back. Thanks to my wings, I was already in the air. One downdraft took me over the cab of the car-crusher and into the textiles division, where I soared briefly, exhilarated, and then remembered the cameras. I dived into a dumpster full of old curtains.

Face buried in dense goldenrod brocade that smelled of cigars, I listened.

No sound of Akele; but I'd been in the path of the cameras, certainly. I wasn't sure if they would pick up my wings. All the same, I refolded them as carefully as a lady folds her fan, trembling with excitement. I wanted to fly again. I wanted to lift bigger things. Much bigger.

As if lifting the car had opened up some kind of access to my origin, then I knew what I had to do. I dug my way through the metal shavings and opened the refrigerator womb. I crawled inside and tried to push through the back of the fridge.

Nothing happened.

Sweat streamed off me; I gasped for air in the confined space, and my hands slipped over the plastic. No traction, no HD.

Did I need to know the open sesame? Maybe the key to getting back lay in the form of a memory trigger, some visual code version of clicking the ruby slippers together and saying, 'There's no place like home.' Maybe—

The refrigerator door opened at my back. Akele said,

'Come out of there now.'

He was angry. A little frightened. I heaved myself out of the fridge, expanding as I went. I didn't dare let the wings out. He looked plenty freaked as it was.

'You been messing with my head.'

I extended myself into his brainwaves. Just a little, so he would feel me. If I'd wanted to play with his head I could have done so much more.

He said, 'You been repairing stuff and leaving it for me to find. Why you want to do me like that?'

In Arabic I told him that I didn't want to mess with him. That I had seen him fixing things himself and I wanted to help.

It was the first I had spoken to anyone. He didn't take the language bait; he answered me in the local American accent with its twangs and dead vowels. There was a faint taste of Senegal in his tones.

He laughed. 'How much you want?'

'How much...?'

'Money! My brothers sell the appliances. I have a deal with Jez Dubowski. I repair and resell, keep a little for myself. It has been this way for years.'

'I don't need money,' I said.

'What were you doing in there?'

'Trying to get back where I am from,' I said. 'I don't belong here.'

He told me he'd seen me throw the car.

'I have to work my muscles. I need it like you need food.'

'You will get in trouble, then I will get in trouble. You can't just throw cars.'

I folded my arms. Of course I can just throw cars.

The man frowned and put his fingertips to his eyebrows like a caricature of Rodin's thinker. His forehead wrinkled.

'I know what you need,' he said suddenly, taking a phone out of his pocket and wiping dust off it. Then he showed me a video.

'Isometrics,' he said. 'East Germans used this method back in the day, but nobody wants to train like East Germans. Their methods got a bad rep because of drugs.'

Baffled, I kept silent.

'You can maybe do isometrics inside a fridge but it's not enough space. You got to push against something you have no hope of moving. If you can lift a car then you need something much heavier. And if you throw cars people will notice. Then you got trouble.'

'Good point,' I whispered. I couldn't believe what I was hearing. He wasn't calling the police. He wasn't calling his boss. He wasn't throwing me out on the midnight highway.

'I wonder if you could move the base of the crane,' Akele said thoughtfully.

# Get Smart

I awakened with charred wings on the sand. The clouds over Viana do Castelo were dense and shapely; I could feel them muffling the town, pressing the sea smooth while light wandered sidelong into the sky. Old men came down the scruffy beach for an early swim, and stray dogs wandered in search of edible trash. A fishing boat spiked the horizon crookedly.

I tried to clean up. The wings kept coming loose from their higher dimensional foldings and it took forever to get them under control. I actually had to reach around and wrest them into my back, squashing them up into HD like a novice air hostess packing a bag overfull of duty-free. My feathers still felt greasy. When I rubbed my oily fingers together I had a funny feeling in the back of my head. Like when you hug someone and walk away with their perfume, their physical imprint.

Only whatever the impression was, it wasn't a person. It was several orders of magnitude bigger.

On the phone Marquita had told me to wait for transport in Viana do Castelo, but even with wings out of sight I was in no condition to be seen. My uniform was torn, stiff with salt water, and generally askew. My hair was all but gone, and there was nothing to cover the rents in the back of my shirt where the wings had broken through. I looked like a disaster survivor, and of course I had no ID or money. In some countries they'll throw you in a van and cart you off to detention for less.

Lucky for me I'm not easy to throw.

At Dubowski's I trained on every piece of equipment I could find. The urge was more than physical, it was an outlet for my frustration over what happened to me. My wings extended into higher dimensions, but I was stuck here with no mission.

Repairing toasters. If I was so strong, how had I been hijacked so easily?

I asked this question of steel and rock and concrete – I pushed and bent and twisted and pulled at the bonds of matter – but I got no answer, just the occasional glimpse of astronomical phenomena like a metaphysical peepshow. Such a tease.

I didn't know exactly where I'd come from or why my component had been stolen, but I remembered very clearly the waveform of the one who had invaded me and ripped part of me out. He had been human when he was scanned. Some AIs of extraterrestrial provenance had been grafted in to his original pattern, and there had been major repairs to one lower leg – but when he took me he had existed only as minor code within my own system. He wasn't technically alive. And he was no match for me in any sense of the word.

The idea of it made me furious. How could I be so easily used? I'm not a mug. I'm not a fool.

Am I?

Akele had the night off and had gone into the city to unload some of the stuff we'd repaired. The relief watchman was sitting in the entrance hut watching the Mets game on his phone.

I was crouching on the metal mountain watching the sky go dark. I was scooping up handfuls of hot metal curls, spilling them from hand to hand. Scraps of sunlight remained in the aluminium, almost enough to burn my skin. I had to find a way back through the fridge, back home. I couldn't give up so easily.

I must have heard a tiny sound because I glanced up. A man was standing at the bottom of the aluminium mountain. He looked up at me, smiling. He was small, unpretentiously dressed in the kind of summer casuals they wear in the Hamptons. He had on sandals, even. A higher-D shadow was associated with his waveform; it was this signature that I recognised.

My hijacker stood before me. I forgot to breathe. I wanted to pick him up by the back of the neck and throw him. I wanted to drop-kick him right over the chain-link fence and onto the highway. I wanted to let him know exactly how I felt about being stuffed inside a refrigerator and left on a junk heap.

But now that I saw him, so small and weak, I found I was at a loss. I couldn't even think what to say.

'I have a request of you,' he said. 'That is why I brought you here.'

I took a long breath. I strode down the side of the aluminium-curl mountain. The metal made a rushing noise as it shifted beneath my feet. He stepped back a few paces. I let my wings out.

'Now listen,' he said quickly. 'It is a simple matter. Do this one thing and I'll make sure you go back where you came from.'

This man couldn't possibly have the power to send me back.

Still. There was that HD resonance. And his left leg, it didn't seem quite right. There was a defect in his skeleton; he should be walking with a limp, but he wasn't. And his brain patterns were all fucked up. Lots of thetas and deltas. Almost looked like a sleepwalker. There was more going on than I could perceive.

'What's your request?'

He pointed over the tree line to the south.

'The beach is down there. You know it?'

Jones Beach. People from the plant went there on weekends. I shrugged.

'If you stand out there you can see the flight path for a particular helicopter that goes back and forth from Sag Harbor to the city a couple of times a week. It's dark green. Flies about 500 metres up, stays a good kilometre off the coast.'

'There must be a lot of helicopters that go past the beach,' I said. 'I wouldn't notice an individual one.'

'You'll notice this one.' He held out a business card. 'Tomorrow from 8:00 pm I want you to be up there. It will be getting dark. The helicopter will come between 8:15 and 8:30. It will have the same insignia as this card. You must get up close so that the passengers can see you. This is very important. You must do this without being seen by anybody on the beach.'

The card said:

## IIF
### Invest in Futures
Finance Initiatives. Austen Stevens, Chairman

I said, 'This doesn't make any sense.'

'You're an angel,' he said. 'Surely you worked this out by now.'

'But I'm not anything of the kind. The resemblance is superficial.'

'That's not for you to decide.'

I was baffled. It would make sense for me to be angry, only I felt like a lion kidnapped by a mouse. Prisoner of my own disbelief.

'I have something of yours. I will give it back if you do this,' he told me.

'What do you have?'

'I think you know. The component I borrowed.'

'Stole.'

'Borrowed. I've stored it safely.'

'Where?'

'Somewhere out of the way.'

Did he mean HD? I was afraid to ask. I hate showing my ignorance. I felt my way inside him using all of my senses, but there was no sign of my waveform launcher being tucked up inside the microscopic structures of his body.

'I will give it back to you. Then you can go and travel anywhere you want. You can return to . . .' He made a spiralling gesture, whirling his hand up towards the sky. I knew he meant HD but I said:

'What? Heaven?'

'Wherever it is you come from.'

I laughed. 'This is absurd. I'm not your toy.'

'And yet you will cooperate.'

'What would make you think that?'

'Because it is your nature to help; that's what you were built for. I am asking for your aid. My intentions are honourable.'

'Then tell me what they are.'

He shifted, rattled his keys in his pocket, wiped his nose with the back of his hand. At last he said:

'I need a person to see you. I need him to believe that someone like you is a possible outcome.'

'A possible outcome?'

'Of his own actions.'

Warily I said, 'I hope you're not playing with causality.'

'No,' he said. 'I'm not playing.'


Just before nine I ventured up into the town. It was Sunday, the banks were closed, and I had no money. Viana do Castelo was crowded with 3D advertisements floating on the air. I could edit those out at perceptual level, but I couldn't edit out the white tourist families who stared at me. I passed a three-legged dog and a bakery that smelled of macaroons and fresh bread. I found a biometric credit machine at a tourist café. I looked into the scanner; it read me and promptly announced an error.

Damn. That always happens. These scanners don't like me. Sometimes they work, but sometimes it's like my HD components interfere somehow with the visible data. Which shouldn't happen, but like a lot of things with me, it does.

'Stupid machine,' I said to the disgruntled German couple behind me, trying to laugh. 'I think I broke it.'

They backed away from my direct gaze. They looked frightened, like they thought I was going to mug them. I wanted to say *'boo!'* in their faces but restrained myself.

I wondered would any driver pick me up if I tried to hitch to Lisbon? Probably not.

Some hours went by. I covered most of the town on foot. I was getting hungry. I wanted to give some wall or pillar a really good push, so I went up to the big church on the hill and worked out on the wall there until I was sweating so hard I became dizzy. I found a half-empty bottle of spring water abandoned on a bench and drank it, tasting the previous person's waveform signature like a hint of lime, and I felt better.

I noticed an old man leaning on a crutch near the entrance to the church. His daughter was fussing over him in Cantonese – I could hear her overtones from twenty metres away, but more than that I could feel her worry for him. He had one hand on the stone and the other held his crutch, and he was shaking. I could feel his faintness and also his disappointment. He had struggled up here because he had read about this church in the travel guides, and he wanted to feel something divine here on the hill over the city and the sea. But all he felt was aching in every joint, and his heart was labouring, and he was so tired. He felt that some essential truth that had once been so close to his heart was now receding further and further. Spirit should be getting closer with age, but it was leaving him.

I couldn't help myself. I reached into his consciousness and I sent out messages that would soothe and strengthen his weary body. I felt his daughter's frustration at her father's insistence on pushing too hard, and I floated patience into her patterns.

They stopped arguing and she coaxed him to an empty bench. The man turned his face to the sun, closing his eyes. The daughter took a selfie of them both with the church in the background. I walked away.

Late in the afternoon I loitered at a bus stand. I was trying to figure out where I ought to go once I'd got hold of some money when a light flashed across me. I noticed a man pacing up and down maybe twenty feet away. He was talking on one phone and had bluetooth in his other ear. The sunflash off his phone had crossed my face, and my first impression was that he'd been looking at me, but he quickly looked away. He was casually dressed, but his red polo shirt looked like some kind of uniform. There was a logo on it for Pace Industries and he had one of those utility belts that holds a phone and tools. He would speak

English with an American Midwest accent. His name would be Jeff. He would fly business class but wouldn't drink. He would fold his cocktail napkin, not crumple it. Neat mind.

He spooked me. I don't know why. I started moving away, not too fast because I didn't want to attract attention, but it was hard to make myself look casual. Everybody was looking at me anyway.

I was crossing the street to get away from Two Phones when I noticed the news display on a screen. Photograph: my hijacker, looking grim. Next to him, a second photo. The old man who had been on the helicopter. The one who had watched me fall.

DOCTOR IMPLICATED IN FINANCIER DISAPPEAR-ANCE

I tripped on the edge of the pavement and lurched forward, crashing to the ground like a tree. A girl who had been sitting on a parked moped smoking a cigarette leaped up and came to help me.

For a moment I didn't know where I was. She was asking was I OK. I said that I was, that I'd only stumbled.

'Stupid shoes,' I added with a snort. She looked at my feet and saw they were bare.

'Is everything all right here?'

It was Two Phones, inserting himself into the situation all square-chested and confrontational. I got to my feet and looked down on him. I started to brush myself off and then realised that the state of my uniform was irreparable.

'Are you American?' he asked me. 'You OK? You look like you've been in a war.'

'I'm an actor.' I gestured at my own body. 'It's for a part.'

He had a mind full of shutters and baffles. Requisition lists. Hierarchies. He found me suspicious.

'I'm looking for coconut milk,' I said, for laughs. 'A lot of it. You carrying any coconut milk on you, Jeff? It's good for the skin.'

'I didn't tell you my name,' Two Phones said.

I smiled. 'I'm a good guesser.'

'So what's yours?' he said. 'You're an actor. What have you been in?'

'My name's Ms Jones,' I told him.

'*Ms* Jones?' he laughed. 'Is that what people call you?'

'You can call me Indiana,' I said.

I was enjoying myself, but I don't think Two Phones was having so much fun. You could tell he had this urge to arrest me and it was frustrating the hell out of him that he wasn't actually a cop. He gestured to my tattered uniform.

'You see, there is the small matter of the aircraft forced to make an emergency landing when a crew member smashed a hole in the hull. Tragically, she was swept outside and died. So did another passenger. What a coincidence that your movie is about the same airline.'

The Portuguese girl had retreated to her moped. Two Phones just had that authoritative air about him, and he had physically cut her off. I stepped around him and, in Portuguese, I said:

'Thank you so much, sorry this man is an idiot. Can you help me and just play along so I can get rid of this fool?'

She offered me a cigarette.

'I'm fine, thanks, Jeff,' I said. 'My sister and I are just going to do a little shopping. See you later. Have a nice day.'

I don't know what possessed me to say 'my sister' but the girl took my arm just as if we really were sisters, and she led me off.

'How do you know my name?' yelled Two Phones, but he didn't follow.

The girl – Gabriela – took me to another biometric machine tucked in the back of a café, and this time it worked. She told me she felt like she was waiting for something to happen, but it never did.

'I got a text. It said you were Resistance,' she said. 'I was asked to take care of you. This is the first time I've ever had anything exciting to do. Usually it's really small things, or nothing at all for months and months.'

I nodded. 'I think that's the idea. Small, distributed actions. Networked good deeds. And hey. You're really helping me out. Thanks.'

She smiled.

'It would be more fun to be you,' she said. I rolled my eyes. She lit a cigarette.

'I want to go to Brazil. There's more happening there.'

'So go,' I said.

'Just like that?'

'What are you waiting for?' I said. 'Somebody to hijack you and take you there?'

She gave me a weird look.

'I never heard of a person getting hijacked,' she said.

I said, 'You never heard of a lot of things, kid.'

# Not one of us

The guesthouse where Gabriela left me was narrow and cheap with a window overlooking a strip of dusty park. After she left I tapped the walls to find the beams. I needed to push. Now, more than ever, if I was going to straighten things out with the hijacker, I needed to be on the sharp.

The building had steel girders so it was a matter of tapping along the plasterboard until I found the places where I could push. I've gotten better at hotel room workouts since Marquita found me the flight attendant job. Back at Dubowski's I'd pulled on the jaws of the crusher. I used to try and stretch and twist pieces of metal, working my spine and limbs from different angles to get the most hit. Isometrics are incredibly tiring, and no one can see how hard you're working. No one can hear a sound. In time I've learned to perform the strength training on myself, using my own body against me. When I train sometimes my wings spring out.

In the hotel room I managed to get some work in just by pressing my body against the wall stud and holding a series of fixed poses. I sat on the wooden chair and pulled up on the seat, against my own weight until the chair creaked and a bit of the seat snapped off. I pushed my hands together and pulled them apart. I bent the towel rack – that was too easy, but bending it back to its original shape without leaving a kink was pretty challenging. By the time I was done with that, my wrists and forearms and deltoids were aching and there were prickling sensations of HD running up and down my back, because when I push really hard I can almost push *through* to HD. Almost.

As we all know, *almost* is the cruellest word.

*

My new phone announced a message from Filippe:

'Stop avoiding me. Come up and let's talk about it.'

There was a Level 3 frequency code that we used for our meetings. Humans like Marquita need cognitive extensions to get to places like this. She told me that the Resistance systems are always set to be a little more sophisticated than contemporary technology, no matter what historical period they are placed in. But none of it seems very sophisticated to me. I didn't need any special modules to access the code. All I had to do was run the simulation on myself.

I locked the door. The bed made extraordinary noises when I lay down. The message was suspiciously mild. I knew Filippe was mad. Did I want to go up with my wings in this state? He was always angling to find out more about them. Ever since I first went to Marquita, and Marquita explained about the Resistance and introduced me to Filippe, he'd been trying to get his sensors on my wings.

I felt bad about the plane, so I ran the Resistance app and dropped in to HQ. I found myself looking down on the interior of the round tower where Filippe kept his office, central to which is the impressive disarray of his sixteenth-century rosewood desk. The light passing through the tower windows attached itself to the curved wall to my right in oblong lozenges like coloured sweets: gold and chartreuse and purple according to the tint of the glass. The colours lit up the bookshelves that scrolled up the wall approximately forever; if there was a top to this tower, I had never seen it. Twenty feet below me the shifting pattern of floor tiles swirled yellow and white like a shoreline of clean bile. The odd slip of paper from Filippe's desk went spinning across the moving floor as he worked, unnoticed by him. He always writes with a quill pen.

I let myself down slowly. There didn't seem to be anyone here but him and me.

'I'll be with you in a moment,' Filippe said without looking up. I regarded his bald spot. He is small, with a curved nose and wide cheekbones and burnished warm skin that shines even when he isn't sweating. I don't know how old he is. Marquita claims he hasn't aged since she first met him twenty years ago, so there seems no point in guessing.

'He's an AI,' she told me when she first sent me here. 'He's an old smoothie, but don't be fooled. He's only a projection of the consciousness of the Resistance.'

That didn't bother me much. I'm only the projection of a something-or-other, and I wouldn't even be in this realm if I hadn't been hijacked.

'I'm sorry about the plane,' I said. 'The situation took me by surprise.'

I meant to imply that he might have warned me what was going to happen, but he just grunted and continued writing. He likes using paper. Says it remembers the trees and the trees remember the soil and the soil remembers ancient times. I don't think this is entirely a metaphor. The paper he uses is probably laced with time paradox just like everything else in the Resistance; the whole place is weirdly conditional. He put some documents in a folder and put the folder in a drawer that was already stuffed with other folders and crumpled tin foil from old sandwiches, and eggshells, and Tic Tacs. The drawer would not close. Irritation flashed across his face. I could feel the tiny movement of the tiles like percolating sand beneath my soles.

I started to walk towards his desk but he stopped me.

'There. That's close enough.'

'You're trying to keep me at a safe distance?' I said, incredulous.

'I don't know if it's safe, but it's a distance.'

The tips of my wings were brushing the round, book-lined walls to either side. It was an uneasy sensation, as though the contents of the books were whispering into my nethermost feathers and insinuating themselves. I retracted my wings.

'The oil on your wings. I can find no record of a recent spill in the Atlantic where you fell. So where did it come from?'

'I didn't get it from the water,' I said. 'It seemed to ooze out from inside my feathers. When the briefcase opened. It was the briefcase that damaged the plane. It's unstable.'

I saw his repressed hostility in the flare of his nostrils as he exhaled through his nose, mouth clamped shut; but he made a note with his fluffy pen. While he was doing this with one hand, with the other he straightened some papers and put an anvil-shaped bronze weight on them. Reciprocally, a stack of folders on the far side of the desk slid to the floor, spilling their contents. I bent to pick them up, but he forestalled me with a gesture.

It's always like this, here.

When I first met Marquita I asked her what the Resistance resisted, exactly, and she said, 'Entropy.' Talk about a lost cause. Filippe files one paper and four others pop into existence somewhere else. I don't know where it all comes from. He's always filing and organising and straightening, and yet this room is always a wreck. And he's usually grumpy about it, but this time his ire was pointed at me.

'What's going to happen now?' I said.

He tapped his pen against his front teeth and looked up, into the blur of light that is the top of the tower shaft.

'You're not one of us,' he said.

'What's that supposed to mean?'

'I told you when Marquita first brought you here that we've never had an angel with . . . all of that.' He waved his hands around, ending with a flourish at me. He was like an overwrought theatre director. 'The wings. You have no records.' He nodded at the archives all around. 'Believe me, I looked. You have no records and you have no mission.'

'So? So what I have no mission?'

'All angels have missions,' Filippe said. 'It's the definition of being an angel. Think of yourself like a delivery system.'

'Delivering *what*? And on whose behalf?'

He threw his hands in the air. 'Causality again! You keep tripping over it. The Resistance is an acausal system.'

'OK,' I said. 'Help me to not trip, then. You say all angels have missions. I have no mission. Ergo, I must not be an angel. Is that how your head is working?'

'Technically, I don't have a head. What you see here is just a sideshow.'

I sighed. He was worse than usual. Seemed to be working himself up to something.

'I did the best I could for you. That was a good job Marquita gave you. Travel the world. Make something of yourself. All you had to do was sit tight and wait for instructions, like every other member of the Resistance. But I knew it was futile. I told Marquita you would never work out.'

I don't think my jaw actually hit the floor, but the fact that he refused to look at me meant it wouldn't have mattered what expression I had on my face. I felt my mouth working as I tried to figure out how to respond.

'Wait,' I said at last. 'Don't you get that I saved that plane? That passenger was up to no good. The guy hijacked me and brought me here and he's got a piece of equipment that screams of HD. Did Marquita tell you what came out of that so-called briefcase?'

'She said you saw a dinosaur.'

'Pterosaur. And I'll tell you something else. I'm wasted up there serving coffee.'

'You're an angel, Pearl. You're here to serve. The whole purpose of the Resistance is to keep it low. Our angels don't do pyrotechnics. They don't fly around performing stunts! They are ordinary janitors and health care workers and truck drivers and waitresses. The whole point of what we do is to tweak causal nature in small ways. Small, unobtrusive ways, Pearl, because that's how the work of the world gets done. But look at you!'

He stood up and came around the desk, planting himself before me, hands on hips. He looked me up and down.

'There's nothing small about you. You're decidedly conspicuous. And it's not just your appearance. People who have met you don't forget you. You have that way of gazing in people's eyes – you're doing it right now. Cut it out! You make me feel like you're looking into my soul.'

'I am,' I said.

'But I don't have a soul. And you know that. No, Pearl, I don't know what you are or where you come from, but you are not one of us and I can't afford to keep you anymore. There was a lot of damage control involved in that flight. Recordings can be fixed, but it's not easy to handwave a hole in the fuselage away.'

'So you're saying...?'

'We're done here.'

I felt myself stagger. Maybe it was just the minuscule movements of the floor beneath me all adding up to unbalance me, but I don't think so.

'Does Marquita know?' I whispered.

'I thought you might want to tell her.' He turned his back on me, stepping over papers to get to his desk, and sat down with a heavy sigh. He licked his forefinger and turned a page.

Coward.

'What is the matter with you?' I cried. 'I believed in you. I believed we were doing something meaningful. I thought we were on the same team.'

Filippe selected one of his official stamps, a large one with a worn wooden handle. He rolled it across a pad of red ink.

'You don't even know what you are, Pearl. How can you possibly know what team you're on? Be glad I didn't just have you taken out.'

He brought the stamp down on the page with a small, clean thump.

# I'd prefer your kayak

The woods gather around you like a winter coat. The fir trees grow right down to the shoreline, and here among them the susurrus of their movement is broken by high-register birdsong dispensing tiny droplets of golden sound. Light-shot clouds of mosquitoes jumble in the weeds that were crushed where something barrelled through the undergrowth at the water's edge, scoring trees and snapping their branches. You remember pain. You remember fear. When you think hard, you remember the briefcase falling open. You were nearly unconscious by then. You remember fire.

Since then, you have been someplace. A kind of cavern or room or hall, a holding pattern; but you can't recall exactly. It's all nebulous. Were you in a cage of blood vessels or were they nerves? A red-hot womb, a star nursery, an array of crystalline forms suspended in gel, a Bayesian probability array. Whatever it was, now there's just nausea and the wreaked-horror aftermath of every particle of yourself having been rendered void and then rewritten in the world.

This is so confusing. If you died out there over the ocean, are you returning to the world in a new body? Aren't people supposed to reincarnate as babies? It's what you always heard.

Between you and the water's edge you see a purplish-brown trail of what might be the faeces of a large animal. No sign of that animal now. It's just you and the briefcase.

Except it isn't you, after all. It's him. Other you.

He stands right up inside your skin, confident. He finds the phone in your pocket – yes, it's still there! Ah! What a mockery of all you've been through, that a phone is in your pocket after falling thousands of feet.

The other one who lives in your skin doesn't power the phone up. He removes the card and tucks it into a hollow space in a rotten stump. Then he throws the casing into the dark water. It flashes twice in the air, then goes under.

There are rocky islands out there, crowned with more fir trees. No boats. No docks. No buildings. The geography looks like Nova Scotia but the light is weak. Scandinavia?

So tempting to dismiss everything as unreal. You can feel the weight of the briefcase dragging on your arm. He is stronger than you ever were. He has more muscle and he has more nerve. Your sweat doesn't even smell of fear. You smell like a man with a purpose: his purpose.

He prowls up and down the shoreline, stumbling over granite boulders in your comfortable loafers. You think of the phone, its GPS. He threw it away before trying to find out where you are.

After a time, he sets off into the woods. You feel it all. Your heart pounds. Your legs work. They are good legs, better than the ones you had when he climbed into you; even so, you are soon weary, yet he keeps going. The light goes slate-coloured but doesn't fade completely. It's getting chilly. He goes on and on, and you feel sure he's going in circles until, ahead, a yellow square of light shows up, broken by trees. He quickens his pace, and your chest burns, and sweat is pouring off you. There is a cabin with a light burning in the twilight, and a break in the trees, and beyond this you see water. You approach. There's a dock, a boat with an outboard motor. A couple of kayaks pulled up on the shore. But no truck, no car. No road, no visible power line.

You come to an outhouse a little way from the cabin. It smells.

He moves slowly now in the blue-grey light. There are voices. Children in the cabin, and a woman's voice.

He goes to the cabin and puts your back to the wall. You begin to be scared of what he will do. You want to scream out a warning to these people. But you can't make a sound.

He turns your head and then he leaves you, just like that. He's gone.

With one eye you look in.

The light comes from a kerosene lamp. Inside, children are lighting a fire. They are talking in Swedish.

You wait. Now that you are allowed to move, you are afraid to move. What if he comes back? What if he massacres them? But he has no weapons, and what reason would he have to bludgeon some random family to death?

What makes you think he needs a reason?

You feel, though, that he has left this one to you because it suits him to let you do the talking.

How unprepared you feel for all of this. You have been seeing ghosts all your life, and now it is as though you are haunted. You should have known they would not let Austen Stevens die without raising their grievances.

They used to whisper to you.

Your father would take you with him on his river taxi. And sometimes he would take oil men. Men in suits and men with boots that looked like they'd never seen a day's work. Nervous over the lack of cellphone signal. They would go to the places where the sump lay in the forest. No one would smoke there. Five miles in the other direction was a village where gas spewed out of a broken pipe and flames burned all the time and on the way you'd pass abandoned villages, places that had been ruined by Pace Industries and the wars it funded, places left behind when people had packed up and moved away.

Up the river in an outboard, and the trees with their overhang of sunbuilt structure over you; they felt just like the school library. Stuffed with possibilities. Shot through with soft, soft light. And full of ghosts, you knew.

Standing near the ponds of oil you'd hear them sometimes, like when you put two plastic cups on a string and talked to your friend: maybe the details were half imagination, but there was a vibration on that string. And there were ghosts in that oil.

'You must help us,' they'd say. 'Don't let us be burned alive. We have knowledge you can't imagine. Make it stop.'

You turned your face down to your hand-me-down trainers, the grime on your legs, the scratches; you looked right through yourself, through the ground and in your imagination it was as if you were looking through the Earth, into the deep places. Out the other side, even, and into space.

The oil company, the soldiers, the journalists, the sickness. The endless fighting. There was something bigger beneath it all.

You thought, when the recruiters came, that joining the militia was the way you could honour the ancestors – for who else could these voices belong to? You never told anyone what you heard. You never told your mother, even when she begged you not to join the fighting. You never told your friends.

But ever since then, even after the war and the near-death experience when the great crow came for you – even after your rescue by the oil company, you hear the spirits: animal spirits, human spirits, things that aren't even from this Earth. When you're near a petrol station or an oil tank or even a coal fire, they whisper to you.

You became a physician to get as far from violence and destruction as you could. You've planned for years to go back, to rebuild, to live well as the best revenge. You made friends who shared your vision, and together you've talked of the teaching hospital you'd create in Kuè as fine as anything in Europe or the States. The fundraising you did. The times it almost came together, and then didn't. The wasted effort, trying to get others to put up the money for your dream.

You tell yourself that was the reason you fell for the old man's job offer: the money. It's always money in this world. The money meant you wouldn't have to wait until you were fifty-five or sixty to get the project off the ground. The thing could be begun now, and you'd be able to do it right. You knew he had his reasons for choosing you; after all, there are things you know about his business, secrets of his. It's not that you kept them quiet out of loyalty. You simply turned your back on that whole mess.

And now here you are. In the middle of a steaming pile of shit. Being framed somehow, for a crime you don't even understand.

You stand by the door, gathering yourself for a while. The briefcase is too suspicious. You leave it outside. Then, feeling like you're in a fairy tale, you go around the front and knock on the door.

They all have green eyes. The grandmother's hair is silver, plaited on one side. The kids have black hair and skin the colour of the walls in detention centres. When you ask the grandmother if she speaks English, she says warily, 'You are a long way from the holiday cabins. Who else is with you?'

'I was fishing with a friend,' you say. 'We came on shore. I fell asleep on the rocks and he must have left.'

'Your friend left you here alone?'

You try to sound lighthearted. 'He's a joker. He's crazy. I thought he would come right back, but it's dark now and I wondered if you have a phone I could use.'

'Phone? No. No phone. No electricity.'

'Cellphone?'

'You won't get a signal.'

They are stiff, watching you with bottleglass eyes. You have seen this look before. The grandmother is thinking that if you can't call for help, neither can she.

'This is embarrassing,' you say. You open your wallet. Your familiar US dollars are still there, which adds an extra layer of strange. Your credit cards will have been cancelled by now but you still have the cash you withdrew at JFK.

'Can I buy your kayak? I have to get ... back.'

You are trying to work out what a kayak costs and at the same time guess where you have to get back *to*. The woman is stiff and you can hear her swallow. You look down at your shoes and it's obvious you aren't dressed for fishing.

It is so tiring and ironic, their fear. No matter how many African people the white people robbed of their lives, still *they* will be afraid of *you*. You fish around in your wallet, come up with your hospital ID card. You show it to her.

'Dr Kisi Sorle,' she says stiffly. And now she leans against the door frame. You aren't a black man loose in the woods anymore. You are a doctor.

Silently you offer the money again.

'Come in,' she says. 'We are just about to have our meal. You are on holiday?'

'Business trip. I won't come in, thank you, I don't want to impose. I just want to get back.'

'That old boat, it isn't worth much,' she tells you. 'But it's a long way to town. If you go a half-mile that way, you'll come to Gustav's house. He has a phone signal.'

If Gustav has a signal he'll have a news feed. You smile and say, 'I'd prefer your kayak.'

# Tool

'The Resistance moves in mysterious ways,' the nurse at Queens Hospital told me after my near-miss with the IIF helicopter. I'd been dragged from the water unconscious by a couple of men walking their dog on the beach. When I awakened, my wings were stowed in HD. The nurse, Chona Navarro, said, 'Your bill has been covered, so that's one thing you don't have to worry about. Do you have a place to go after we release you?'

'I guess... I don't actually know Akele's number, but he works at Dubowski's Recycling... Wait a minute. Who paid my bill?'

Chona handed me a business card. On one side it had a picture of an open suitcase with vacation snapshots spilling out. On the other was printed

*Destiny Destinations*
*Marquita Roumain*

'That's not the logo I saw on the helicopter.'

'The helicopter? Oh, right. You fell out of a corporate helicopter. IIF, was that it? We informed the police. They'll probably come talk to you soon.'

I was still bleary. The bed was too small, and the room was hot and cramped, and I could feel the pain and distress of people in beds on either side, and in the hallway, and across the room. I thought of the hijacker, so dapper and contained, with his gimpy leg and his misshapen waveform. He had told me to fly and I had flown. I had seen the passenger in the helicopter: an old man. The bags under his eyes. I'd felt his spiritual frailty like a quaking feather touch. The downdraft off the helicopter blades caught me. Then the iron-dark sea.

'I don't understand,' I whispered. 'What's going on here?'

She put her hand on my wrist. I felt her compassion. Her embarrassment.

'I'm not supposed to say.'

'Why not? What's the big secret?'

'We're just ordinary people,' she said, smiling. 'We do really simple things. Say you shared your computer out to solve a big problem. Well, this is like sharing yourself out. Letting yourself be guided on a time-share basis.'

Then she closed her mouth and pretended to look at my chart.

Now I was sitting on the edge of a hotel bed while the Parisian dawn melted over the plate-glass window. The glass was almost soundproof. Everything outside this room seemed remote.

'*Taken out.*'

I said it to Tsubota, Marquita's snake.

'Filippe said he could have had me taken out. Does that mean taken out like you take out the trash? Or does it mean taken out, like, off-with-your-head? Because if it's the second one, he's kidding himself. I'm not that easy to take out. Who is he to say that to me?'

Tsubota was stretched along the climate vent that formed a ledge at the bottom of the window, basking in its warmth while his tongue tried and failed to taste the view of Notre Dame.

Marquita was sleeping, sprawled on her back with her mouth open, a slug trail of saliva tracing gravity's vector from the corner of her mouth. Her brightly-beaded braids were splayed around her in a semi-circle like the head of a paintbrush that's been jammed against the paper. Or a halo. The hotel's Egyptian cotton sheets were tangled with her legs, but one foot had managed to escape and its painted toes twitched in her dreaming. She wore a shell necklace that wouldn't have looked out of place on a mermaid and, even though the fine wrinkles on her neck and around her eyes showed the drag of the years, she had fucked like a storm all night.

Marquita was a small, economical person who could command

any given room. She had glided her electric body over mine like a sea creature, her fingers holding me open so that her tongue could lick me into other realms. She had melted and consumed me, and when my thighs clenched and my legs wrapped around her in my extremity, she laughed and bit the insides of my thighs and I thrashed her off the bed. I'd rubbed her whole body with shea butter. I found the limits of her by sound and weight. Her moisture had soaked into my skin by morning, and I knew her cells and the clacking of the beads in her hair. I found one of her pubic hairs in my teeth and I swallowed it. I'd missed her so.

My heart sounded like a gong this morning. It needed work to do, and so did I. But I'd been kicked out of the Resistance. If I pushed into the immovable bulk of the world, where would I go now? At Dubowski's, equipped with Akele's training advice, I'd pushed against the base of the crane. Every night I pushed. I pulled against the jaws of the crusher. I ripped at the wheels of the biggest truck in the lot, committing ligaments and tendons and all the electricity of my body.

That's when I started getting glimpses of HD. The spaces inside things parted for me like a curtain. This happened for milliseconds at first, in the extremity of my exertion. Then I learned to identify the state and make it last longer than my muscles could sustain the effort, so that there was an afterglow of this feeling of being open to something that had no name – maybe it was beyond naming. The opening went down and down and out and out, higher-dimensional space branching like the inverse of twigs or dendrites. Even after I stopped pushing I floated there with every sense standing upright.

There was a presence in this emptiness, a sense of habitation, of immanence or intelligence. I felt like I had my fingertips to the silvery snail trail left behind by something I'd never seen.

I was listening for probability waves, searching frequencies for a signal. A trace of what had made this invisible realm. It was like a distant scent of home.

After a few days I came to anticipate the opening of HD,

so that my sensory modules started upcoding even before the day was done. At the end of the shift I would stand behind the warehouse or under the shadow of the car-crusher and wait for the yard to be closed up. One night the crane operator was working late. He'd fallen behind and had to transfer a pile of wreckage closer to the crusher to be ready first thing in the morning. He'd been told off twice by his supervisor. Everyone else went home. The operator kept working. He kept making mistakes. He swung a taxi too hard on the end of his hook and it crashed into the side of a big metal receptacle with a gong that sizzled in my occipital bones and down to my heels.

At last he was done. I was desperate by now. I had begun to yearn for the dissolution I felt when I was straining against the immovable. I craved it.

The operator climbed down from the cab. He took a swig of an energy drink and blotted his forehead with the sleeve of his T-shirt. It was an awkward gesture, and it seemed to trigger a release of emotion. I felt his knees weaken. A part of him just gave up. He sagged against the base of the crane. Back then I didn't know how to put together the reasons for his feelings, the ways in which his life was falling apart; I just felt the effects like ripples rolling over him and over me at once. His jaw worked.

I pressed the heels of my hands against one another. Pressed myself against myself, and watched him. I sensed the angles of his bones and I felt the ground beneath him, holding him in place, and I felt the aching in his gums that came from weariness because he hadn't been sleeping. I wanted to help him. I pressed harder.

The act of pushing seemed to activate something in me. In between the electrical signals of the man's nervous system I found a constellation of apertures – thousands of them. I inserted my consciousness in between these pulses like a drummer inserts a syncopated beat, like a swimmer reaches down a toe to feel the bottom. There was no bottom. In between the beats of his electrical activity there was a great stillness, there was a long, lightless ocean, and it was exerting a faint but perceptible force on me. I could fall so easily.

'Pearl!' Akele was standing on tiptoe, craning his neck to get up into my line of vision. 'Pearl, come back!'

I took a step away from him and steadied myself. The otherness faded, or maybe I should say it receded, as though all of the extra sensations and thoughts suddenly scurried to hide like electrons hiding behind one another to escape the Coulomb force.

I was aware that tears were streaming down my face and my breasts were bouncing up and down because my diaphragm was in spasm and I was a little lightheaded.

'My friend, what has happened?'

He took my arm and led me away, out of sight of the crane operator.

'Turn off the flashlight,' I said. When he hesitated I said, 'It's easier for me if I can't see you.'

He switched it off and now the lumps and curves of recyclables took on tones of grey and violet and blue in the darkness, and the sound of the maple trees across the fence became sharper and full of the words that trees speak to the air, and I smelled the damp underside of a stack of wooden pallets that had been left out in the rain. I could feel Akele breathing.

'I have a problem,' I said. 'I don't know which parts are me and which parts are my environment and which parts are ... other beings.'

There was a silence. He coughed. Then another silence.

'I saw this on daytime TV,' he said in a stiff, serious voice. 'Boundary issues, they call it. A common problem. What you must do is set limits. This is what I understand, anyway. You can't just give yourself away, Pearl.'

'Why not?'

'People will use you.'

I laughed. 'Use me? What, like using a thunderstorm or using a mountain?'

He shrugged. 'Don't put it past them. It's the way of the world.'

In Paris I realised that Akele had been right. The hijacker had used me, but I had scraped together a little bit of identity. A job. A girlfriend. These were my efforts to make peace with my situation. I thought I belonged with the Resistance. I can't say I felt fulfilled serving coffee to transatlantic passengers – but it had given my existence some kind of meaning. Now I'd come so close to recovering the stolen component, maybe even finding my way back to wherever I came from and, instead of helping me, Filippe was throwing me out.

I felt like a tool.

Just then Marquita farted and woke herself up.

'Wasn't me!' she declared, propping herself on her elbows and looking around, uncannily alert. There's never any slope between Marquita's levels of consciousness. She's discontinuous. 'What's for breakfast?'

I poured her juice from the room-service tray. We hadn't talked last night. There would have been no point. Sometimes the body has more to say than the mind; but now I had to pull myself together. Something was going to happen now.

I observed her swallow the juice, her foot already jigging with the energy she can't seem to keep down. She wasn't looking at me.

'Does Filippe know you're here?'

She shook her head.

'Any mango?' Tsubota moved at the sound of her voice. I watched him trying to find his way down from the top of the heater.

I brought the tray over and let her choose what she wanted. She ate with precision and speed. She didn't linger. She would walk away from me; I could see it now. Too efficient to do anything else. Filippe must have rubbed off on her.

'The Resistance didn't predict anything that happened on that plane,' she said, spearing chunks of mango on her fork. 'I don't know why your shift was changed, but it was and now the whole trajectory of the future has been altered. It's like a hole in causality opened and everything we're working to build is starting to unravel.'

'The briefcase is … it's a thing that used to be my component. It's supposed to be a part of me. It *is* me. And he stole it.'

She put down her fork. 'It's a briefcase, Pearl. What do you mean, it used to be your component?'

I hugged myself.

'You wouldn't understand. It was … like my bone marrow, or my lymph. That briefcase isn't just a briefcase.'

'So I gather.' She leaned back in her chair, sighing. Her eyes flicked from point to point on the cityscape outside the window as she thought. 'Look, Pearl. Filippe is scared. No one knows what you are or where you came from. He feels like something is coming up on him from behind. Nobody likes that feeling.'

I snorted and stood rocking on my two feet.

'He should have talked to me straight, then.'

Marquita waved her hand in the air like she wanted to erase something.

'I'm not getting in the middle,' she said. 'I'll tell you what I know. I won't tell him I saw you. What else can I do?'

Someone had hardlined a coral reef on Marquita's toenails in exquisite detail. The effect was holographic, and when you looked at her toes it was as though you were seeing through a window into the undersea, and the fish were swimming. I kept glancing away and then looking back quickly, trying to catch the algorithm behind the trick; but I couldn't. It was very convincing.

'You talked me into the job. You really didn't know this would happen?'

She laughed. 'I talked you into the job because I thought you would be happier up in the sky than on the ground. When I met you, you seemed so lost. I wanted to help you.'

She poured coffee. I said:

'Do you think I could be one of those women who love too much?'

'Not from where I'm sitting,' Marquita stroked my calf with her holographic toes.

'Seriously. I fall in love with you all. Random people. I just look at them and I want to get all up inside them, I want to go with them and be them only *more* somehow, I want to... I don't know what it is, like provide some kind of enhancement. Tell me honestly. Is that *eww*? Should I be thinking about the ethics of this?'

'Love is attachment. That's essential for the survival of the species. Women who love too much? What the fuck is that? The whole idea implies that love is a pathology. So now women are devalued because we can attach deeply.'

'I still wonder if I'm violating boundaries by letting myself reach into people like I do.'

'Maybe it's not love at all,' Marquita said. 'Maybe you're training your mirror neurons. Learning the species by empathy.'

'Then why do I feel so... hooked?' I almost added, 'I find it hard to say goodbye.' But I caught myself.

Marquita gathered up her braids and began to wrap them up in a cloth.

'You still haven't figured out your mission.'

'I'm waiting for you to find my file.'

'I think you're going to have to write your own file, baby,' Marquita laughed. 'According to the airline's statement, you and Kisi Sorle were both blown off the plane when a ceiling panel came off. They made an emergency landing at Reykjavik,' she said. 'The airline's being investigated for its maintenance record.'

'The passengers saw me.'

'The passengers were oxygen-deprived. Besides, everybody's focused on the missing billionaire and the fact that the man who shot his daughter got blown off a plane before the authorities could catch him. There's way too much going on for anyone to worry about you.'

'So the Resistance isn't staging some sort of cover-up?'

She looked uncomfortable.

'Not in the sense you mean, no. We don't coerce anyone to do anything. You know that. The Resistance is about all of us working in small ways for a better future.'

'You sound like a propaganda movie.'

She gave a sea captain's belly laugh. 'It's very rare for people to be aware of what they're a part of. The Resistance just gives little nudges.'

'And the technology?'

'I already told you I don't understand it. I think it comes from the future or something. Here, I want you to look at this.'

And she showed me Dr Sorle's file. She spread it all around the room; the Resistance has a technological edge over its contemporaries. There was his life story. His education. His family connections. His spending profile, online activity, political record, neurological patterns, DNA . . . everything you could think of, except—

'Do you have his waveform signature?'

She gave me a funny look and sucked her teeth. I realised I'd overreached the technology available to the Resistance. Damn.

'So what can you tell me about the briefcase?'

Her mood headed south. She bit off each word as if it pained her.

'It's. A. Problem.'

'You're telling me. What was that animal?'

'You would know that better than I would, Pearl. You saw it. What would you say it was?'

I shrugged. 'Looked likes one of those quetzl things from the mid-Cretaceous. Really big specimen. Question is, where did it come from? The briefcase must be folded into HD. That's the only way it could open up like that.'

Every time I said 'HD' there was a flicker from her. I don't think she quite believed in higher dimensions. It was like Akele walking around the back of the refrigerator to see if there was a hole in it, like a magician's prop. I let it go.

Marquita got up and opened the bathroom door. She crooked

her finger to me. Inside was a big, kidney-shaped sunken tub. She bent over and fixed the plug in place, then started filling it.

'Take out your wings,' she said.

''Scuse me?'

'You heard me. You said there was oil. You had to fold them to stop them burning. So let's see them now.'

I was afraid. Afraid of the pain if I let them out. Afraid the oil had ruined them. Afraid of something else, something undeclared, masked. The look on Marquita's face was sharp, wary. She wasn't afraid, exactly. But she was something. Eager? Hungry.

That was it. She was hungry.

I stood looking at myself in the bathroom mirror and saw what Marquita saw: a fifty-something woman of indeterminate not-European ancestry, her denuded head wrapped in an orange cloth, her weighty breasts moving as slow pendula even in the tightest exercise bra. Shoulders like a linebacker. Traps so steep they looked like one of those road signs that warn trucks to use a low gear. Legs bowed and springy, feet large and high-arched. A nice thick layer of subcutaneous fat: no chance of this one passing as a ripped-up bodybuilder. She was packing power.

Marquita looked at me with open adoration, but I always look at myself with surprise. There's so much I haven't figured out yet, and most of it is myself.

I didn't know what else to do, so I unfolded my wings.

They filled the whole room. My feathers, normally a ménage of black and grey and dark brown and bronze, were now uniformly sludge-coloured. The oil had soaked right through them.

Marquita let out out a hiss of breath.

'Lay them in the tub one at a time. No, you get in.'

'It's not big enough,' I said. They were curled as tightly as I could curl them and still they were painting the wallpaper with oil. There was a strong smell of it.

'We'll get this done, if we have to do one feather at a time,' Marquita said grimly, pulling on a pair of latex gloves. She picked up a bucket and sponge. 'Come here.'

Oil dripped on the floor. Marquita scraped some up and put it in a black vial with a bar code.

'What are you doing?'

'I'm going to send it to the TEM at Edinburgh,' she said. 'They can look at the molecular structure. I'm curious.'

'Why Edinburgh?'

'Because that's where you're going after we leave here.'

'It is?'

'That's where Dr Sorle was last headed. He was going to meet Liam Forbes, who is a digital finance maven heavily involved with Stevens ever since Stevens left Pace and put out his own shingle at IIF. You didn't hear it from me.'

'How do you know that?'

'His phone records.'

'Yes, Marquita, but how do *you* know that?'

'Same as ever. Resistance.'

'So, you're not giving this oil to Filippe.'

Marquita has a poker face. It even works on me. She just stared at me, daring me to doubt her.

I sighed. Then I reached out and pulled out a pin feather. I gave it to her. She looked surprised.

'Go ahead,' I told her. 'Tell Filippe to knock himself out. When you figure out what I am, be sure and let me know.'

She held the feather up to the brightly-lit shaving mirror and squinted.

'It's soaked right in. We really need to get this stuff off of you. It's not going to do you any good.'

'Just pretend I'm a seagull in an oil spill,' I said. 'But it's going to take you all day.'

'Well, I can't really run you through a car wash, can I?'

The concentration on her face as she worked. There's a magic about Marquita. She's fierce and focused. The flesh on her brow lies in little waves.

'Keratin is used a lot in nanotech now,' she informs me. 'They make plastic with it. The structure of a feather is complex and extremely durable.'

I laughed. 'Is it now, Wikipedia?'

'A feather would be a very good storage device,' she told me. I laughed again.

'Are you trying to find out my secrets?'

'I'm just saying. Your wings are for more than flying. We know that, even if we don't know how they work.'

'They have components in HD,' I said. 'If you stick my feather under a TEM you're only going to see in three dimensions plus time-development.'

'Yep. And I'm betting that will be plenty interesting in its own right.'

She scrubbed and scrubbed. She sang Ella Fitzgerald songs. An hour went by. She looked like pit crew and the hotel bathroom smelled like sulphur. The biblical irony was not lost on me.

Then she said, 'About Kisi Sorle. There's more than one story.'

I widened my eyes, to goad her. She said slowly, 'I mean, literally. Filippe looked into him.'

'Go on.'

'Kisi Sorle has two trajectories. They seem to have split from one another during the unrest in Kuè, when he was just a teenager. Austen Stevens was in charge of global operations at that stage. Kisi was part of a peaceful protest movement against Pace, but there were militias active in the region at that time. He was badly injured, had his leg blown open by a landmine. One of him was saved by some Pace Industries engineers who had wandered into the wrong area by mistake, and he ended up being taken in by a woman in Imo who kept dozens of orphans. She sent him to school. She convinced him to try for a scholarship funded by Pace Industries and he was educated in London. He's an orthopaedic surgeon now with an American wife and children. Stevens subsequently left Pace and became extremely wealthy with IIF, his financial company based in New York. Then, in a very strange move, Stevens hired Dr Sorle as a personal physician. Recently Dr Sorle has been making a very good living doing basically palliative care.'

'And the other Kisi Sorle?'

'Ah,' said Marquita. 'Impossible to say. He comes from somewhere else, like you. He's either an AI or something projected by an AI. We don't know how he accesses Dr Sorle's body.'

I felt my face doing things it's not supposed to do when you're in control of your emotions.

'Do you think Filippe could have sent him?' I asked. I tried not to say it through gritted teeth, but I've never been much good at hiding what I'm thinking.

She laughed.

'Filippe doesn't have that kind of power! He's a paper pusher.'

'Marquita, tell me for real now because it's only you and me here. Did you know what had gone down at Austen Stevens' house when you changed my shift and put me on that plane?'

'No!' she barked. 'And you know very well that I couldn't have known. That's not how we work. You have to let go of this idea of predictable outcomes. The Resistance isn't an extension of the body the way a tool is an extension of the skeleton. It's an extension of the mind.'

'With respect – you have no idea what it's an extension of.'

She said, 'You're mad at me. This isn't my fault. I've told you before. The Resistance is based on probabilistic predictions, and the system is governed by what we call the Austen Correspondences.'

'I don't have that in my archives. Are you sure it's a real thing?'

'That in itself is worrying, Pearl, but nobody knows how your archives were built or when or where. You're missing my point.'

'Am I? What's your point.'

'The name, Pearl. The *Austen* Correspondences.'

'What? Austen Stevens? Seriously? He invented them?'

She made a pffff sound. 'They are named after him. Maybe. Maybe, maybe – I don't know! There are things that can't be known with certainty. It's the nature of the system.'

'You think this Dr Sorle – one or both of them – do you think they are trying to manipulate causality using my equipment? Are they trying to control these Austen Correspondences? Take over the Resistance? What?'

'I don't know what their motive is. It could be revenge on Stevens himself. Kisi Sorle has every reason to hate Austen Stevens for his policies in Kuè. His people's land is more than an economic possession, it's the whole basis of their culture and identity, and Pace trashed it. They killed and lied about it. It's not the kind of thing you just forgive. So no, I don't trust the good doctor any more than I trust his violent alter-ego. He's not standing deathwatch over the old man for a paycheck. There has to be something more to it.'

'Well, if someone is trying to take over the Resistance using one of my components, then can I just say that Filippe is a jerk to treat me the way he did. I loved being in the Resistance and I don't appreciate being thrown out.'

'I know,' Marquita said softly. 'Filippe has reasons for everything he does. But we'll probably never know what the reason was.'

'I'll tell you one thing, Marquita. I'm not going to be just moved around like this.'

She laughed out loud. 'You have no idea what's moving you. No idea. At least just admit it. Why did you confront Dr Sorle like that? You could have waited for the plane to land. You could have done so many things differently. You were grandstanding. You went batshit.'

'The briefcase was unstable! I honestly thought he could bring the plane down.'

She shook her head. 'No,' she said. 'Just no.'

We looked at each other. She had many secret places. I liked that.

'You're drawn to Sorle because of his damage,' Marquita said gently. 'It's your nature. That kind of mess, though? In a person? His shit will mess you up. You know that, right?'

'I'm bigger than he is,' I said.

'Be careful, Pearl. This thing you do with people. This devotion.'

I never blush, but when I'm embarrassed I do look at the floor. It's not normal, what I do. It's not expected. Maybe it's not even welcome. I wonder if I am some sort of aberration.

'Pearl. Choose wisely the ones you throw your weight behind. You haven't been here very long. You lack . . . '

She paused, because my eyes were saying: *What do I lack, dear Marquita who is leaving me out of obedience to the principles of the Resistance, whose love crumbles in the face of a stiff breeze? What lack I?*

' . . . judgement,' she finished. Then she squeezed out her sponge and went back to work on my feathers.

'The oil company wants Stevens,' she said after a while. 'They need to expose his skimming and figure out what he's done with the money he made – because he made a lot of it in the 1980s before regulation. He doesn't care about anyone and he isn't afraid of anything. He has battalions of lawyers. They travel in sevens, nines – you never see just one. I keep waiting to get word that one of our agents can do something. It's so hard waiting for the right tweak to come down the pipeline.'

I said nothing. I still wasn't clear on what the pipeline was. I knew that the system worked roughly like this: angel gets tip from somewhere in the pipeline. The tip is like a mini-mission coordinated by the Resistance. Sometimes the tip is something morally neutral, like, 'Stall your car in the middle of such-and-such intersection at 10:26.' Other times it's like a Secret Santa: 'Buy a meal for that guy who tricks on Lambert Boulevard.' Other times it's just straight-up being human to someone else: 'That kid at that table over there needs some extra attention, find out what's going on.' The angel does the thing. It seems random, or maybe a tiny act of senseless kindness, but actually it's contrived. According to Marquita, each of these actions is possibly a minute tipping point that sets in motion a chain reaction to advance humanity.

I never could see it. The idea that this principle should work makes it sound like the universe is made of Swiss clockwork, not fickle electrons that might as well be leprechauns. The butterfly effect isn't real in the sense people think it is; chaos is chaotic, right? You can't manipulate it by flapping a particular butterfly on a particular day. The only way you could make the butterfly effect work, to interfere in a chain of events, would be to run against the grain of time. And that really *would* be resistance to entropy.

But the funny thing about entropy is that it loves order. Entropy loves order because more order burns everything down faster, and the universe is standing there like the ring of idiots that stands around a high-school brawl, yelling, 'Fight, fight, fight!' because all that metabolic heat means we all go down in flames just that much sooner.

Irony in my eye teeth, that we build high because it gives us farther to fall.

Marquita said: 'Accept it. We're all just servants, Pearl. We're all mugs.'

Mugs for *what*? That was what I kept wondering. No one pretended there was a god, not in any centralised or personal sense, anyway, so where was Filippe getting the insights as to who should take what action for *the greater good of what*? Remember, the greater good is a subjective business, yo. Marquita never wanted to talk about that. She took her work on faith, and when I failed to do the same she looked at me like she thought I had a fever.

'There are some people on the ground in this world who do great things, invisible things. But it isn't enough when it comes to what Pace Industries did in Kuè. We're up against too much greed and too much history. Something big is going to have to happen to change the patterns.'

'Do you think that something is Kisi?'

She just looked at me, all sadness in her face.

'I can't talk to you anymore,' she said. 'I told you everything I know. But it has to end now.'

How can I explain about Marquita? It'd be like explaining the sun. I remember when I first called the number on her business card. She took me back to her seedy apartment in Queens with its smudgy windows and sink full of dirty dishes. Jars of spices everywhere. She had a heating pad that she kept near the window for Tsubota, and she had what seemed like a forest of house plants. She had stacks of old paperback crime novels and all the furniture was covered with Mexican horse blankets and random pieces of dyed cotton. I can still smell the place.

She fed me and she lit incense and she took out a guitar that she'd covered with stickers, price tags and labels from all over the world. She told me she was addicted to travelling and then she played me songs she'd heard in different countries.

'I have perfect pitch,' she said. 'I remember everything I hear. So that gives us something in common.'

Then she held out her hand to me and I knew what would happen. It was simple. No discussion; no buildup. Just: us.

We started out in that scruffy apartment in Queens and now here we were in a swanky hotel in central Paris, and it was ending exactly the same way it began. Sudden and symmetrical and perfect, like some fucking Mozart chamber music.

She had to leave me now. It was simply the way of things.

I tried not to cry. My face scrunched up and I had to blow my nose in a piece of toilet paper. It came away sulphurous, stained with oil.

'Don't be like that,' she said.

I tried to laugh but a sob came out.

'I told you. I get attached.'

'And I told you. You're here to learn. You learned me now.'

She tapped her fingerprints to mine, so I could feel their faint grains and whorls. The abundance of her smile broke over me.

I wanted to kiss her but she was too fast for me.

'Au revoir,' she said, and left me standing in the traces of her perfume.

Me, I smelled of complimentary hotel soap. Also hell.

# Can't touch this with a barge pole

Your face is everywhere. On TV and newsboards. On people's flow.

You were blown off the plane, presumed dead. So that's good. But the story of the old man's disappearance means questions. The public loves a mystery.

Liam Forbes has arranged transport for you, and he has set up a meeting at the Balmoral Hotel but you don't go there because you're not a fool. You cut your dreadlocks in Gothenburg with a feeling of doom because you'd grown your hair the way you'd grown your spirit, and what was it for? Your beard is coming in; no one will recognise you, but you can't shake that hunted feeling.

You go to Liam's townhouse at 3 am, hoping to catch him unawares. No one is on the street at this hour, and darkness settles upon the rooftops and the gutter pipes.

Dogs bark. A youngish woman opens the door for you. The two of you have never met, but she knows your face.

'Hurry up and get in, Doctor!' She strains to hold the collars of two Dobermans. 'You shouldn't be here. Liam's not home.'

You step inside and wait while she locks the dogs somewhere else in the house. You can hear their nails clattering on the parquet floor. You have so very little choice in all of this. The other self is right there with you, he has locked in on you, he looks through your eyes.

She lets you into the library. It has a massive fireplace, heavy floor-to-ceiling curtains, a discreet monitor. She is calling Liam on the screen.

'You need to come here now,' your voice tells his image.

He fidgets. He's in a hotel waiting, but he's not in Scotland. Wherever he is, it's daylight. Did he think you wouldn't come here? Or were the dogs meant to protect the woman? She stands behind a Louis XIV armchair, blunt-nailed fingertips thrumming against the upholstery.

'Pace Industries is on to you,' Liam says. 'We can't do this now. They'll come in and take everything. They've been waiting for an opportunity like this.'

This is when you throw the other one out of your skin long enough to say:

'It's simple. I'm not going to prison. I want private transport to my own country, no questions. I want the bequest I was promised. I don't care what you do with the rest.'

Liam swings his head in a show of regret.

'I'm sorry, mate. I can't touch this with a barge pole. Too dangerous. There was no bloodletting in our original arrangement.'

'I made no arrangement with you.' Your legs shake with effort. The one inside you is getting angry. You have upstaged him. This gives you courage, but strangely you aren't really certain whether it's you or he who says: 'Don't you care what's inside *this*?'

Your arm hoists up the briefcase like a trial exhibit before a witness. If Liam recognises it, he doesn't let on.

'Just go, Dr Sorle,' he insists. 'I'll stay out of your way.'

You can feel the woman's agitation. Liam has abandoned her here, with you, and in their minds you are a murderer. He must know how angry you will be. Has he no concern for her well-being? Is she bait? Does she understand the position he's put her in?

You push past the presence in your throat, and with your own soul you say to her: 'What do you think is going to happen right now?'

Her pupils dilate.

'You can't be seen here,' she whispers. 'Please go. I'll erase the security footage. No one will know you were here.'

You can feel the other self gathering force.

'I have Mr Stevens,' your voice says, without you. 'As agreed. I am late, but inside the contract window. He sent you the codes; I saw him do it. He is here. There is no judgement call for you to make. I am delivering the briefcase and the scientists will have instructions for how to store it. Your part is only to release the funds and set this thing in motion.'

The woman edges away from you.

Liam says, 'My instructions were to set up the money and infrastructure for a low-profile scientific foundation called the Resistance. The Resistance has a mission to develop artificial intelligence with a global humanitarian outlook. The human resources groundwork has been done by others, but I have done the finance side. I set up an intricate system of funding that relies on offshore economies and that is not linked to any one government, as Mr Stevens requested. I have, of course, minimised tax impacts as well. I have received instructions from Mr Stevens to set this in motion, but hours later the news broke of the shooting in his house. I will not be party to it.'

Your armpits are damp and pent aggression coils in your legs. You try to keep it back but the other self is too strong; he rolls over you like weather.

'You're a fool and a coward,' he seethes. 'You were told it would be messy. You were told. What do you think the reason for all the codes and secret handshakes was? You know I am doing precisely as Mr Stevens wished.'

Liam is shaking his head. 'I think you should leave my house now. There's nothing more to say.'

Bitter bitter laughter.

'I see now. It's simple. Pace has got to you.'

Liam sighed.

'Stevens was a deluded old man, deranged by his illness. He believed he had already been marked to live forever and some kind of time-travelling ship was coming to take him away to the future. If I'm a fool and a coward, then you're a con artist. But good luck to you. I haven't got anything to do with the will. If you want your bequest you have to talk to his executor. There will just be the small matter of proving you didn't kill Stevens yourself.'

'If he was a deluded old man then you won't mind if I open the briefcase I took from his house.'

'Actually, I think I do mind. I'm going to ask you again to leave.'

Your sure hands set the briefcase on the floor and in your voice he says, 'Watch this.'

He puts your hands on the latches. There is a struggle over control of your hands and eyes and spine. Just as before, you lose.

It's the story of your life, losing.

You lose, and you see none of what happens then, and you wake up much later in the mist among the stones with your head pillowed on the briefcase and bloodstains on your clothes.

# The cupboard under the stairs

Maybe I was just in a bad mood, but I took an immediate dislike to Edinburgh. The light was weak, spineless. Half-hearted. The sun never seemed to make it all the way over the top of the buildings. It sulked on the lowdown like a rumour. Light lay like melted butter in the faded turquoise sky, sun-fingers picking out ironwork shadows on the pavements of Heriot Row where Liam Forbes lived. The vibe was too stiff, too deserted – not my thing. One of the houses had a brass plate discreetly noting that Robert Louis Stevenson lived here as a boy. Played in the neighbourhood gardens, apparently, having adventures and maybe dreaming up Long John Silver. Now the gardens were locked all day and when I looked through the bars the sodden, mushroomy lawns were empty except for birds.

What the hell was I doing here? I missed the sky. I missed the airports and the clash of accents, the smell of spices, the robes and the duty-free and people hugging each other on arrival from faraway. I missed the nightclubs and the music and the pheromone smells, the packed humanity of my former life. Already I felt I was going to shrivel up like old fruit.

I walked up to the imposing black door of 44 Heriot Row and knocked. There was an immediate and powerful sound of dogs, barking. Big dogs, barking like the horns on trucks, scrambling towards me with a cracking of claws on tile. Enough noise for at least seventeen of them. I stood quaking on the doorstep. The street was deserted. We were five minutes' walk from the biggest shopping street in Edinburgh, but nothing moved on the cobbles of Heriot Row and the nearest pedestrian was a speck.

Two large bodies struck the door: *Thump. Thump.* Scrabble of claws. The brass mail slot wobbled and flipped back, and I glimpsed the tip of a black snout. The barking stopped. There were only two of them; they started whining with hopeful sincerity.

Nothing new about that. Animals love me. What can I say? I'm lovable.

I waited. No one came.

'OK, guys,' I said through the door. 'See you later. Looks like I gotta come back when somebody's home.'

As I started to turn away, the door snicked open. I heard panting. A dark nose came around the corner and a moment later a full-grown Doberman had worked the door open and with a wriggle, burst out. He leaped at me. His paws hit my chest and I staggered backward and down one step while he licked my face joyously. I shoved him off, and he bounced off the other dog, an almost-as-large female. I'd shoved him hard enough to take him almost off his feet, but both dogs seemed to regard this as me initiating some kind of game, because they rebounded at me, wagging and panting and bouncing. Meanwhile, the door was swinging wide open but there was no human in sight.

I shoved one dog away with each hand and stepped into the gloom.

'Hello? Anybody home?'

The house was spectacular. The entrance hall had chessboard tiles and a dripping-crystal chandelier and a wide staircase that swept up into darkness. No lights were on, and the rear hallway was shadowy and silent. There were no shoes, no coat racks, just a small ornamental table with a mirror over it. The place was a show home. The dogs escorted me in, and the female actually closed the door behind us with her long snout.

'So it's like that, guys?' I said to them, patting their heads absentmindedly as we went from room to room, looking for a person. No one was here. 'You know how to open doors? Thanks for letting me in. Now what should we do?'

That's when I saw the blood smeared across a white chessboard tile.

It wasn't that big of a deal. Truly, I've seen nosebleeds that were worse. But my hackles were up and my ears went on high alert. I couldn't sense anyone's pain; couldn't sense any person in the house at all. There were smears of blood and little puddles of a foamy, translucent fluid on the tiles of the hall, and I followed them into the house until I could see through an open doorway into the big reception room that overlooked Heriot Row. The place had been ransacked. Cushions were off the sofa, papers were on the floor, the drawers of an exquisite cherry-wood desk were sticking out like crooked tongues. The firewood bin was tipped over and a bowl of cut flowers had spilled on a Turkish rug.

I looked the room over for several seconds before I noticed the bloody remains of a strange animal on the hearth. I squinted at the gutted mass of its body from several angles and finally decided it was an exceptionally large frog. My opinion of its species was based mostly on its legs; the rest of the body was mangled. It was blue, and its blood was sort of purplish. Organs were scattered on the stone. The blood smears seemed to originate here; blood had been tracked across the room and into the hallway.

I didn't want to think what I was going to find if I went any further. I thought about calling emergency services and then remembered that I am emergency services, being an angel and all.

One of the dogs was nudging me with his muzzle, whining.

'What is it?' I said. 'Does somebody need help? What are you trying to show me?'

The dog took off down the hall, claws slithering on the smooth tile. Avoiding the wet patches, I followed her to a narrow door in the right-hand wall, the kind that led to a cupboard under the stairs. It was open a crack.

When I opened the door and tugged on the light string I fully expected to find a dead body. Instead, I found a sick cat. It was huddled on the stone floor of the pantry, wedged between a big bag of kitty litter and a bigger bag of dog chow. It had vomited on the floor and over a dustpan and brush, and when I came in it tried to move, but there was something wrong with its hind legs so that it could only drag them. It was trembling, eyes black with fear, breathing harsh breaths with a noise out of proportion to its size. I could smell its urine.

I stepped away, putting my hand on the dog's head as I returned to the corridor. I kept walking back through the deep house, passing an empty dining room with locked French doors looking out on a patio. At the very rear of the house there were spiral stairs going down. I found a big kitchen done out in gold and white and inhabited by two more cats. These were perfectly healthy, sitting on the sill above the sink chattering at the birds in a window feeder on the other side of the glass.

There was a beautiful green leather bag on the kitchen counter. Keys. Wallet. Phone.

I went out the back door and called into the garden.

'Hello? Is anybody there?'

It wasn't a big garden. Everything was done out in stone and pebbles. There were a few potted plants in what might have been an attempt at minimalism; or, judging by the way the dogs were now careering around the space peeing and squatting, maybe plants couldn't survive with these guys around.

At the back of the garden was a small, arched door. It was shut but unlocked, and led into a narrow alley that led in turn to Gloucester Lane. I found the key and locked it. Then I went back upstairs. I searched the whole house but found nobody. I was keyed up. At least there was no corpse, which was what I'd been expecting since the moment I saw the blood. But how much relief could I feel at the thought that Liam and his girl-friend had been abducted?

I couldn't call Marquita. She'd explicitly told me not to contact her. So I went to the phone in the green bag and found

Liam's number. It rang several times before a muffled-sounding man picked up.

'What now?' he grunted.

'Liam Forbes? This is Pearl, I'm a friend of Bethany.'

'It's not a good time. What do you want?'

'I'm really sorry about this, but it's urgent. I came to see Bethany and the front door was open, the dogs are here but she's gone.'

'Are you serious? She probably just stepped out.'

'No, listen. Her bag is here. Her keys. Her phone. It looks like somebody's been in the house. There are drawers open, stuff thrown around. I'm concerned for her. I think I should call the police.'

'What? No, wait.' There was a noise of shuffling and movement, then a silence. He came back on sounding sharper. 'Look... sorry, what did you say your name was?'

'Pearl.'

'Pearl. There must be some mistake. We have an alarm system. We have two big dogs.'

'I know, they're with me now.'

'But how did you get in?'

'The door was shut. I knocked on it and the dogs came—'

'And they let you in, right? Leonard knows how to do that. But if the alarm system wasn't set, then that means Beth probably just went down the road to get some milk or something and she'll be right back.'

I didn't know what to make of it. I know I'm not human, but if somebody called me to tell me my house had been ransacked and my girlfriend was missing, I think I'd be a little more upset. There was something in his tone that seemed to suggest I was wasting his time, spoiling his beauty sleep...

'OK,' I said. 'You don't want me to call the police. You sure?'

'How do you know Bethany?' he said.

'What?'

'I don't remember her mentioning a Pearl. I take it you're American?'

I winced. My default Long Island accent. I should have modified it.

'I'm here on vacation and she said to look her up. Look, I think the best thing is for me to wait a little bit, and if she's not back soon I'll call the police and they can come around and see what's gone on here. Oh, and the cat is sick. Throwing up blood and stuff like that.'

There was an audible groan.

'Can you just not call the police, all right? I don't want Bethany's parents to get involved. I don't know how close you two are, but she's a lively girl and she can be a little ... unstable.'

Why didn't I believe that?

'She may have just thrown a wobbly about something,' he went on. 'She's been known to go off on the odd adventure. And if the house is a mess, it's always possible the dogs have done it. Let's just take this one step at a time.'

'Sure,' I said. His fear was strong enough to haunt his voice over the crackling line. It was a specific kind of fear. Fear for his girlfriend's safety? Mmmm ... no. Fear of losing control. 'When are you going to be back?'

'Me? I'm in Singapore, I can't get away.'

So if Dr Sorle had been hoping to meet Liam Forbes, he was going to be disappointed. Had he been disappointed enough to abduct Bethany?

'What about the cat? Looks pretty sick.'

'Oh, there's a card for the vet somewhere in the kitchen. Best thing is probably to get them to come collect it.'

*It.* How nice.

'Do vets make house calls?'

'I don't know. Bethany has an account with them. They know us. Thanks, and sorry you've got caught up in all this. I owe you one.'

The line cut.

'I don't believe this.'

I stood in the kitchen with its softly ticking clock, the dogs at my feet gazing up at me hopefully.

The lilty-voiced woman who answered the vet's phone said she couldn't come out until after office hours. I found myself promising to bring the cat to her surgery.

Being at death's door didn't seem to have an effect on the cat's refusal-to-get-in-carrier-fu. Even though it was partially paralyzed, it managed to resist all my efforts to cram it into the plastic cage I found in the pantry. I ended up returning to the ransacked front room and fetching a pair of heavy-duty fire gloves to protect my hands. The dogs wagged and barked as I shoved the cat in, both of us hissing. I was sweating by the time I got the cage closed.

I really don't know what people think is so charming about these creatures.

# Teacake

Bethany's keys led me to a Land Rover parked neatly outside. In the glove compartment there were receipts from shops on Princes Street, a broken 3D projector, and a cherry chapstick. Also a stash of Maltesers. The dogs both tried to claim the passenger seat, which must be a normal occurrence judging from the state of the tartan throw Bethany had placed there. I banished them both behind the metal grille in the back. The cat was still retching intermittently, but the struggle to get in the carrier seemed to have worn it out and it lay on its side, breathing fast and shallow.

I started the car. I don't technically have a licence. I never needed one, flying from city to city. I had to pull on my archives to get the subroutines I needed for operating the vehicle, and even so I found the cobbles disconcerting. I plugged the vet's address into the satnav and off we went through the back streets of Edinburgh's New Town. It didn't look very new to me. They could have filmed *Amadeus* here. A lingering sense of sadness – maybe even grief – oozed from window frames and stone, and at the same time a feeling of resistance. *Stalwart*. That was how the buildings felt. The streets were narrow and sometimes I passed other cars with only inches to spare between our wing mirrors. I could feel the whites of my eyes popping out, but the other drivers waved cheerily like, no biggie.

We ended up going downhill into a scruffier, damp neighbourhood with a school, a Morrison's and a line of shops surrounded by terraced houses. On one side of the vet's was an off-licence and on the other an off-track betting outlet, a launderette and a kebab shop. The dogs rushed in ahead of me. I opened my mouth to apologise for them but found myself in an empty reception area sporting posters advertising wormers, diet cat food and flea remedies.

The places I find myself.

'Hello, what have we here?'

The ethereal voice floated ahead of the woman. She was stout and sixty-something, with a ruddy face, curly grey hair and very small purple-framed glasses. Her voice was high and clear and its sound made something shine inside me.

'I'm Alison. I gather Teacake's poorly.' Her accent made 'poorly' made sound like Pearly, and I was thrown for a second because I thought she'd said my name, and I hadn't told her my name.

'Uh . . . I guess.' I found myself tongue-tied. I don't know what it was about her. 'I came to see Bethany, but she'd gone out and I found the cat like this. He's been trying to be sick but nothing comes up, and . . . Well, you can see how he's breathing.'

She had taken the carrier and now she went back to an examination room. Teacake was unconscious now; she poured him out of the carrier like syrup. She examined him with a thoughtful, abstracted expression on her face. She asked what he had eaten, how long he'd been like this, and I had to explain that I had no way of getting in touch with Bethany to find out more.

'Lucky for him you came when you did. I'll just pop him back in his carrier and take an X-ray. Be right back.'

And she was off. I stood looking at the sweaty marks Teacake's paws had made on the formica table, thinking about Liam. There was something fishy about him, but it was hard to tell what that was over the phone. I can read people much better when I'm in physical proximity to them. Anyway, I didn't like him and I didn't think he liked me, either. How was I going to get him to open up to me about Pace Industries and Dr Sorle when I couldn't even get him to show the slightest concern for his missing girlfriend?

No two ways; I should call the police.

If I did, I could forget about Liam ever talking to me about anything.

'Well, then,' said Alison, returning after what seemed like forever. 'There's no gut impaction, no signs of injury internally or externally, so the most likely explanation is poison. His symptoms are symptomatic of having eaten, say a poisoned mouse or rat for example. You could check his environment and try to find out what he's gotten into. I can't give an antidote if I don't know the poison. For now I've pumped his stomach and put an IV in, and we'll look after him and hope he recovers. I'm afraid it could go either way.'

'Oh, my...' I said. I never say *oh my god* because as yet I've had no contact with this so-called god. In my mind the phrase sounds like 'Oh my (blank)' but people just hear 'Oh, *my*.'

'You could try reaching Bethany again.'

'That may not be possible,' I said uncomfortably. The vet folded her arms and fixed me with a canny gaze.

'Don't tell me she's finally left him.'

I didn't say anything. She picked up the idea and ran with it, though.

'I always thought it was only a matter of time. She was only with him for his money. But I can't understand her leaving and not taking her animals. She really does love them.'

I fumbled for a response. I am the world's worst liar. A three-year-old can lie better than I can. But Alison was already trundling out into the reception area, where I found both dogs chewing on giant rawhide bones that had been placed on high shelves for sale. Various pieces of furniture were overturned and a poster displaying the life cycle of the heartworm was hanging half off the wall. I put everything back the way it should be and then a girl walked in carrying a rabbit in a basket. Both dogs lunged toward her, wagging, but I checked them. Nobody drags me.

The screen in the waiting room was filled by Dr Sorle's face and my own.

AIRLINE TRAGEDY UNDER INVESTIGATION

'What?' said Alison as I froze to the spot. 'What's the matter?'

'Nothing.'

I moved so that I blocked the screen.

'Call me if you find what he got into. I'll keep a close eye on him and ring you around ten tonight, after my last check.'

I could feel this deeply practical woman staring at me openly after I turned my back. I tried not to be paranoid about that. People stare at me all the time. I'm six inches taller and substantially broader than most women in these parts. I have the shoulders of a rugby star and my skin is dark brown. People stare even when I'm not on the news feeds.

She watched me manoeuvre both dogs out on to the sidewalk. This involved a lot of slobber and shed fur. I stood on the pavement in the gathering gloom, breathing deep the cool, yeasty air.

That's when I saw Two Phones in front of the estate agent's across the street, pretending to look at 'To Let' ads.

# Colonel Mustard in the library

'There goes the neighbourhood,' I said loudly. Two Phones was pretending not to notice me, so I walked straight up to him. The dogs felt my mood. The male gave a whuffling bark as we approached.

Two Phones didn't know what to do. He looked right, he looked left. At a loss, he brought one of his phones to the ear that didn't already have a device in it.

'How's it going, Jeff?' I said.

'Ms Jones,' he said. He squared up to me, contracting his delts so that he puffed up the way animals do when they're trying to establish dominance. This was a mistake. I'm bigger. Plus the dogs.

'If you have Bethany Collins then let her go,' I said.

He bent and ruffled Leonard's ears. 'Hey, Leonard, how you doing, buddy?' he said.

'No, I haven't seen Bethany today,' he said. His eyes gleamed behind little crinkles at the corners. There was a faint pink line on his neck. High blood pressure. 'I was just speaking with Liam, actually. Are you concerned about her?'

The way he said it was odd. He had such a rigid head, I couldn't get inside his emotional patterns.

'It's very clear to me, Ms Jones, that you are working in concert with Dr Sorle, who is a murderer and, in all probability, a fraudster. So let me come clean with you. I work for the oil company that Mr Stevens skimmed for decades. It's my job to find the money he stole and recover it for my company. As soon as my team found out about the home invasion in Amagansett and the subsequent event over Iceland, we started checking biometric data on passengers and crew. So imagine my surprise when you – supposedly dead – tried to take out cash in Viana do Castelo, where I just happened to be at the time because I was on my way to an offshore rig.'

'This is supposed to explain why you were creeping around me?'

He laughed. 'Creeping? That's not a very nice word.'

'You didn't talk to me openly. You sneaked around spying on me. And now you're following me.'

'No, you're following me. I let you go because we had another lead on the whereabouts of Dr Sorle. That's how I got here to Edinburgh *ahead of you*, so, sort of by definition, I can't be following you. I'm not really interested in you unless you do something to make me interested. Right now, you're making me interested. If you annoy me, I will take appropriate action.'

Up in HD my feathers stood up a little. An auto-shop smell crept up from my own skin, like I was oozing metal and grease.

'If you had such a great lead on Dr Sorle's whereabouts, what are you doing following me?' I said. 'You know what I think? I think you poisoned Bethany. Maybe you're trying to hold something over Liam, something to do with this money.'

He laughed, then rubbed Leonard up and down the ribs so that the dog's skin moved into wrinkles over his muscles. Leonard licked his face in return. I still couldn't get any read off what he was really thinking or feeling. This is frustrating for someone like me.

'I don't think you heard what I said. If you get in my way, I will take appropriate action.'

By this point I'd realised I would make a terrible TV detective, but I was already in the conversation up to my elbows. I'd been relying on my ability to sense what is going on in people's emotions and to pick up fragments of their visual imagery in order to maintain control of an interaction. I couldn't do that with Two Phones. He had probably been trained to control his reactions, and he seemed to know I was bluffing my way through this. I felt my confidence slipping.

He stood up and dusted off his chinos. Both of his phones were vibrating.

'Don't hurt her,' I whispered.

He shook his head.

'You're being ridiculous,' he said. 'Go back to your car.'

I went back to Bethany's car with the dogs, and I drove back to the house with my eye on the rear-view mirror, but there was no sign of him. While I was driving I got a call from Liam.

'Listen, I hate to ask, but is there any chance you could look after the dogs just until tomorrow? Beth had to go out of town. Our usual dog-walker can take over, so they just need to be let out tonight and so forth.'

'She had to go out of town.' I loaded my voice with irony.

'Yes. Can you? If not, I'll start making calls.'

'No, it's fine,' I said. Now I was starting to think they were in it together, Liam and Two Phones.

I had shut the library door so the dogs wouldn't molest the corpse of the giant frog; now I put on gloves and transferred the whole thing to a series of plastic bags. I put it in the freezer.

OK. So it's like a game of Clue. A locked room mystery. I needed the security footage. All I knew was that Bethany had been here and had left her bag behind. The door had been left open, or someone had a key. Someone had come in. There had been a struggle, or the appearance of one. A giant frog had been introduced to the scene (unless it was already there – but no sign of a giant frog habitat or giant frog kibble in the larder). Teacake the cat had been poisoned.

I considered what I knew about poisonous frogs. Most contemporary species came from South America and all were tiny. The only record I could find of a giant frog referred to a prehistoric example.

OK. Let's just leave that there, shall we? Because reasons.

Then I started checking on Stevens and Dr Sorle. Stevens had worked for the oil company beginning in the 1970s as an engineer and rising to senior management. During this time he had spent significant time in Cameroon and Ghana as well as Kuè, where he was director of operations, and he'd later had executive roles in Aberdeen and Rio. He had retired after the turn of the century, founding a financial services company that catered to international executives like himself. He had been investigated four times by the IRS on tax evasion but nothing ever stuck. He had four ex-wives and ten children scattered across continents. Two of the children were involved in his business. He was considered a philanthropist and had given large sums of money to research on life-extension technologies.

'This is ridiculous,' I said to the fish tank in the kitchen. I fed the fish and then I found my way around the password in the security system.

There were multiple cameras, and it took me a while to find the beginning of the incident. The last shots of Liam in the house had been taken the day the news broke about the disappearance of Austen Stevens. He was carrying a garment bag and a laptop case when he left. It was clear that Bethany had been here alone with the animals just this morning. Only hours before I'd arrived.

I watched Bethany let Kisi Sorle in. He was carrying the briefcase in both hands. I paused the recording more than once when it seemed to me that I saw the briefcase jerk in his grasp, as though something inside it were trying to get out.

I remembered very well how it had torn through the fuselage of the plane like butter.

They moved into the front reception room. She switched on large screen in the corner. Dr Sorle addressed himself to it.

I heard the words that were said. 'I am delivering the briefcase and the scientists will have instructions for how to store it. Your part is only to release the funds and set this thing in motion.'

He opened the briefcase. There was a roar, a flare of light that swamped the image, and the camera cut.

I cross-referenced with other recorders in the house. Oddly, the camera from the rear hall didn't pick up any flashes even though it was in a position to catch bright light emerging from the open doors of the library. So the flare of light must have been a fault inside the camera itself.

Bethany was seen running out of the room and up the stairs. The bedroom camera showed her fending off the dogs that had been locked in the room. She was going through her closets and drawers, searching for something. Downstairs there was a noisy crash, as of furniture falling over. A glass-mounted painting in the hallway was seen to move as the reflection of light in the glass stirred. A man's voice shouted, 'No! Not here!' Then a series of bangs and thumps.

Locking the dogs in her bedroom, Bethany came back down, carrying a small bag. She edged around the closed doors of the library and hurried into the kitchen, cringing as a hair-raising sort of animal squeal came from the library. She rummaged in her handbag, then dropped it on the kitchen counter and ran outside barefoot.

The camera lost her halfway down the garden.

As Bethany reached the kitchen, Dr Sorle came staggering out of the library, winded. He was bent over, dragging the briefcase as though it were a loaded sledge. He hauled it through the kitchen and down the garden. Out of frame.

There were no cameras at the back of the garden.

I could see the garden from here in the kitchen. I switched on the security lights. There was the door I had closed and then locked when I'd first come.

I went back outside with a torch. I looked around the door at the back of the garden for any evidence. I listened with all my senses. There was just no way to know what had happened.

The dogs had followed me and they whined to get out of the back of the garden, so I got their leads and brought them with me. The alley was empty except for some recycling bins. I walked the dogs around the block and let them into the locked gardens across the street. The gardens were empty and silent, and I was wondering how long I could keep up the dog-sitter charade when I noticed something.

There was a radio signal pulsing from the iron fence around the gardens. I prowled through the bushes, looking for the source. Finally I spotted a tiny camera attached to a holly branch.

'Amateur,' I muttered. Staying out of its line of sight, I reached up and crushed it between my fingers like a roach. Then I went back inside and heated up some instant soup. I closed the shutters and turned off most of the lights. The dogs fell asleep.

Two hours later I was still thinking. I prowled the house looking out of windows and feeling paranoid. When I knelt at the mail slot on the front door, I could detect a new pulse coming from the same location as before.

'Come on, guys,' I called to the dogs. 'Walkies. Bring your noses.'

# Notes on upgrades

Archives retained in older versions will be automatically compressed for use in upgrades. In default mode waveforms must be individually selected for deletion/editing.

To change from default mode and enable automatic deletion of older generation archives see Section 4.5a.

Upgraded versions of the application can be set to run as older versions under selected conditions. Cautions must be observed due to the risk of waveform **Corruption** and in rare cases **Leakage**. Symptoms of **Leakage** include but are not limited to sonic emission, weather disturbance, unintentional cognitive synchrony and disruptive interference with similar waveforms. When waveforms share 98% or more similarity **Leakage** can escalate to **Resonance** or **Identification**.

These conditions are usually self-correcting.

Risk of the above syndromes is very low for pristine samples collected and stored without editing. Edited waveforms are thought to be prone to the phenomenological protrusion **Identification**, which can result in loss of administrative control of the unit. The percentage of material altered through editing is roughly proportional to the risk of **Resonance** and **Identification**.

To assist in evaluating these risks a table of constants of proportionality under a range of environmental conditions is provided in Appendix F.

# A prosaic tearing sound

I took the dogs to the place where the camera had been installed. 'Do you smell Jeff?' I said to them as they sniffed all around and took turns peeing on whatever they smelled. 'Go find him.'

They dragged me across the garden and out the other side, their enthusiasm compromising my rotor cuff until I gave up and broke into a jog. They were on a scent.

I called the vet on her mobile.

'What do you know about poisonous frogs?' I said. 'Do you have an antidote for that kind of thing?'

'No,' she said sharply. 'Do you think Teacake ate a poisonous frog?'

'Maybe.'

'What kind? Depending on what it was I could try an anaesthetic...'

'Giant. Prehistoric,' I said, then realised I'd been an idiot for saying that, hung up in embarrassment, and turned off the phone. As if that would fix things.

The sun was already gone. As we crossed over the tram line at Princes Street Gardens a mossy perfume of atomised rain drifted more or less down. Eventually I realised we were making for Holyrood Park and the rocky uprising of Arthur's Seat that owned the town. The green and grey wave of rock surged towards the sky and reminded me how very old the world is, for real. As we came closer I could smell the magma. Could feel the emptiness down below where the chamber was, where the heat of the earth turning itself inside out must have boiled up to give rise to this landscape. If I quietened my mind I could hear the bass drone that signified a great energy that once was.

It's the *was* that gets to me. Because it's all gone now, and yet somehow I can't accept that. My *now* seems to enclose other *nows* in a way that I don't think Eckhardt Toll would approve of.

I spotted Two Phones ahead. He set off up the main path. There were other walkers and dogs, some with torches, and in the ground light I could see veils of mist scrolling down from Arthur's Seat. The scene was spooky, but it never occurred to me to feel scared. People don't frighten me in the slightest. Marquita was always telling me off for it.

'You are not Batfink,' she'd say. 'Bullets *can* harm you. And your wings are not a shield of steel, OK? They're more like a trans-dimensional extrasensory resource, as I understand it.'

I never paid attention to her. Humans didn't seem capable of aggression toward me. Before I got the airline job I had worked in a prison for a while and I had worked cleaning buses at the Port Authority, and I had done the work of the Resistance there, too. I had cleaned up people's puke and I had given them a helping hand and a boost of courage, and I had noticed their humanity even when they couldn't see it anymore themselves. Nobody ever tried to hurt me. I'd like to think it's because the ones who are the most dangerous to themselves and others are also the ones who need me most.

Then again, when you are my size it's hard to take physical threats from humans seriously. Even with my wings furled and my power body folded, I'm a commanding presence. That was one reason why it was tough to follow Two Phones without making it obvious I was following him. I let him get too far ahead, and then I lost sight of him in the darkness. The dogs had stopped straining at their leads.

'This is not going well, guys,' I said to the dogs. 'We didn't lose him, did we? Did we?'

I let them off their leads and they bounded off through the rough grass purposefully, but in different directions. Great.

I stayed on the path, which led through a sort of valley and then came out on the side of the hill. It wound around the spire of Arthur's Seat, overlooking different parts of the city as it made its rising circuit. I found myself climbing the south-west side with the university campus and its observatory visible in the distance, breathing deep as my legs felt the ascent. I looked at the ground before my feet, until something told me to look up.

Dr Sorle was standing on a rocky outcropping above me. A few pieces of scree tumbled down and bounced at my feet. Wind thumped into my chest like it wanted to play.

Two Phones was on the path between me and Dr Sorle, and because of the way distant yellow streetlights blurred the damp air he was almost invisible in deep shadow. I shrank into myself, edging sideways and out of the doctor's line of sight. I watched him carefully when he moved. He was not limping even a little.

'I'm not coming in,' he said in a rumbling, musical voice. 'Turn around and go home, and don't send anyone else. That will only make it worse.'

'If the briefcase contains everything you say, we won't need you,' Two Phones said.

'The briefcase contains everything you could possibly need to convict Austen Stevens,' Kisi Sorle said. 'It contains all that and more.'

'We'll establish that ourselves. If you're telling the truth then we're in business. If you're not—'

'See for yourself,' the smaller man said quietly, lifting up the briefcase. It swung from his hand, and I thought what a risk he was taking. I remembered how it had torn open the hull of the plane; I half-expected it to fly up in the clouds or plummet into the earth.

Two Phones said, 'Put it down on the rocks, just there.'

It was hard to see the details of this because of the light and the angle of the rocks that were above Two Phones and me. I had the impression that Kisi stooped and I could see his heat rising from the general area, even though I couldn't see him. He must have been bent over for several seconds.

'Now open it and step away,' commanded Two Phones.

This was too easy. I waited for the man with the briefcase

to make some sudden move, but he was no longer visible. Two Phones didn't even seem to be armed. He stood on the path with his weight on one hip so that he looked almost casual, but I could see one hand by his side, trembling. 'Come and get it,' Kisi Sorle called. Two Phones shifted his weight from foot to foot. One of his phones rang and he killed it. Then he set off up the rocks. He looked awkward in his chinos and his too-tight polo shirt, and he seemed reluctant to put his hands down to steady himself. He moved as if he were used to climbing stair machines, not real hills.

He got to the top.

The heat profile of the area around Kisi Sorle abruptly grew bigger. I felt the briefcase open as if it were my own throat, and for an instant I saw and heard and felt and understood certain things very clearly—

—for one moment like a suspended droplet I got a postcard from home and I remembered my own origin in a vibrantly dense flash of information—

And then it was gone and I had no time to think about what I'd glimpsed. No time at all, because the rocks around the place where Kisi Sorle had been stretched their boundaries and became very large and entirely different. I saw teeth. Heat blossomed out of the stone as the clouds above were blotted out by the near wing of the qzetzlcoatlus. Great darkness, smelling of metal. I saw one long, silvery eye before Two Phones was seized in jaws that might have been made of steel and they might have been made of efreeti smoke. Anybody's call.

There weren't any screams. Only a prosaic tearing sound.

# Lemme see you walk

I was tripping over myself to get away – backward, side on, you name it. I heard barking. Below, both dogs came into view as though unglued from the background darkness. They converged on me and I pushed their heads down as they tried to get up in my face and sniff me. In silence the pterosaur had melted down to become a small inanimate thing, indistinguishable from rock and shadow, but I could feel a tugging sensation on my skin that made me... Well, *uneasy* just isn't the word.

*You'll be next, Pearl*, I thought. I was too angry to fly. Damn Filippe for not believing me. A man was dead and a quetzlcoatlus was roosting smack in the middle of a city and I'd been left to cope on my own.

I looked up at the crags. Rain fell in my eyes. I started climbing.

With the dogs surging either side of me I pulled myself over boulders, scrambling across patches of grass, up into the darkness and the wet. I found one of Two Phones' phones lying on a tussock. It still worked. I slipped it into my pocket and opened my senses. I could feel movement inside the old granite that had been heaved up from our mother's breast to lie now in moonlight like spilt milk. He was hiding in stone. Dr Sorle, or the quetzlcoatlus, or both.

'Where are you, Dr Sorle?' My voice came out in gasps. 'Come out. I want to talk to you.'

Nothing. Not even a heat signature. Rain began to fall in earnest, and my fingers went numb and failed to grip the rock. I stood up in a patch of long grass surrounded by boulders, and that's when I saw movement. A hot blur of a man, sliding off to the left.

I threw myself forward and tackled. He gave a harsh scream,

and I winced at the thought I'd attacked an innocent dog-walker. We hit the ground; then his lithe body twisted beneath me and he threw me off. Dr Sorle dragged himself away from me and put his back to a tall rock, holding the briefcase behind him like a child trying to hide a box of cookies. His voice cracked as he said, 'I am not your enemy.'

The dogs had arrived from off to my right. They charged him and he shrank back, now holding the briefcase above his head. It must have been heavy from the way his arms were shaking from the effort of it – or was he afraid of the dogs? The white apparition of my own breath rose up before my eyes and blew west.

*What was in that freaking briefcase?* He obviously thought I knew.

'I want Bethany back. Immediately.' I sounded so confident, but already I was considering the likelihood that Bethany had already met the same end as Two Phones. I mean, Jeff. I realised I didn't even know Jeff's last name, nor the names of his family who would now never know what ending he had come to.

Dr Sorle was looking at me with . . . I don't even know what it was. A composure bordering on serenity. In this gloomy old place he looked like a monk of some undiscovered religion.

Not that I was fooled. I didn't take him at face value, because he was not as he seemed. And the briefcase, rain-smeared and scuffed with its locks safely shut, it was not a briefcase. It was a piece of my essence.

'There are two of you,' I said. I was remembering Marquita's words to me in the hotel room, and an ache for her absence sprang up in my body. 'I need to know which one you are. Lemme see you walk.'

I called the dogs to me and he took a few steps, straining under the weight of the briefcase. There was a slight drag to one leg.

I sighed. Dr Sorle.

'Let's just put the briefcase down and talk,' I said.

He lowered the briefcase until it rested on the ground. Then he set it flat on the wet grass and sat down on it. His trouser leg rode up in this position, exposing a diamond-patterned sock. So much for being dangerous.

'I'm sitting on it because I am afraid of what may come out of it,' he told me, misinterpreting the line of my gaze. 'When you threw me out of the plane, for example. And just now.'

I stopped breathing. There was a ringing in my ears.

'Tell me what you remember about the plane,' I said softly.

'You went berserk.' His voice cracked. 'You took it from me and swung it right through the ceiling.'

'I know that part. What then?'

'I was sucked out of the plane. I fell. The case came open. It's been open before, at Austen Stevens' home. But I didn't open it that time.'

'Who did?'

'The other one. It is as you say. He can come into my body and control me.'

My first thought was the Resistance.

'How. How does he control you?'

In an instant his eyes became like blades.

'He . . . he . . . he fills me up from inside. When it first happened I lost consciousness. Now I can sometimes remain present. The things he does are ugly.'

I could taste the bitterness on his tongue. Too close; I pulled back. That's not how the Resistance operates. When the Resistance guides a person, it's just a hunch or a small impulse. Always towards kindness. No possession and definitely no kung fu whatsover.

'Go on,' I said. 'The case came open as we were falling. You know that I came down after you, right? I was trying to catch you.'

'I saw you pass me. The case was flapping open and I thought . . .'

'You thought?'

'I thought, man, if I am dying then I may as well try and get inside. To where they went. Because it can't be any worse than hitting the ocean at terminal velocity.'

'That makes sense,' I said. I just wanted him to continue.

'So I grabbed it with both hands and I put my head inside and then I seemed to turn over somehow.'

He stopped.

'Don't stop. What then?'

'Can't say. When I regained consciousness I was hundreds of miles away. And wanted by the police internationally. I had to cut my hair. I had to hide.'

He was on the verge of tears.

'Tell me the whole thing,' I said. 'I know you were educated on a Pace scholarship. But why did you go to work for Austen Stevens last year? You're an orthopaedic surgeon. He had cancer. What was the point?'

'About Pace. People think I was bought but this is untrue. I took the offering but I did not forgive. I thought about what to do with the opportunity. I went into orthopaedics, maybe because of the surgeons who put me back together after the land mine. Ultimately I wanted to go back to Kuè, maybe to my own family on the river, or maybe to Imo where my foster mother lived. I wanted to practise medicine there. But then I met Ayeisha and her roots are in America. So we settled there.

'In my mind it was only temporary. I spent many years building my career and my reputation, sending money back, bringing my family over for education. I became my own man – more than my own man, because I was with Ayeisha and we were blessed with two daughters whom I love beyond imagining. With them I was as close to happy as I have ever been.' He paused, and the pause lasted long enough to load a cannon.

'And then he contacted me.'

I knew who 'he' must be, but I had to hear myself say it. 'Austen Stevens.'

Dr Sorle nodded.

'He offered a large salary – the sort of money that naturally makes anyone suspicious. He said he had come to regret his actions in the delta. Time had shown him he was wrong. He showed me his medical reports; his illness was terminal. He showed me his will. There was a substantial bequest intended to make amends in my community – to be administered by me because he trusted me not to steal it or lose it in speculation. It was more than Pace ever paid.

'I already knew he had resources because in my youth Pace Industries used to bring me back in holidays to work security on the ships. Stevens had been skimming for years; he had clever people to help him with his money and he'd created a web of shadow assets that gave him considerable power, not just financially but politically – if the two can ever be separate.

'There was only one condition. I had to take care of him until his death.'

Dr Sorle's words stopped.

'This was a kind of torture for you,' I said. 'Like twisting the knife, after the killings in your country. The sickness.'

'He was messing with my head,' Dr Sorle said. 'What was I to do? A part of me wanted to walk away utterly, put it all behind me. I had chosen to live a small and meaningful life. I had chosen to build something real and I thought I was at peace with that choice. Until he came walking in with his money and his desire for forgiveness – or so he said.'

'So you decided to work for him.'

'Yes. I treated it as a test for myself. That even if it sickened me to look after him, I would hold my own humanity paramount. And at the end of it was this promise, something on a scale I could never do myself, money that I could carefully administer. I made plans for how to use it. Who to deal with. How to make this project work for the whole community. But I think you can see where this is going.'

'He tricked you?'

Dr Sorle made a glottal sound, as if engaged in a small struggle.

'People will say I had a psychotic break. That I could not hold the tension inside me and I snapped. I might have believed that myself, had it not been for you.'

'Glad to be of service,' I said. 'You didn't have a psychotic break. You have another self. An alternate path, if you will. He would have been you, if things had gone differently.'

Dr Sorle shook his head. 'That can't be so. During the bad times as a young man, some of my actions lay heavy on my heart. But I was never a murderer of innocents.'

'You were at Bethany's house. You opened the briefcase there, didn't you?'

'I was there, but I didn't open the briefcase. He came. The other one.'

He was trembling. I studied him. I saw Dr Sorle in his human beauty, and filling the great space behind him I saw another intelligence, calculating and obscenely vast. A deathstar of a mind.

He stood up. I stood up. He was holding the briefcase in his right hand but I was on his left.

'Where is Bethany?' I said with an effort.

'I. Don't. Have her.'

I threw myself at him, knocking him over.

I don't know why I did it. Reasons are just the thoughts we retroactively apply to explain what we do. Most people don't act out of reason. They act by instinct and then try to justify what they've done. I'm no different. I tackled him. The dogs came running, barking, growling, as Dr Sorle and I struggled. He was a handful, but no match for me. I broke his grip on the briefcase and took it from him. The whites of his eyes gleamed, and his breath was hot.

'I have no wish to quarrel with you, Pearl,' he whispered. 'Give it back at once.'

He didn't move. I hefted the briefcase. It was about as heavy as half a motorcycle.

'How did you get this through airport security?' I gasped, panting. 'I'm surprised the plane could take off at all.'

'Sometimes I think I want to destroy it. You don't know how I pray for the strength to restrain myself.'

'Something ties you to it.'

'You will see,' he said. He stood there, a simple animal. Breathing. I could feel the heat and moisture coming off him. Suddenly I understood how completely unable to escape his situation he was. He couldn't step up outside himself. He couldn't step down inside himself. He was stuck right where he was, with his mind beating on the walls like a butterfly with eyes on its wings. He was stunned that I didn't buy his pose, because he didn't know what I know: that there was exponentially more of him just on the other side of his perception. The eyes on his wings were real. He was an iceberg.

'Give Bethany back safely. At least tell me where she is. That's the only way I'd be willing to help you deal with Pace.'

He sighed. 'I told you, I don't have any hostages. I don't know what he did to her.'

'He.'

The briefcase weighed so much, I swear my right arm was already a couple of millimetres longer than my left. I passed it to my other hand, swinging it like it was a kettlebell.

'The other self.'

'Yeah, well. Pass on a message to your alter ego. This thing belongs to me. He has stolen it. I'm taking it back.'

Then I turned and sprang off the rocks.

# Post-Event Adjacent Reality Launcher

I flew. I was stunned and hurting in parts of myself that I hadn't even known existed. I clutched the briefcase to my chest and it didn't seem to weigh anything at all. *You are mine*, I thought. *We are together now.*

There had been a suspended moment when the briefcase opened and Dr Sorle was replaced by the quetzlcoatlus. In that moment I had an experience as thin and sharp as a papercut. When you get a papercut sometimes you don't start to bleed right away. It's like your flesh is shocked and forgets to part even though it's been cut open.

And you wonder if you imagined it but you didn't. The pain follows you at a slight distance, and in just this way the memory was following me. As I flapped awkwardly with my seldom-used wings, as I breathed hard and then glided, giddy with my own erratic motion through the air, the papercut started to catch me up. I passed over houses and pubs and cars and the tram line, through the rain-salted cold air of October's dark tea-time, and the visions flew alongside me. A flock of visions of my home.

As I banked to the west and glided over the Haymarket the papercut overtook me and I saw it all again, a slowly unfurling impression rich in detail and uneasily different to anything on Earth.

In the place where I come from there are nested functions. Deep-throated fliers, some with curved beaks and some straight. Some have bright crests and some have modest heads whose feathers lie smooth as glass; some are headless. Which is a shock. They sit with claws warping around furry luminous threads stretched taut across the sky like telephone wires. With fat bellies and ruffled feathers they survey the ruin, clever eyes scanning what is below. Some flap slowly; others hover and flit.

They have woven this place from the wreckage of metal structure, from the scrambled desiccation of life forms reduced to dust and rime. From silicon and gold. The birds sift through the detritus with their beaks; I believe they transmute some of what they find into the threads. I don't understand how this is done.

With clever beaks and wingtips the beings who made me compile masks made of human skin, made of feathers, made of biological circuits: mitochondrial turbine engines and electron pumps. Their masks are made of darkness pregnant with radio, the slow deep turning of long wavelength light. They wear these masks and they hop around a ragged fire that drinks up the foreign atmosphere.

They wear these masks when they turn their beaks to the sky, where the plasma field shudders and sparks with the impact of more debris, where wreckage of worlds collides with the shield of the sky.

Their nights are numbered. They have no days.

They are calling me, calling with a sound like black-backed gulls lost inland. I can hear home in their voices.

I want to go to them. I want to feel that mud between my toes. I want to feel the distant charge of that plasma sky. The roaring silence seems too close sometimes, as though in my sleep I could accidentally fold up and disappear into an HD drainage grate in the cosmic scheme. Who would miss me? No one here even knows who I really am. Least of all my self.

Long ago my bird mothers used to grow creatures in their gardens powered by magnetic gradients. Now they make baskets. They make garments and shields. Three of them are making a boat. The boat is crafted of sumac and resin from a colonial organism two degrees of abstraction removed from these here parts. It's woven of nano-infused clay and Fourier synthesis. One of my mothers carves the molecular faces of fire deities into its bows with his razor-edged beak.

'Mother,' I say to him. 'Where will you sail this boat? You can't take it past the plasma shield.'

'Come home, Pearl,' he replies, looking at me with one eye. 'We need you. Come while you still can.'

When I look back at my mother I don't know what I'm seeing. I want so badly to learn. With their clever toes the bird mothers put together the inescapable, one layer over the other. Carefully limning the edges of the containers with a lick of spit. Sometimes they could pass for people.

Especially when they wear the skin masks.

Sometimes they could pass for builder robots. Sometimes they could pass for clouds or tissue paper in a shoe box. I can shine through them. I can rumple them. I can forget about them if I let myself. I don't let myself. These bird mothers are all I have. The mud of their nests is made of life stories.

I can smell Kisi's childhood on their breath. Who else have they eaten alive?

When I was hijacked, they were distressed. If there had been a chat session between them it would have gone something like this:

Lady God I: Thing got out.

Va: Is the plasma field OK?

Horsebird: Of course. But Thing has taken the Post-Event Adjacent Reality Launcher

Va: That's not good. I knew we shouldn't have modified Thing. It's so risky.

Horsebird: The alternative was death by attrition.

Va: So now it's just death.

Lady God I: We can crunch ourselves and go out as seeds.

Va: Like I said, death.

Horsebird: How much time have we got?

Lady God I: The uncertainty is wider than the time frame itself. Maybe enough time to load. Maybe not.

Va: Can't see the point in loading. There's nowhere to hatch the eggs.

Horsebird: Let's see how the PEARL reacts to theft. It may surprise us.

Lady God I: Prepare the nest. It's all we've got left.

# Not Nevis

I was only a couple of miles away from Holyrood when I remembered the dogs. Reluctantly, I tore myself from the information that was now fizzing through my consciousness. I had to turn round and labour my way back through the soft rain to Arthur's Seat. I alighted on the rough dead grass not far below the point where I'd taken the briefcase off Dr Sorle; there was no sign of him now, but it was possible he was still up in the crags. I was braced for a fight but not seriously worried. The only reason Kisi Sorle's waveform had been able to steal my launcher in the first place was because his pattern had been stored inside me and I hadn't seen the hijacking coming. Back then he'd had the advantage of surprise. He didn't scare me now – at least, not as a human being. Whatever bigger intelligence I'd sensed just beyond him was another matter.

I folded my wings and whistled. Soon dog noises could be heard, shadows that panted and wagged their stumps for tails and breathed meaty delighted breath when they found me again.

I got out of there. I put them on their leads and we walked back through the town, but this time we avoided Heriot Row; instead, I used an online map to find a way to the vet's office. By the time we got there it was after 9 pm, and Alison had said she was checking Teacake around ten. I stood outside for ten minutes looking at the lit windows over her surgery before it occurred to me that this might be Alison's flat. I could smell her dinner faintly through the open window.

I knocked on her door and she opened it with a round cross-stitch frame in one hand and bifocals on the end of her nose.

'What's happened now?' she said sharply.

I was finding it hard to speak. It was as though what I'd seen on Holyrood could somehow pour out of my mouth like horror movie blood. Not that I knew exactly what I'd seen; and that fact was probably the worst of it.

She stepped back and I went in. Her flat smelt of beans on toast. There were cats on the sofa beside a squashed place where Alison must have been sitting. She brushed biscuit crumbs off the broad shelf of her bust and put her embroidery away.

'You're really worried about Teacake, aren't you? Come on, I'll take you down and you can see for yourself.'

I followed her down an interior staircase to the back office, where she flicked on a desk lamp. The rest of the practice was dark and smelled of urine and antiseptic. The dogs were sniffing and wriggling with excitement. *Pull it together, Pearl.*

'Since you think it might have been a poisonous frog, I've tried an anaesthetic that decreases the permeability of the cell membrane and blocks the receptors to some of the most common batrachotoxins. It may help. The good news is that his heart rate is stabilising, but he still can't move his legs. Is there anything left of the frog?'

Why can't I lie? She looked at me like I was a little kid holding a broken vase behind my back.

I said, 'Do you think Teacake will live? I mean, without a specific antidote?'

Soft empathy in the curves of her face. 'I don't know. He's made it this far. We'll just have to see what develops overnight.' She was watching me carefully as she spoke. 'There's something else, isn't there? What do you need?'

This kind of offer isn't unusual. People tend to go out of their way for me. I don't have to ask. They offer. Usually they aren't so up front about it, though.

'I think Bethany may have been abducted from her home,' I said heavily. 'I would have called the police, but I'm not convinced they could do anything.'

She pointed her finger at me.

'I knew you weren't an old friend!' She lit up like a sparkler. 'You're some kind of government agent, aren't you?'

Heat flared in my face.

'What makes you say that?'

Alison laughed out loud. 'It's just you're packing some muscle there, and look at you carrying that briefcase... But I get it. You're undercover. I won't say a word to anybody.'

I looked at the briefcase.

'It is kind of a giveaway,' she said gently. 'So what is it you need?'

'There's something I have to take care of. Can you keep the dogs here? And, if I'm not back by morning, could you check on the cats at Bethany's house?'

'Of course. Is that all?'

Two Phones' phone announced a text. My heart rate spiked.

She was excited. I sensed the way her muscles trembled beneath her skin. I let her take me back upstairs and make me a cup of tea. I watched her dunk an Abernathy biscuit with the enthusiasm of a child. I closed my eyes so she wouldn't think I was staring at her. I soaked in the feeling of her instead. Emotionally she felt like a bruised peach, but I could feel her protection as a real warmth around me.

'Thank you,' I said softly.

She frowned.

'How are you going to find Bethany?'

Another text on Two Phones' phone.

'Excuse me.'

The first text said:

**Wife going to parents for weekends with kids. Advise.**

The second text was from a different number.

**Not Nevis. Maybe Singapore. Raratonga.**

The first one could be innocent but I couldn't help thinking of Dr Sorle's wife and kids. I wrote back: **Don't touch family. Everything under control. Delayed.**

I didn't know what to say about the second text without giving away that I didn't know what it meant, so I didn't answer.

'Ben Nevis is a mountain,' I said aloud.

'It is that.'

'And what does it have in common with Singapore and Raratonga?'

'Rara-who?'

'Tonga.'

'You got me.'

I closed my eyes. I couldn't think rationally anymore. Too much had happened. I could feel the briefcase, so close to me– and yet so far. I needed to find a way to put it back into myself. The birds in that strange world with its plasma sky, they would know what to do. They would know how. But where were they? Inside the briefcase, somehow...

With the fire.

And/or the quetzlcoatlus.

Putting myself back together clearly wasn't going to be a straightforward thing. The thought of opening the briefcase was intimidating. I needed a metaphysical bomb defusion kit.

'Penny for your thoughts,' Alison said.

My eyes jumped open. She was refilling my tea cup.

'I should go,' I said. But I didn't want to. I wanted to stay in the warmth of Alison's living room with the cats and the softly ticking clock.

'Do you want to crash here tonight?' Alison said. 'I know you were planning to stay at Bethany's but if you're worried about being alone...I mean...I don't know what I mean.'

We looked at each other. I don't know what she was feeling because it wasn't any of my business to touch her mind that way, not in these circumstances, so I restrained myself. I wasn't a part of the Resistance anymore, and I wanted to be a person with her.

'That's really nice of you,' I said. I was feeling disloyal to Marquita. It wasn't even sex I wanted. I just wanted to lie my head in someone's lap and be safe. Even for a moment.

'But...?' said Alison, smiling.

'But there's something I have to do.'

'There is! And you came to ask me to look after the dogs and I said I would. And you're going now.'

She stood up, flustered. She thought she had overextended herself. I wanted to hug her.

'Actually,' I said suddenly. 'Do you think I could just use the yard out back for something?'

'The *yard*? Well, yeah, sure. Use the yard. I'll show you out the back door.'

She let me into the yard and switched on the porch light. The rain had stopped but it was chilly and there was a faint smell of diesel from the road. The yard was enclosed by high stone walls on three sides and the practice building itself on the fourth. Alison's van was parked to one side and there were two recycling bins, but this left a square of wet asphalt about six feet on a side where I could lay the briefcase down.

'Could you switch that light off?'

'I promise I won't look,' said Alison. 'I'm going back to my needlepoint. It requires ferocious concentration, you know.'

'It's not you,' I said. 'It's them.' I indicated the buildings that overlooked the yard. She shut off the light and left me out there in the darkness. I heard her go upstairs.

I wiped my palms on my trousers. The briefcase was strobing slightly in the ultraviolet and I couldn't be sure, but I kept thinking I could hear sounds coming from inside it. The sounds were faint and hard to distinguish from the hum of the boiler in the veterinary practice and the soft singing of the electrical equipment in the yard next door and the sibilance of traffic moving through puddles. I might have been imagining it, but the presence of the briefcase somehow seemed to organise the white and almost-white noise of the environment and convert it to an implied music. Oh so softly, the briefcase was calling a tune.

I knelt and put my palms on the naugahide surface. You are mine but you've been made into something else. I am yours but you don't know me anymore. How do we put ourselves back together? Where to begin?

The briefcase wasn't locked. It didn't even have one of those flimsy combination locks on it. All it had were brass closures to either side of the handle, each of which flipped open with a small brass button that slid in a groove. There was nothing to it.

I put my thumbs on the buttons and tried to slide them.

The buttons did not move. At all. There may as well not have been a groove.

So I tried them one at a time, in different sequences. I grabbed the closures and tried to pull them out of their sockets, but I couldn't seem to get a good grip on them. I had big fingers and they were small devices. Small but strong.

I could hear the air coming out of my own nostrils in frustrated little snorts.

Damn!

I should have known, of course. Trying not to be angry, I sat back on my heels. How can you not be angry when someone steals a part of you and then turns it against you and locks you out of it? How can you not be angry when someone locks you out of yourself?

OK. Maybe I was a little angry now.

I put my fingers on the seam where the top half of the briefcase met the bottom. The hinges weren't particularly strong. I could probably rip it open, though I wasn't sure I wanted to. I decided to part the halves of the briefcase by just a crack, get a glimpse of the inside without damaging the structure.

I couldn't get my fingers into position. They kept slipping off. I sat back and manoeuvred the briefcase between my legs so I could get a better grip on it, but no matter how I turned it I couldn't get my fingers into that crack. I worked on the hinges. I dug into the naugahide with my nails – it was already damaged in places – but I couldn't seem to make a dent in it.

I stood up and looked around. There was a utility room between the veterinary practice and the yard, just big enough for two people to stand in. It had a washing machine, a deep freeze, and some shelves with odd things like horse-shoe picks and dog leads, gardening gloves, a screwdriver—

A screwdriver. I picked it up and went back to the briefcase. I put the sharp end into the joint of the briefcase, but again I couldn't get a purchase. I found a piece of broken brick and tried using that to drive the point in, but I missed and hit my own hand.

Sucking my own fist now, I was starting to feel really foolish. How had Kisi Sorle opened the thing? Did it have some kind of open sesame? If it did, how come I of all people didn't know it?

I grabbed the handle, about to reposition it for another assault, but the briefcase had suddenly become heavy. Heavier than lead. I couldn't move it at all.

It felt like somebody was pulling my cock and I don't even have a cock. Like that.

On the other hand, a heavy object is always a challenge to me. I set myself up to lift it. I had something to prove here.

When you move a big weight, the heavy effort comes first, your fast-twitch fibres sprinting for their lives, burning themselves out while the slower ones catch up, en masse, moving the load. And then, suddenly, there's a point where it's easier to move than not move. Easier to keep going than to stop. Sir Isaac's inertial mushrooming of events. Statistically, that one point where the pebble starts the landslide, that point is the answer to everything. Imbued with a deep magic. And yet: so what? Because without the heavy lifting and the long incremental endurance you got nothing. You. Got. Nothing.

As always when I lift, the world parts like a pair of lips and I can see its language emerging from the mouth of the cosmos, I glimpse realities that are folded up dimensions of where I am. It's a rush better than flying, better than sex.

But even as my consciousness drifted down into the realms deep within my atoms, my ligaments were hitting fail point. Capillaries in my eyes broke and my vision blurred. As the effort went on and on I realised that if I tried any harder I would tear muscle off bone, pop a joint.

I let up. Walked in a circle, away from the briefcase and back, staring at it like it was an alligator.

Then I went back in and grabbed it again.

This time instead of being heavy it was light. Too light. I picked it up like it was air, lost my balance, and fell hard on my left side as the briefcase tugged at my right hand just as it had done on the plane. The muscles of my hand were spent; involuntarily I let go and the briefcase sailed across the yard. It hit a metal recycling bin with such force that it punched right through the side of the bin and crashed into the contents leaving a hole behind. Empty plastic bottles poured out and rolled on to the pavement like a little noisy sea.

I charged over to the bin, lifted the lid, and dragged the briefcase out. It was undamaged and had returned to a more normal weight.

'Who is making that infernal noise?'

A pale chubby face appeared at the top of the yard wall. Unshaven. Nose red with drink. Flashing eyes. The man's white breath floated away from him and vanished.

I set the briefcase down but put one foot on it just in case it was thinking of going anywhere.

'Oh!' exclaimed the man, pulling himself higher and setting his elbows on the top of the wall. He had a can of cider in one hand, and he waggled it slightly as though judging how much was left inside. 'Sorry about that. You're a person. I thought it was those bloody cats again. Everything all right over there?'

I narrowed my eyes. 'Everything's fine.'

'Where you from, then?'

'Long Island,' I said in my best Long Island accent.

'Right, well, I hate to sound suspicious, but is that actually yours?'

'Of course,' I said – and I didn't even convince myself. What must it look like, me with my screwdriver, my brick, and my temper trying to open a briefcase in a back yard at ten thirty at night?

'Well, because, you know, I am in fact an expert locksmith,' he said, and actually winked. He smiled with a mouthful of yellow, jumbled teeth. 'I sleep on the street purely out of inherent honesty. I could get into any building on this road. Any one.'

He gestured with the cider can left and right.

'I can pick any lock. Truly.'

I picked up the briefcase and walked over to him. He was a mess in the way of a bombed-out house. In his interior there were personal possessions, good furniture, books, music, clothes – but they were thrown everywhere and covered with dust and rubble, and rats had moved in. It was a sad place, but someone was still living in the ruin.

'OK,' I said simply. I reached up and clasped his cold, dirty hand. He looked startled; then he held my gaze. His eyes were bloodshot and the pupils were overlarge, but he was trying hard to focus on me. I tugged and he kicked and he came scrambling up over the top of the wall and tumbled into the yard. The cider spilled in a foamy splash.

'Never mind,' I said. I leaned into his emotional patterns. So much wasted ability. The urge to repair was strong. 'You don't need that. It doesn't even work.'

'No,' he said. 'It doesn't fucking work.'

He picked up the can and slurped up the remainder of it, then chucked the empty tin back over the wall. 'It doesn't work. But it's what I do. Let's see your lock. Christ, it's dark over here. Dark for dark business, is that it?'

'I can see fine,' I said.

'Right, well there's no lock here, is there?'

'I thought you could pick any lock.'

'There has to be a lock.'

'I've seen someone open it. It opened for them. Just not for me.'

'Well, there's no lock.'

120

'There is.'

'Isn't.'

It went like this. Then he said, laughing,

'Listen, you silly cunt. It's not locked at all. It's fucking glued. We need a cunting knife. Sorry, excuse my manners. We need a *sharp* knife.'

He reached into his pocket. I gripped his forearm like a vice. He yelped and stared at my hand on his arm, which he now could not move at all.

'No,' I said. 'No knives. No cutting.'

'I was only going to get a cigarette. I'm unarmed. Reach in my pocket and see for yourself.'

I let him go. I wasn't afraid for myself; my reaction had been fear for the briefcase, for what would happen to me if it were damaged. Don't know what possessed me to think it *could* be damaged; nothing was making much sense by now.

Shaking, now, the man took out a packet of cigarettes and put one between his lips.

'Suicidal, I know,' he said, lighting up. 'We're all going to die, anyway.'

The back door of the practice opened and the light came on.

'Conor?' sang Alison. 'What are you doing here? What is going on?'

# News from Mars

'Yo, Alison,' said Conor, blinking in the sudden light. 'We were just having a friendly discussion about the art of lock-picking.'

Alison came outside in her slippers. She calmly took in the sight of the screwdriver, the spilled bottles, and us. I had hastily gotten to my feet, keeping hold of the briefcase, but Conor winced when he tried to get up. I put out my hand to help him. He was cold and his back hurt. There was other pain, too – nebulous, non-local, but no less real. Before I knew what I was doing, I'd looked deep into his neural architecture to see if I could help. Sometimes in the past when I'd done this, the simple fact of me being there had been enough to cause a change. It seemed that my presence caused a shift in a person's attention that initiated some internal process in them. Some part of them could take it from there and they'd feel better. Other times I used to use the geometry of HD to give a bioelectrical nudge.

Since I'd been kicked out of the Resistance I'd been wondering why I was still doing this. It was a kind of compulsion to try to help people; but what if they hadn't asked for my help? Conor was rickety on the inside, intensely strong in some places and perilously weak in others. His addiction had entwined itself around him like a choking vine, but worse than that he was blindingly lonely.

'It's a chilly night,' Alison said to him. 'You didn't sell the sleeping bag, did you?'

He wiped his nose and shook his head. 'I've still got it. Could do with a dram, though, if you're offering.'

'How about a sandwich?'

'How about both?'

'A sandwich, I think,' Alison said.

*

After she'd made Conor a sandwich and argued with him about the whisky and after he'd got angry about that and then apologised and then got angry again, we showed him out through the yard gate to save him climbing the wall. Alison went inside to check the animals one more time. I stood at the front of the practice and watched Conor walk away with his head down, kicking at invisible objects on the pavement and muttering to himself. I wanted so badly to get up inside his brainwaves and re-tune him like a piano. I didn't know anymore whether I should, and after my failure to open the briefcase I wasn't even confident that I could.

'Teacake's a fighter,' said Alison, coming outside with me. Conor was gone by now but I was still thinking about him and considering the possibility that he might hurt Alison one day if the addiction got the better of him. 'So is Conor. His dog died last month. He says he doesn't want a replacement, but I'm going to find him a rescue dog soon. He does better with a dog, honestly. He used to busk and he did all right for himself, considering.'

I nodded, but now I was thinking about the briefcase with a rising sense of frustration. I felt impotent. If only I could re-install it maybe I'd know what I really was, where I really belonged, and what my mission was supposed to be. Who was I to be an angel to any person when I was a lost soul myself? I was thinking of Bethany, of Jeff, of Dr Sorle. I was mixed up with all of them somehow and I had to fix things but how? What was I even going to do now?

'Hey,' said Alison, nudging me. 'It's been a shit day. Best if we just go to the pub.'

Alison's pub was called the Cock Inn. It was half-full and pleasantly scruffy, and we didn't have to wait long to be served. We took our drinks to a corner safely out of the way of a friendly darts competition but within sight of the giant screen TV. I couldn't see the door from my position. Cowboys and spies always sit with their backs to the door, don't they?

I kept the briefcase trapped between my calves.

'I'm not a drinker,' Alison said. 'Don't let me overdo it. I have to get up early to check the animals, yours included. I'm normally in bed at this hour. Perils of not being fifty-nine anymore.'

Her manner implied we were confederates in ageing. I didn't want to touch this, because technically I was only two years old. My hair was showing some grey and my kneecaps throbbed from all the walking, but I didn't have the experience that Alison did.

'I'm planning to retire when I find someone to take over,' she said during her second drink. 'It has to be the right person, though. I can't hand the practice to just anyone. My clients trust me.'

'What will you do when you retire?'

'Ah, that's easy.' She finished her shot and chased it back with a long drink of bitter. 'Travel. So many places I've wanted to see but could never take enough time off. My own children have seen more of the world than I have. Maybe I'll even go to Raratonga, speaking of paradise kinds of places.'

She winked at me. Then her expression turned serious.

'I guess you can't tell me what it's about, this Ben Nevis business.'

'It may be something to do with Pace Industries,' I said carefully. She had no visible reaction to the name, but she couldn't be unaware of the Austen Stevens news story.

'Hmm. Raratonga. I wonder if Pace have any holdings there. Can't find anything much in common with Singapore unless you count maybe a relationship with the British Empire. No mountains. I don't suppose you can give me any more information?'

'Not Nevis,' I said. 'I wonder if the connection is something to do with Liam. Singapore, that's connected to him. What about the other places?'

'I don't picture Liam climbing Ben Nevis, if I'm honest.

Bethany always complains that he doesn't even use his gym membership.'

'Ben Nevis is the only Nevis I could think of.' I got up to buy another round. I really should dig a little deeper in my memory. Maybe there were others. Some town in the American midwest, or . . .

When I came back with more drinks she had her phone out. So much for my archives. She said, 'Nevis is an island in the Caribbean. So they are both paradises, Raratonga and Nevis. Singapore, not so much.'

And what did they have in common?

Tick. Tick.

I had nothing. But I could feel the briefcase touching the outside of my calf. I drank my orange juice while Alison put down a couple more shots and another half-pint of beer.

I wanted to dissolve into the moment, be part of the bar and the crowd and the air and the alcohol. Not have to think.

News from Mars was in the air. Money problems, as usual. Everyone had an opinion.

'We have to fund these things,' Alison said. 'The space program is the pinnacle of our achievement as a species.'

I shook my head, silent.

'What? You disagree?'

I shrugged. 'More than one way to skin a cat.'

'Yeah? What other way of going into space unless you, basically, *go into space?*'

I looked away, whistling.

Alison thumped her half-pint glass on the counter.

'So what are you saying? No spaceships? Why not?'

'Because spaceships aren't practical. Would you send a bicycle to Mars?'

'What kind of question is that?'

'It's no dumber than expecting to get to another star system or another galaxy using some version of the rockets you use to get to Mars.'

125

'What about a gen ship? There's a game about a gen ship, isn't there? Murder mystery, I think.'

The bell rang for last orders. Alison lunged for the bar. For someone not planning on overdoing it, she'd already had five or six units pretty quickly and it showed. I wondered what she'd remember of this conversation in the morning.

'There are games about unicorns, too.'

'Unicorns are imaginary! There are real rockets, there is a real space program, and some guys at MIT are working on a warp drive I think. Something about relativity.'

'Rockets used to be imaginary until someone built one. Everything's imaginary in the beginning. And unicorns can be built.'

'Unicorns. Can be built. Uh. OK, I guess you got me there. You're funny, Pearl.' She leaned into me and pressed into my shoulder with her finger as though to push me away. She pushed herself away instead, and I had to grab for her before she fell off the chair. She batted her eyelashes and said, 'Next thing you're going to tell me you've seen one.'

I shrugged. 'You never know what someone may take it into their head to build.'

Even a dinosaur. Even an angel. Are we that sexy? Maybe somewhere there are hacked trilobites and fungi. I'm starting to wonder. Pterosaurs? Prehistoric frogs?

'So if spaceships aren't practical, then what is? What's the alternative?'

'Shhhh!' I said. 'Listen!'

There was a news report about Austen Stevens' firm: Invest In Futures Foundation, aka IIF. Receivership, they were saying. Or a hostile buyout. Money was missing. So much money that nobody was saying exactly how much. Austen Stevens had authorised transfers into accounts that were now shut down with no trace of their contents and there were rumours that hidden offshore assets had also been tapped.

*We are keeping all avenues of enquiry open with respect to Mr Stevens' disappearance.*

'Here on Wall Street they're calling him the Six Billion Dollar Man because he vanished, taking an enormous sum of money with him and throwing IIF into chaos.'

'Aha,' said Alison, suddenly very clearly. 'What do Raratonga and Singapore and Nevis have in common? Offshore money laundering.'

Just as she said this, I felt a hand on my shoulder.

'Yes,' said Kisi Sorle in his low, intense voice. 'They do have this in common.'

# You can hear the dead

I stood up, shaking off his hand.

'Let's step outside. I don't want any trouble in front of my friend.'

'Why don't we walk your friend home, and then you and I can have a quiet talk?' I wasn't listening to the plane of intention that stretched behind his words, cracked and pitted and fuming in places. I was listening to the timbre, the bass fur that shivered the air beneath my feathers.

How was he superpositioning himself on Dr Sorle this way? The resemblance between the two of them really was superficial. He was like an evil twin – if not actually evil, he was everything that Dr Sorle wasn't. Confident. Arrogant. Hard.

Alison drained her glass.

'This is very exciting for a Tuesday night,' she said. I put my arm around her protectively as we left the pub. I was sure he had done something bad to Bethany. I wouldn't put it past him to take another hostage.

I don't know what the three of us looked like bumbling along the pavement to Alison's flat. Two of us were brown and one of us was over six feet tall and a hundred kilos, and it wasn't the dude. Kisi said nothing, but strolled along with his hands in his pockets as though just taking in the air. I waited for Alison to unlock her door. She went in and then before she shut the door she put her hand on my forearm.

'I am going to text you in ten minutes,' she said with the excessive care of the inebriated. 'I want to know you're OK.'

'Lock the house,' I said as I left. I was pretty sure she'd be asleep in ten minutes.

Kisi Sorle stood right where Two Phones had stood earlier,

outside the estate agent's. I shivered, but I walked over there like I wasn't bothered.

'You can't open the briefcase without me,' he said. His magneto eyes his banshee soul, the light on his skin always moving and I was angry.

'I know you're not Dr Sorle. You just used him. And me. I'm getting sick of being messed around by you.'

He started walking away from Alison's surgery, gesturing for me to go with him.

'Where are we going?'

'We can't stand here arguing under a lamp post,' he said. 'Someone will hear us and call the police.'

'You wouldn't want that, now, would you?' I snorted. But I walked with him. He took three strides to every two of mine.

He said, 'Did you try to open the briefcase yet?'

'Why?' I said sharply.

He smiled. 'I am the only one who can open it. Biometric latch, nature of the security on it.'

'But it's my launcher! Why can't I open it?'

'It's only a part of you,' he said. 'And it happens to be a part to which I have the key and you don't.'

'Don't you get how creepy that is?' I said.

'It might be creepy if you were a real person. But you're not.'

I had to look away because I was about to cry and I didn't want him to see it. I couldn't let him break me.

'So, Pearl Jones,' he said. 'You have the briefcase, but you can't get it open. So what use is it to you? Without me, you have no way to get back home. And that's all you really want, isn't it?'

I shook my head. 'You held that over me before and you never delivered. You're going to send me home? You and whose slingshot?'

He laughed.

'In the matter of slingshots, you would never believe me if I told you. But if you have reason to resent me for borrowing your launcher you might want to consider the trouble you have caused me in turn. You nearly caused that flight to crash, and you delayed me from reaching my destination. I was on time-sensitive business. I was on a mission.'

'What kind of mission?' I said sharply.

'I am in the process of setting up the Resistance.'

I made some inarticulate noises. 'The Resistance has been around for centuries—'

'Because it works with causality and it's based on the Austen Correspondences which as you may know originate in another frame.'

I recalled Marquita talking about the Austen Correspondences but she'd sounded as if she didn't have all the information, with all of this 'technology originating in the future' stuff. I felt a little queasy hearing the term again in this context. I thought the Resistance functioned by statistical interpolation, but I had to admit it would be more effective if it used higher dimensions to coil back and forth across probability spectra. Crudely put: if it used time travel.

I said, 'I told you not to play with causality.'

'I wanted to build something,' he replied. That low voice like velvet, smoke. Saffron. 'This is important. This is meaningful. This is a way to make sense of all the suffering, all the ruin, all the pain inflicted on my people and the environment, the land where I was born...'

'How?' I said. 'What does your country have to do with the Resistance?'

'There are technologies out there that you can't imagine. Some of them are in you. And you have no idea. This man's money can be the beginning of our species getting access to higher-dimensional manipulations and when it does, past and future will be laid out before us like a map and we'll be able to move them around, create alternatives, run models...'

'Wait. *When* it does? What do you mean, when it does? The Resistance is already here.'

'It is right now. Tomorrow, if these transactions don't go

through, the Resistance may never have been. All of its work could be undone. I came here with a series of authorisations that were meant to move money into a series of nest accounts from which it would filter into the IIF Foundation, which was Austen Stevens' brainchild created with a little help from me. But I got here late, after the news reports of the violence in New York. I was late thanks to you, Pearl. Forbes lost his bottle. I need to get him to change his mind, or the Resistance will never come to pass. Especially with Pace Industries running after him trying to recoup the money Stevens hid in the islands.'

The islands. *Not Nevis.*

'Does Liam Forbes know what you're really doing?'

'He knows the investment company is a front. This business of using dirty money to set up a research organisation, it began as a sort of decoy or shell game to see if he could outmanoeuvre the authorities... Stevens didn't *really* believe he'd live forever until he saw you fly past his helicopter. I was going to give the briefcase back to you as soon as the funds transfer went through. I still intend to. But we're running out of time, and if the oil company picks up Forbes before the transaction is complete, there will be no Resistance.'

I stopped and put my hands on my hips.

'So you got rid of Jeff the oil guy. I didn't like him much, either, but I wouldn't say he was asking to be murdered. So why did you eat him? From where I was standing it looked like you went not just medieval, but prehistoric, my friend.'

He waved his hands loosely, like it was all a joke.

'No, no, no. That's ridiculous. Dr Sorle does not host me willingly, but he has no choice because our waveforms are already so similar. Imagine what would happen if I tried to project myself into another species! I would be... untranslatable.'

'I saw what I saw. But even if I believe that you don't moonlight as a quetzlcoatlus, Jeff is still dead. You meant for that to happen. And you've dragged Dr Sorle into it, too.'

'What do you care about Jeff?'

'Killing is killing.'

'I know what killing is,' he said sharply. 'I have seen enough of it. But I was only going to store him in the briefcase.'

'Store him? In this?' I swung the briefcase wildly for effect. 'What kind of briefcase is this?'

'Surely you've worked out what kind by now. It's a waveform launcher. It used to be yours. Maybe you can explain how that creature got in there.'

'Don't look at me,' I said. 'I don't know shit since you stuffed me in that old refrigerator.'

It was a half-hearted rebuttal, but I was still reeling at the idea that the Resistance could go up in smoke at any moment. 'You knew enough to try to take the briefcase off me,' Kisi said. 'As I told you before: your actions endangered not only the passengers but all of the Resistance and its work.'

'Yeah, I hear I'm a real loose cannon but you're a saint.'

There was a deeply unhappy pause. Rain began to fall.

'We have to try to repair the situation,' he said. 'Keep walking.'

We kept walking. I was aware that we were going back up into the New Town by the same route I'd driven with Teacake, earlier. My knees were feeling it, going up the steep hill. Cars passed us on the cobbles with a rushing sound. Then he said:

'You are a recycled piece of junk from a dying civilisation, and when I rose up inside you I found you being picked over by crows. They cobbled you together out of extinct animals and nano-libraries and you were always a fool's hope. You scanned me when I was only a boy, but you got more than you bargained for because I'm not a person who just lets things happen to them and doesn't do anything about it. You scan me, I launch you. We're even. So if you are looking for something profound, don't. You will only be disappointed. Better to know the truth and then no one can own you.'

'Why? Why would you hijack me? If you had asked me . . .'

He laughed in a falsetto. 'Ask? Ask? I shouldn't have to ask. Did you ask before you took my soul? Did you ask before you spewed thousands of copies of it out across the galaxies, like scattering grass seed?'

'I don't know what you're talking about. I have no knowledge of any of those things.'

He wasn't listening. 'I want to make something great. Here on Earth. I want our species to level up. And you're going to help me.'

There was a field of agitation around him. Shadows were moving in the bright sweat on his face. I could see his pores, the stubble where his beard was growing in, and he was rubbing his palms on his thighs as if to wipe something off them. Sweat, maybe, or maybe something else.

'Make no mistake, Pearl. Pace Industries will come for the briefcase. They think it contains information that will lead them to IIF's hidden assets. They'll come after you and they won't stop until they get it. So you have to decide: do you want to save the Resistance? Or do you want to run around carrying an unstable artefact from a lost civilisation hoping it won't spit out a pterosaur next time you open it?'

I made a face.

'There are always other choices,' I said.

'Like what?'

He was up in my face and I smelled his breath. Something familiar there. Something I could understand; it took me back to some unspecified past moment of— Couldn't be peace. No.

'Please,' I whispered. 'Don't take over this man's body. Make your peace with Dr Sorle. There has to be a way to make this situation better.'

'What do you know?' he snapped. Spittle flew from his lips and his bloodshot eyes flared intimidation. 'What did they tell you? That you're here to ease the suffering of the living? What about the suffering of the dead? I can hear them, you know.'

'You can hear the dead.' I kept my voice carefully neutral.

'Since I was a child. I could hear them under the ground in the oil fields. In the pipes. In people's houses. I can hear them in petrol tanks. How would you feel if you walked into a petrol station to buy a Diet Coke and the fuel in somebody's Citroën started whispering to you? You probably think that's funny, don't you?'

I didn't dare think anything. He was freaking me out. I'd folded my wings down out of sight, but I let their knowledge hold me and give me strength. I was here for a reason, and until I found out what that was I would have to hold the line. If only I could see it his way, maybe I would know what to say to him.

'They were there long before we were human. Long before. History has taken them from the ground and sent them into the sky, and we breathe them in. They live in leaves and deadfall. Is it any wonder both of us have ghosts in our bones, Pearl? We come from the dead. And we don't have free will.'

I noticed that I'd edged away from Kisi because I couldn't take the intensity of being near him physically. We were a block away from Liam Forbes' house. What had Kisi done with Bethany?

'You can't fight me,' he said. 'I have history on my side. Give me the briefcase and let me close this deal. I'm running out of time.'

'I don't believe you. You lied to me before.'

'Why do you think the Resistance kicked you out? They're afraid of you. They know you blocked me from bringing the briefcase here. They think you're going to destroy them and they're right. You are. Unless you give me the briefcase now.'

'I want to see you open it. If you can open it and show me what's inside, then maybe I'll consider helping you. I don't promise anything.'

He sucked his teeth with a sharp hiss. 'We don't have time for this.'

'Because you're on the run from the law.'

'And because I've barely got Forbes on the hook. He's agreed to meet me. I have to show him proof that his boss isn't dead, that everything is going to plan. Then he will release the funds. That's how the deal was set up.'

'The proof is in the briefcase?'

He threw his head back and laughed, exposing the columns of his throat.

'Pearl, Austen Stevens is in the briefcase.'

# Forth

Sweat sprang on to my palms. I don't know why. I mean, it's not like the briefcase was big enough to hold a body. If it had been a bowling bag with a guy's head in it, or even a garment bag... Ugh, but no.

'He's not dead,' Kisi added. 'I wish he was, but he's not. As far as I know. I promised him immortality.'

'You scanned him,' I said. 'You stole my scanner and used it to scan somebody right before they died. But where's the body?'

'Oh, the body is in there. He's captured. He isn't dead or alive.'

I guess that makes Alison Schrödinger's veterinarian.

'I'm coming with you to meet Liam Forbes. I need to see this for myself.'

'I can't bring you with me.'

'Why not?'

'You might spook him.'

'Good. How about I open my wings? That should spook him real good.'

We took Bethany's car because the meeting was in Queensferry. Kisi said Forbes hadn't wanted to meet him but had been persuaded it was in his best interests.

'How did you persuade him?'

'You don't need to know that.'

Bethany. It had to be. Kisi was holding her hostage somewhere. How could this cold, angry man originate in the same boy that had grown up to be Dr Sorle?

'He is afraid to be seen near his own home. Pace has investigators looking for him. We must get the deal done before he's picked up for questioning.'

I concentrated on my driving. The inside of the car was a well of darkness. I could see only the whites of his eyes and a faint reflection of streetlights off his skin; the lines of his expression were lost to me.

We were a third of the way over the Forth Bridge when the first two bullets punctured the rear window and lodged in the stereo and the air vent, respectively. I braked and there was a jerking thud as we were struck from behind. The car spun out. The bridge moved sideways, the sky turned, headlights moved laterally in my vision as I tried to hold the wheel.

My wings exploded into the car. Kisi ducked. Windows broke. The wheel juddered and came off in my hands. I saw the whites of Kisi's eyes as I handed him the steering wheel like it was a birthday present, and I felt a wild, futile smile break across my face.

We were sliding along the rail that separated the main carriageway from the pedestrian walkway. There was a big, predatory 4WD behind us with its headlights set to dazzle. It hit us again and this time lifted us up on its bull bar. There was a crunch as Bethany's car was jammed against the rail. The 4WD reversed and then rammed us again. Metal buckled and gave. We were bucked over the guard rail and the car landed on its side and spun. I ended up trapped on the downside of the car, with my door pressed against the ground. Kisi above me was climbing through the broken passenger window on to what was now the topside of the car.

The car juddered to a halt. The rail was broken and the car was now in the pedestrian area, stopped by a second guard rail. I could see the dark waves below through the hole in the windscreen that my head had made. I felt no pain. The other vehicle rammed us again. Nothing between us and falling but that piece of metal. Clinging to the surface of the car, Kisi reached in for the briefcase.

'Oh no you don't,' I said. 'Don't you give it to them.'

He reached in for me.

'Take my hand.'

'Go, Kisi. My wings are stuck. I can't get through that door.'

'Take my hand. Now!'

I drew breath to argue. He grabbed my arm and pulled. My wings were jammed against the doors and ceiling, protruding halfway through broken windows, and my head was sticking out of the broken windscreen; I was wearing this car like an aluminium coat. I had the briefcase in my left hand and I thrust it ahead of me. The 4WD struck us again, and at the same time three shots punched through the briefcase and into Kisi. I felt him take the impacts.

His body trembled. He gripped my forearm tighter; then his hand slid out of mine and on to the briefcase, clutching – there was a jerk as the whole car moved again, and in a second he was gone from my field of view.

I thrashed like a dog shaking off water, kicking myself upward. The car fell away from me. My wings spread wide, aching; I surged up, out over the tossing waves of the firth. I saw people get out of the 4WD, and more were running towards the scene from another vehicle. I stroked past the central support tower of the bridge, and I could taste the briny undersmell of its structure on the back of my tongue.

From on high the scene looked insignificant. The car was crumpled. What little traffic there was at midnight had stopped and clogged up the bridge, and people were rubbernecking. The distress of frightened drivers was decaying to annoyance. I couldn't see Kisi anywhere.

But he'd been shot. He wasn't on the bridge. He had to be in the water. I vaned and let myself drop, searching. More shots popped off, but nothing hit me. No Kisi. In those few seconds while I was preoccupied by escaping the car, he had disappeared.

He must be in the water. I flew in spirals, scanning the waves for any sign of him on my visible spectrum; there was none.

What if he was not swimming? What if he was under the water, unconscious or worse?

And the familiar feeling came over me, the sense of being behind the beat. The bullets had gone through the briefcase, too. I knew what happened to that briefcase any time it felt threatened. I didn't need to look for a man. Not anymore.

# Come back

I headed east, away from the searchlights, and then I saw it. Over the railway bridge the ancient animal glided black and lunar, like a cracked piece of sky. As its shadow flickered through the bridge's ironwork a train was rolling out of Edinburgh and I saw passenger after passenger coddled in the carriages' pillbox windows. None seemed to sense the entity that passed over their heads.

As I flew after it along the Forth, making towards open sea, an image of its desire opened in my mind. Oil rigs. Fire on the water. Mayhem.

But not tonight. Too much pain. The bullets had done harm.

The quetzlcoatlus went down on a strip of shabby beach. A lacework of trees broke up such misted light as came from street lamps. At the top of the beach a concrete hut bore a large notice-board spelling out parking restrictions and assorted prohibitions, most of which had been spray-painted over. A length of buckling pavement skirted the sand. By day people would jog here, walk their dogs, take the air. Now the sirens' drunken singing floated from the bridge, and there were no dogs in sight. Good thing for them, because the pterosaur had landed splayed in the shallows, where it alchemised the surrounding water to black steam. An acrid, frightening odour stained the back of my throat, and I coughed as I landed on the wet sand, tripping as though my feet didn't remember how to stand on the earth.

The creature looked like forged emptiness. It breathed smoke and the vast unlit places between stars. On the ground it seemed amplified. Its wings made a hard wind with even the most casual movement, and its breath rebuffed the waves. A pheromone fume seeped from its fur. There was a disturbing hum in my occipital bone, a sensation of drag on my consciousness. Like magnetism. The sensation was out of all proportion to my physical body. I felt I could be reeled, wings and all, into a single one of the quetzlcoatlus' black-hole pupils and never be found again.

'Dr Sorle,' I said. I didn't look at its eyes, but I could feel their pinpoints roving over me like the sights on a rifle scope. 'Dr Sorle, I know you're there. Come back. We have to talk.'

I didn't expect a reply; in fact, my whole effort at dialogue had gone over the top of bravado and down the other side, a Jack-and-Jill tumble into sheer idiocy. *We have to talk:* like characters in a soap opera, like someone writing cartoon-bubble expressions on a depiction of the numinous – a blasphemy. As soon as the sound of my words had punched their way quivering through the air, I knew there would be no talk. Talk is cheap.

There would be this other thing.

This:

When you were a boy you picked through the sump of oil in the lowland. The smell of black smoke and a glimpse of flames, so alien against the lush green, an ugly show of power.

You used to wander away to watch the fires. In the smoke you saw bright-feathered dinosaurs. You saw pterosaurs. You didn't know what they were at the time. You saw other things that you couldn't name or even describe. You guessed they were demons; certainly they were terrifying. It was only years later, trained in the simulators of the birdmasters, that you learned that dinosaurs and angiosperms *were* the oil. Their echoes had infected you even then, rippling backward to the small boy you used to be.

Ancestors used to come out of the fire, too. They'd look at you and they'd point. Wordless accusation. You could never forget that. Not in all the years. The fish-hook weight of their gazes. The birdmasters would never explain, and by the time you learned how you'd betrayed your ancestors, it was too late.

After the black-winged bird fell out of the sky and turned one silver eye on you as you lay bleeding, after the boy you used to be was scanned up, the birdmasters didn't hesitate to tell the boy how dead you would be. They told the boy that in the great scheme of things, you were supposed to die. The birdmasters told the boy they had saved him, because he was special.

That was the beauty of their plan. The birdmasters knew how to borrow against the past. They took for agents the ones who were doomed anyway. The ones who wouldn't live long enough to leave descendants or make a ripple in the stream. The ones who could vanish and never be missed. They took the boy and the boy was supposed to be grateful.

The boy was grateful. At first.

Now with everything that happened you'd think sincerity would be outside the curve. But the boy used to be grateful *and* sincere. Learning to hate came later.

*We outrun the bleeding edge of time,* the birdmasters boasted. *We play parkour with the higher dimensions. We transgress on the unused spaces and one day we will find our way back to the Immanence that abandoned us.*

Who wouldn't want to play parkour with the higher dimensions? The boy took the bait. And nobody expected you to live. But you did.

There was a sound like thunder. I stepped backwards into the cold water, my heart jamming in recognition. The pterosaur's body seemed to pulse in synchrony with my blood, but I couldn't take this in.

I didn't recognise myself. Never again the same. In my brain a thicket of dendrites were standing on end in dark and terrible welcome: nervous impulses that cried out, *I know this story! I lived this story.* That black-winged bird dropping out of HD and into the jungle, it was me. I scanned, I stole, I flew away, I carried away the injured boy's waveform, I returned to the nest, I was broken down for rebuilding, it was me. Except it wasn't. That was some predecessor of me, some aspect but certainly not the whole. Nothing is so tidy. Yet somehow I am in all of it, I am of all of it, I am and was and will be there, and maybe

I'm getting sucked into something twisted but it's too late and it has always been too late.

Kisi's story is also my story.

I thought about this a second. Then a twitching coda of a realisation tapped me on the shoulder like a Scooby-Doo ghost:

*He stole me but I stole him first.*

Breathing. Shaking. I was afraid. Kisi Sorle had been shot, and I had to help him. My teeth ached.

'Dr Sorle.' My voice emerged bald and crumbling. 'I can help you. Come back. I'm here. Come back.'

But Dr Sorle was not coming back. He was leaving. The quetzlcoatlus seemed to grow, until I realised that the space between me and the world around me was growing, and the beach was stretching away, and the sky was unpeeling from itself so that everything was becoming more remote from everything else. 'Kisi, don't go. Don't let it master you. You have to break away.'

Nothing so feeble and dim as human intention in the face of that sucking darkness. But I picked up my sluggish feet, hauling myself through the shallows even as it seemed all things were becoming increasingly far from all other things. The quetzlcoatlus reared over me and a crushing weight came down.

I staggered backwards, wings vaning for balance as I braced up against it. Muscle heated. I willed my tendons to hold.

When I got in the car I never expected this. One minute, the most you're dealing with is a steering wheel and traffic, maybe a couple of bullets; the next, the ineffable is bearing down on you as if to crush you beneath its casual, steel-shod heel. No real warning. It was on me now: power and more power, clearing the world off me like a vast original wind from the heavens, blowing water away from my ocean floor, exposing the cracks in the deep.

I felt like a matchstick but I held fast and I held and I held and just when it seemed certain I would be crushed to diamonds and steam, there was a snapping sensation. The world rushed back in and darkness lifted and the human form of Dr Sorle collapsed, bleeding, into my arms.

# All creatures old and new

Alison picked up the phone on the seventh ring, groggy. She didn't ask me for explanations, and she listened to my description of where I was.

'Sounds like Cranleigh,' she croaked. 'On my way.'

I carried Dr Sorle up the beach and lay him on the sand. He was still holding the briefcase against his chest, his hands curled around it in a sort of spasm. There were three bullet holes in the briefcase, and they were smoking.

We were both soaking wet. I tried to keep him warm with my body, and with my wings I called up all memories of his waveform when it was whole, overwriting the injuries as best I could – but I was out of my depth. It must have been fifteen minutes before Alison's 4WD spun into the car park, and all I could think was that Dr Sorle was a part of me and I was a part of him and I wasn't going to let him die.

Then Alison's headlights flashed over me; I waved to get her attention. The 4WD manoeuvred between posts and buildings and bumped out onto the beach. It stopped ten feet away with the headlights on us and Alison came staggering over, the wind whipping her hair sideways into jagged lines.

She had her phone out. Kneeling down she took one look at him and declared the need for an ambulance.

'No! Alison, please. It's complicated.'

She was feeling for his pulse, and she tried to turn his wrist over. He curled on his side, teeth bared in pain, and his hands tightened on the briefcase.

'Dr Sorle. Kisi. Stay with me. We're trying to help you.'

His eyes were squeezed shut. But his fingers found the latches and before I realised what he was doing, the briefcase sprang open. The briefcase that I'd battered and thrashed and prised at to no avail, it opened for him with a big pale smile. He put his hand inside.

Before my visual cortex could process what was inside the aperture, a wall of hard flesh hit me in the face. I was thrown back, stunned, landing on my ass in the sand. There was a woof of violently relocated air, and the quetzlcoatlus now crouched where Kisi and the briefcase had been. Its head was as big as the body of a horse. Its wings splayed across the sand and up on to the concrete walkway.

'Oh my *god*.' Alison had been thrown against her vehicle; her leg was blocking one headlight.

'He's full of bullets,' I told her.

'I know I'm still drunk,' Alison said. 'But I've never in my life dropped acid.'

'Can you help?' I said. 'Because if you can't, no one can.'

'How am I supposed to get near it?'

'Leave it to me.'

I approached the quetzlcoatlus and knelt by its head, in line with the left eye. It was like a laser in some sort of reverse; I could feel the thread of light not drilling into me, but pulling me in to the quetzlcoatlus' labyrinthine mind as if it were a fishing line.

It was as though this creature could suck me in just by perceiving me.

I shook my head to throw off the bad thoughts that were gatecrashing my mind. Instead, I told myself this was a miracle, and I reached out. At first when I touched the animal I was only halfway believing it was there, in the sense of blood and guts anyway. The muzzle was fever-hot, almost too hot to sustain a biological process that relies on enzymes, and lice were crawling through the faint soft fur under its long jaw. I flinched when one of them crawled on my hand. Some past participle of air blasted through the vertical slits of the quetzlcoatlus' nostrils, a gas far too ancient for any human.

Where had this thing really come from? What was it, really?

Alison was cracking open the blister-packs of whatever medical miracles I'd been silly enough to think she could work. Alison wasn't screaming and running, but I could feel her body trembling from two metres away.

There was more going on here than Late Cretaceous tomfoolery. The scalloped edges of its nostrils with their tiny hairs. One black fang, like a sliver of night, like volcano glass. I touched because there was no other way to believe it was true.

My skin was singing discordantly with awareness of pain – the creature was burning up from the inside, too much kinetic energy coming from this world or some other. I can't ignore suffering. Not built to turn away. I took a deep breath, knowing I could put my lips to this animal as if the burning place were a snakebite and I could suck out his pain.

'Pearl. Give me a hand. Can you hold its ... claw ...?'

Why. Isometrics. Are. Useful.

Let me count the reasons. Number 47: because you never know when your obliging vet friend will ask you to hold an unconscious pterosaur's leg out of the way while she roots around with her forceps, looking for the place where the bullet chatters against the bone.

I'm not trying to move something, I'm trying to hold it still. Isometric effort. People make a fuss about the lift, the magical gravity-defying surge when spectacular change happens. But everything has a history, and the sweet spot is only one moment in a continuum.

We begin by not being crushed to death and progress from there.

There's a thing Marquita used to tell me about the philosophy of the Resistance. She said, 'If human beings didn't want to find the magic, the shortcut, the underlying truth, then we wouldn't have the big brains. We'd just have the big biceps, Pearl.'

Good thing I got the biceps right now, that's all I'm thinking as I hold the mofo heavy paw up out of the way. Sweat peels away from my skin and falls on the cold grass.

146

A couple of teenagers were walking along the beach, talking and smoking. I brushed them away with my feathertips, sending them west towards a chippie. There was a faint smoke rising from the pterosaur. One of the kids was troubled about his parents' break-up. I bolstered his faith in himself where I could.

Multi-tasking. It never ends.

'Hand me those big calipers,' Alison said. 'It's in there deep.'

I leaned on the animal's shoulder and watched Alison. She was crouched on the ground, head bent in and torch trained on the wound, her right hand gently exploring the edges of the torn flesh. Where she touched the creature, instead of flinching from her, it felt better. I felt better looking at her, too. Her curling grey hair was clean and blew in ragged wisps, and I could smell the brand of washing powder she used on her clothes. I liked the way her tendons lay against her bones. I liked her skin. It had fine lines like waves leave on the sand after the tide's gone out.

Alison didn't have a mission. She was a healer. She was a human who knew what she was doing and why she was doing it. She wasn't afraid to put herself on the line, but she didn't just throw herself in front of the bus for people, either. I could learn a lot just from observing her. I'm not sure when exactly I realised I was in love with her. She was so small and gentle, but also so confined. I wanted to make her feel things she'd never felt before, take her to places she never thought she could go – except I had no idea what those were or how to find them for her, and the thought of it brought a trembling, as of a memory of the future.

I wanted to fix her but she was already perfect. Just looking at her made me ache and feel whole at the same time.

I don't like admitting my need, because it seems creepy. As if I get off on people being damaged. It's just what I do. Toasters, microwaves, humans – I'm a fixer-upper. I tried to find some gap in Alison that would indicate what possible help I could offer. The only problem with her was that she was resigned to a small life, when she was cut out for big things.

'Pearl!' she snapped. 'Pay attention! I said, pass the antiseptic, please.'

I let go the leg with one hand and got her the antiseptic.

We exchanged glances over the bleeding wing as she took the bottle. Her eyes said, *How crazy is this?*

And mine said: *It's what you were born to do.*

# Fucks like a gerbil

After the bullets were out, the quetzlcoatlus lifted its head and tried to break away from me. Sand flew in great sheets as it swung down the beach with the gait of a person on crutches, using the claws on its wings as forelimbs. I clung to the edge of the left wing by my fingertips, pulling the animal off balance. Its head came round and its mouth opened, foul and meaty.

I wanted my component back. I thought of Dr Sorle, so easily overwritten. I wasn't going to settle for this.

I curled my fingers around the bone on the leading edge of the wing. I put all of my effort in, firing motor neurons and raising rate coding in my cortex until HD opened and I could see the minute passageways that connect and sustain reality like a coral reef sustains life. And once again, the quetzlcoatlus folded and collapsed into a briefcase in the arms of Dr Sorle.

My fingers were numb.

'Help me get him in the car,' I gasped. I managed to get the briefcase off him this time, and between us we rolled Dr Sorle unconscious into the back of the 4WD.

'He can't go to A&E,' Alison said. 'But my flat's not big enough, either. I don't even think the yard is big enough. And it's cold.'

I was already piling horse blankets on top of him. His body was softer than the other Kisi's, and I was worried about shock.

'I'm pretty sure the damn briefcase is to blame,' I said. 'I don't think anything will happen if we keep him away from it.'

'I hope you're right,' Alison said. 'My insurance doesn't cover acts of pterosaur.'

We turfed the cats out of Alison's spare room and I carried Dr Sorle to the bed as if he were a sleeping child. Spots of blood showed through his bandages, but he didn't wake.

149

I took the briefcase into the bathroom with me and washed the blood off my face and hands. Alison threw my clothes in the washing machine and started a cycle, bringing me a too-small pair of pj bottoms and a hoodie that one of her sons had left behind. It was gloriously soft and roomy, but I couldn't stop shaking. While Alison was letting the dogs out and checking the sick cat one more time, I made us tea and brought it upstairs. I set a chair by Dr Sorle's bed, positioning the curtains so I could watch the front of the building without being seen from outside.

My teeth hurt. And my eyes hurt. I was running what had happened on the bridge through my mind, trying to draw conclusions. The people who rammed us weren't doing it for effect or intimidation. They didn't simply want to grab the briefcase or capture Dr Sorle.

They hadn't been law enforcement. They might have been working for Pace. They might have been working for IIF.

Or they might have been Resistance. According to Kisi, the Resistance saw me as a threat. I watched him sleep. In the amber lamplight I noticed the sparkle of pale sand caught in the hairs on his forearm that lay outside the duvet. His body had slipped in and out of HD so beautifully, but not in time to dodge the bullets. There was a little of his blood on the briefcase where he'd held it.

I no longer knew who the bad guys were.

Alison and the dogs came in. She passed me the biscuit tin, then sat down heavily on a wooden chest at the foot of the bed.

'I knew you were going to have trouble with him,' she said. 'And I didn't text when I said I would. Not that I could have done anything. My god. I hardly know where to start.'

'I'm sorry to bring this all on you,' I mumbled through the biscuits I was wolfing down.

'Yeah, well. So when you said "prehistoric frog" you weren't taking poetic licence.'

I smiled. 'It's really late. We're both shattered. There are things you want to know, and I can't explain them to you.'

'You could try.'

I lifted up the briefcase and showed her the bullet holes. 'Look inside the hole and tell me what you see.'

The briefcase wobbled as I passed it to her. She braced it on her knees and peered into the hole.

'It's... That's funny. I can't seem to— I thought it was dark, like a hole, but it actually seems to disappear when I look right at it. It becomes a slit and then it disappears. Like an optical illusion.'

She tried to poke her finger in.

'Don't—' I began. But she couldn't do it.

'Ooh, it's like trying to put two magnets together at the wrong end. It won't let me. Feels like ... swimming against a current.'

I reached over and took it back from her. 'Maybe better not to do that. Just to be on the safe side.'

She said, 'I see from the local feed that Bethany's car has been smithereened on the Forth Road Bridge. Should I expect the police?'

'Maybe, if they talk to Liam and he connects me and you. But it's not the police I'm most afraid of. I need to get Dr Sorle out of here as soon as possible. I just don't know where to bring him.'

Alison focused on her tea. Lamplight put deep crags in her face, and fainter lines, too, like the script of some language spoken far away. She was thinking. I didn't intrude, though I desperately wanted to know what she was thinking.

'You can't bring him anywhere right now,' she said. 'I'm going to bed. Call me if he wakes up, or if you need anything. I put an extra toothbrush in the bathroom for you.'

She put a hand on my shoulder before she went out. I have no idea why, but when my body felt the warmth of her hand I nearly burst into tears.

I turned off the lamp and sat listening to the soft breathing of the dogs and Dr Sorle. My insides were trembling. I had never had enemies before. I knew they were out there, hunting me or my component or both of us, but I couldn't see them and I couldn't even be sure who they were. It made everything worse. Everyone had become a potential threat. If I was right about the attack on the bridge, I had been mistaken for a stain that needed to be removed, a weed that should be pulled, an insect that must be poisoned. My existence was no longer required.

But I felt the opposite. My existence was very much required by me, and I wasn't going to be stopped so easily. I sat watching the street and waiting. Before it was light, the morning traffic started up little by little. A delivery van pulled up to the Spar across the road. Then a taxi coming from the direction of the New Town pulled up outside Alison's. The back door opened and a man got out. He looked like a professional wrestler. I stared, my blood surging up. He held the door open and a slim young woman with blond hair got out. She looked up at the window where I was standing and took out her phone.

I heard Alison's mobile go off from the sitting room. I ran to silence it, waking the dogs. They piled after me down the interior stairs to the hall shared by Alison's offices. I looked out the window beside the front door and saw the big man looking up and down the street warily. The woman was leaving a voicemail. Then she looked up, straight at me.

We both jolted when we saw each other. I fumbled to open the door.

'Bethany!' I cried. I had to restrain myself from throwing my arms around her and rejoicing that she wasn't dead. The dogs were ecstatic. Even as the big man stepped between Bethany and me protectively, they rushed outside, surged around him, and budged up against her, wagging. She glanced once at me and then bent to attend to them.

'Oh, my ickle wickle babies!' Bethany cooed. 'So this is where you've been. Mummy's come for you.'

She straightened and looked at me with quite a bit less affection. 'Where's Teacake?'

I gestured for her to come in. She looked at me darkly.

'Get Alison, please. I don't know who you are. Apparently you've been in my house. Pretending to be a friend. I've never seen you in my life.'

Alison was already coming down the stairs, tying her dressing gown.

'Well, that's a relief,' she said. 'We thought you'd come to harm. You ran out of the house without your bag or anything.'

Bethany said, 'It's complicated. I just got back from St Kitts and found the dogs missing and Liam told me Teacake had been poisoned.'

So she'd spoken to Liam. I wondered if he'd really been waiting for us in Queensferry or if that had just been a story to draw Kisi out. There had been something so random and excessive about the attack on the bridge.

'Come on, you can see Teacake,' Alison said. 'Pearl, could you put the kettle on. Again.'

The big man stepped into the house first.

'I need to check for threats,' he said, but I stood in front of the door to the stairs.

'That's my flat,' Alison said firmly. 'I assure you there are no threats up there. Come along. Nothing in the back but a sick cat and a couple of rabbits.'

I left them in the surgery and went upstairs to check Dr Sorle. Then I put the kettle on. I could hear Alison and Bethany talking down in the hall. Murmuring, really. I crept down the stairs and listened.

'At first I thought you'd finally left him, but when Pearl said she found the house wide open we were really worried.'

'Pearl! Who is that woman? She's posing as my friend.'

'It's a bit complicated. She's a sort of government agent.'

'Oh Jesus fuck, well, keep her away from me. I'm so done with all of this. Do you know, I nearly got killed that day I took off? I grabbed my other passport and got out of here.'

'Other passport? To St Kitts?'

'They gave me a passport when I invested in property down there,' Bethany whispered. 'Liam's been involved in this crazy offshore deal. He asked me to use my citizenship to open an account, and I did, but then he messed me about. He fucked off because he's afraid of some American psychopath who poses as a doctor. He didn't warn me. I was completely unprotected. I swear, Alison, the guy came to my house and threatened me. It was a near thing!'

'Yes, how awful . . .'

'I've had it with this rubbish. I was going to leave Liam anyway. He fucks like a gerbil. I went down and moved the money.'

'You how?' Alison yelped.

It was all I could do not to jerk the door open and go crashing into the hall. The Resistance. She had moved the money that was intended to establish the Resistance.

'Shhhh! I don't want *her* to hear.'

'Sorry,' Alison whispered. 'What a dangerous thing to do.'

'I was going to leave him anyway. The whole deal they set up is falling apart since Austen Stevens disappeared. Liam's bound to get caught, but there's nothing to connect me to any of it because the money was all secret anyway. No one knows where it is.'

'Hen, this sounds like a handy way to get yourself killed. You want to rethink your plan.'

'Liam's the only one who knows, and he won't kill me. And I've got Kostya. And the dogs.'

After that I stopped listening. I went back to the guest room and called Marquita. I had to warn her about the Resistance. Even if Filippe had put out a hit on me, it wasn't Marquita's fault. What would happen to Marquita if the Resistance unravelled?

When I dialled her number, the line was already dead.

# Hilda Doolittle

I don't give up easily. I could find no trace of Marquita's travel agency, and her social network profiles placed her in Mozambique working for an NGO. Her privacy settings were locked but it was easy to get through and find out that she was married to a Mozambiquan political activist and had grown children in Florida, had adopted three more in Maputo. Her face was the same but her hair was different.

I pinged Marquita on video.

She didn't answer right away, and when she did I almost didn't recognise her. Gone were the braids; her hair was cropped short, almost shaven, and she was much too thin.

'Hello? Who's this?'

'Marquita, it's me. Pearl.'

'I'm sorry, who? How did you get into my contacts?'

'Come on, don't be like that.'

Her voice was the same. My chin was quivering. I wanted to run into her arms.

'I'm not going to say anything about anything,' I said. 'I just need a sign that this isn't as bad as it looks. Any sign.'

There was a small silence.

'I'm sorry,' she said slowly, gently. 'I think you've got a wrong number.'

'I don't have a wrong number, Marquita.'

'Well, then I'm going to have to hang up. I don't know what this is about, but please don't contact me like this again. I can't help you. If you need help you have to approach my husband through official channels. I'm not involved.'

'Wait!' I said. 'There's nothing sinister here. I'm not looking for a handout. Please don't hang up.'

Small children were clamouring in Portuguese: 'Mommy, Ishaan pushed me.'

'She touched my porridge!'

'He looked at me.'

'Stop that, you two!' Marquita turned away from the camera and made shooing motions. To me, she said, 'I'm so sorry. I have to go.'

Tears were streaming down my face.

I didn't say anything, but I listened to her scold the kids for a moment or two before the line cut.

She was gone.

I sat looking out on the blue-tinged morning, at the blurred pools of amber surrounding the streetlamps, at the rising tide of rush-hour traffic. I tried to take in what had happened, but I felt numb. Soon another minicab pulled up to the kerb. The driver rang the bell. Dr Sorle stirred at the sound, and I watched him awaken even as Alison showed Bethany and Kostya out. She took the dogs with her.

Dr Sorle was in pain. He managed to sit up anyway.

'We didn't dare take you to the hospital,' I said, offering an analgesic. He didn't take it.

'What happened to the briefcase?'

'It's OK. Unlike you.'

'I'm not going to any hospital.' He started the slow process of putting on his shirt. 'I'm going to turn myself in to the police. I've had enough.'

'No, sir,' said Alison from the doorway. 'You shouldn't be out of bed.'

His face was strained. 'This can't go on. My family are in danger.'

I said, 'They went to your wife's parents.'

He stared at me. 'You—'

I held up Two Phones' phone. 'You're right to be concerned. Pace is certainly tracking your wife. But I don't think they'll lash out at your family in America.'

I felt his reaction to the slight emphasis I'd put on my last two words. His nostrils flared.

'OK,' Alison said mildly. 'We can involve the police if that's what you want.'

'I have to take a leak.'

'Come on. I'll show you.' Alison led him to the toilet. Once the door was closed, she ducked into her own bedroom and I heard drawers opening. She careered back into the hallway and positioned herself outside the bathroom. Dr Sorle emerged tentatively.

'There you go. Back in bed for now. Come on, you've lost quite a bit of blood.'

While she was talking she had taken his arm and was gently leading him back to the bed.

'I can't. I have to go.'

'Of course you do.' She pressed him back until his knees caught on the edge of the bed. Her right hand went into the pocket of her dressing gown and grasped something.

'No, honestly, I need to—'

'Do you feel faint? You do, don't you. Just lie down for a moment.'

As she was talking, Alison brought a syringe out of her pocket; in a practised manner flicked the safety cap off with her thumb.

'Just some medication to help with the pain,' she murmured as she plunged the needle into his glute, right through the fabric of his boxers. He grabbed her wrist too late.

'I don't want any medication. I have a high pain threshold,' he snapped. 'What is that? What are you doing? You can't just . . .'

He'd jerked her off-balance and for a moment I thought they were going to have a wrestling match over control of the needle, but he soon subsided on to the bed, mumbling.

'I'm a vet, Doctor,' Alison said, standing up and straightening her clothes. 'We don't go in for the niceties. Sorry.'

I stood there gaping.

'Alison, you shouldn't have done that.'

'Maybe not. But we need a chance to think this over, and if he calls the police then they'll take him into custody and what happens if he... you know, if he changes into 20,000 leagues under the sea in a police cell?'

'And his family?'

'If his family are in danger, it isn't because of the police. It's because of Pace, and Pace won't be any happier with him in police custody.'

'I'm not sure of that,' I said. 'Pace might own the police.'

'Own the Edinburgh police? Get real. This isn't America, you know. We haven't privatised everything yet. And have our own oil, thank you very much.'

We left him sleeping and went downstairs. Alison made coffee.

I put my hands on the brick wall of Alison's kitchen and I pushed, as if I could get back to the Resistance somehow, to Filippe. Far away, high up, I could feel big spaces brush my wings. Emptiness feels like emptiness, it has no reality at all, no matter, no energy, nothing where the Resistance used to be, not even boundaries, not even edges, not even hints. I couldn't get there from here anymore, and I felt queasy for trying.

Alison was looking at me carefully out of tired green eyes. In this light her upper lip looked shrunken like a desiccated slug, so that her mouth was more of a slit.

'Pearl, what's upset you so? You look like someone died.'

I said, 'Bethany embezzled the money that built the Resistance and now it's gone.'

Alison was quiet for a time. She spoke carefully.

'When you say Resistance, what actually do you mean?'

I told her. Best I could. Which was not very well. She took in the information with wrinkled forehead and silence. Eventually she asked, 'So you're saying this organisation is controlled by an artificial intelligence.'

'It's controlled by an emergent intelligence,' I said. 'The thing doesn't operate according to human logic. I think it has HD elements that allow it to slip time. It can model consequences of specific actions and find points in a chain of events that are vulnerable to small influences.'

'What kind of small influences?'

'Usually helping someone in some way that isn't very costly or difficult. Providing access to information, or sustenance. Think of "for want of a nail" sort of thing. The Resistance will step in at a point where the provision of a nail would be critical to some desired outcome. Or it might be a case of preventing something from happening. Like stopping someone and talking to them – you might do it because you feel compelled to, without knowing the reason. Maybe the reason is that they miss their bus, and then they avoid getting killed in a crash. But no one knows. The nature of the Resistance doesn't provide information about the path taken. It's just inputs and outcomes.'

'But this person has to be special in some way, right? Would the Resistance intervene for just anyone?'

I shook my head. 'It's for people whose actions down the causality stream are valuable to the whole.'

'According to whose judgement?'

'Good question. I'm not sure what exactly it's programmed to do. Dr Sorle said something about humanity levelling up.'

'And this money transfer was going to make the Resistance possible. But how does that work? If the technology hasn't been invented yet, then how can it exist for you to tell me about it?'

'HD,' I said.

'Hilda Doolittle? High definition?'

'Higher dimensions. Think hyperspace.'

'Ah,' she said, nodding. She thought for a while. Then she said, 'This whole Resistance business doesn't make a whit of sense. You can't orchestrate kindness. The whole point of kindness is that it doesn't give you anything back. Kindness is like feeding the birds. You offer seeds and don't control where they go or what they do. The idea that you would only do certain good things on certain days or at certain times because of strategy – that's madness.'

'Trying to optimise outcomes is madness? But it's what we do in all sorts of ways. Whenever we share information with each other, provide resources, we're doing it in the expectation that something beneficial to us will come out of it, even if only indirectly. How is this any different? The Resistance just acts across time instead of distance.'

'What if you helped someone and then found out afterwards that you had enabled them to do something unconscionable? Would you not take back your kindness?'

'I don't know what I would do,' I said. 'But you can't control everything. The world is chaotic. You can't predict outcomes with certainty and it's lunacy to try.'

'Exactly,' Alison said. 'Which is why you won't convince me the Resistance is a worthwhile enterprise.'

I had to look away because my eyes were flooding with tears. Where was I in the causality stream of the Resistance? Kisi Sorle had stolen my component and launched me here to convince Austen Stevens to invest in futures that Stevens thought would be immortality for himself, but would really become the Resistance. I had been used to offer proof of a thing that would now never come to pass, thanks to Bethany's tampering.

And Bethany had pulled her money out on account of the violence committed by the Kisi Sorle I had scanned. Violence that was only possible because of the briefcase again: my component, the part of me that held me here, kept me from inhabiting all of myself, kept me in ignorance of my true purpose.

But the man who represented Pace Industries and its crimes in Kuè? Still in the briefcase.

How messed up is that.

# Plant

The drug is keeping your consciousness down and you can't seem to fight it.

You dream you're in the garden with your wife and daughters. You're planting vegetables. And he's there, on the ground. All cut open, so that his guts are spread out but he's still alive. You're sowing unusual seeds in his body. The old man will lie on the ground, his flesh bursting with these potentials. He will be in agony as they curl and dive through him, consuming his resources, ending his ego's hegemony over mute flesh. His mutinied cells will talk back to him in many languages across worlds and times, and there is nothing he can do about it and you feel so happy, for the first time you can remember since you were a boy you feel that the world is right. Doctor, he will cry out. First do no harm. And you will break your oath like breaking the sound barrier. You will hear nothing of his cries. Nothing but blue sky when he's gone.

# Superunknown

I knew what I had to do. And now that it was upon me, I was scared and vaguely aggressive. I felt like a jockey before a race.

'He won't sleep long,' Alison said. 'I didn't give him enough, and he's liable to fight it and try to get out of bed even though he's sedated.'

'Good,' I said. 'I need him to be awake. He's the only one who can open the briefcase.'

Her eyes lit up.

'I'm going to have to leave you for a while,' I said to her. 'I need you to keep an eye on Dr Sorle and the briefcase. Try to keep them apart. I think the pterosaur only happens when he gets into it.'

There were blue shadows under Alison's eyes; beneath the mask of freckles, she flushed.

'I'll get my assistant to cancel my appointments for today. And maybe I'll call my colleague Gunther for backup... You know that the police will be looking for Bethany now, because of the car.'

I shook my head. 'Don't say her name to me. She's a vandal.'

So much careful, delicate work. So many sacrifices. And now everything Kisi Sorle had done would be for nothing. Because of her stupidity. The irony was that I'd feared for her safety, had pursued Two Phones partly because I had been afraid for her. If someone had killed her before she got to St Kitts—

'One other thing, Pearl. On the phone the other night you said "prehistoric frog", didn't you?'

'Oh, that. Yeah, I put it in the freezer at Bethany's house. What you really need to know about the briefcase is that it's unpredictable. I don't know where the frog came from. I can only guess it comes from the same place as the pterosaur.'

'And the briefcase has a pattern of bullet holes identical to what was in the pterosaur, and the wounds in Dr Sorle.'

'That man upstairs isn't necessarily Dr Sorle. He ... You should treat him like a multiple personality case.'

'There's no such thing as multiple personalities, that whole line of psychology was wrong—'

'Just treat him like that anyway, OK?'

I handed her my phone.

'I won't be needing this where I'm going.'

I got myself cleaned up while Alison was talking to her assistant downstairs. Then I dragged the briefcase over to the bed where the man was tossing and moaning. He was feverish, semiconscious. He was also subtly different. This wasn't Dr Sorle anymore. I braced myself.

'Maybe I should give him antibiotics.' Alison came in wearing chinos and a cardigan over a Dogs Trust T-shirt. 'I'm reluctant to involve a doctor. I'm already criminally liable. This could end very badly indeed for me.'

The briefcase was looking quite a bit worse for wear, and the bullet holes were leaking what I first thought was smoke, but actually seemed more like a gas of light. Or plasma...

Just for old times' sake I tried the latches. Still locked.

The man in the bed opened his eyes. He brought his right arm to the bandage wrapped around his ribs, then to the bandage on his left arm, then to the one on his shoulder. Three wounds. He grimaced and sat up.

'Oh no you don't,' Alison said, moving as if to press him down again. He ignored her and got to his feet. Dr Sorle had yielded easily, but this man shot a hostile look at Alison that stopped her in her tracks.

'Kisi,' I said. 'What are you doing? You're going to wear out your body.'

'Don't be absurd. I am healing the body.'

He peeled back the shoulder bandage and took a look at the injury. It was getting better very quickly.

'My waveform is much more efficient than his.'

'Lie down anyway,' Alison said. Then she added, 'Please.'

He sat on the edge of the bed as though compromising.

'I feel like hell,' he said.

'The Resistance is down,' I told him. 'The funds were moved. I don't know if there's a way to get them back. Probably not.'

Actually, there probably was. If you had it in you to force Bethany back on a plane, take her to the bank under threat and make her put the money back where she'd found it. I didn't have it in me and I didn't want Kisi to have it in him, even though he probably did.

Kisi's face had closed. He was somewhere between rage and despair and exhaustion. Just looking at him was scaring me.

'It's over,' I told him. 'You're unstable. The briefcase is unstable. You were lucky last night when they shot you. I still can't believe you're not dead.'

He caught sight of the briefcase and gave a rough guffaw, then winced as his ribcage moved too much.

'Dead would be easier.'

'Kisi. You owe me a debt. Are you the kind of person who uses others the way you've been used? Or will you honour your promise?'

He was shaking his head.

'I don't know how to give it back to you. It looks different here than it looked in HD. It looks like a physical object but it isn't that.'

I said, 'I need you to open it.'

Alison said, 'Pearl, you can't seriously—'

I held up a hand without looking at her.

'Be quiet, Alison,' I said. 'In fact, it might be better if you left.'

Her eyeglasses flashed as she tilted her head sceptically.

'That depends. What are you going to do?'

'Whatever I'm going to do, you don't need to see it.'

Alison snorted. 'Look, I'm the one who's going to end up cleaning up whatever mess you make, so let me have a little respect. This is my home and my business. Whatever you're going to do, you can't do it here.'

Kisi pushed himself to his feet, hissing.

'You're right,' he said. 'Do we have a car? Let's just go.'

I had been running all the permutations of what might happen and how easily we could be stopped, and I had already decided we were at a dead end. We could go out the front of the house and be taken – or followed. We could go out the back alley and it would be the same. I couldn't call Marquita for backup, I couldn't disappear into HD leaving the briefcase behind because that would solve nothing. I had to take the chance that this would work, and the briefcase would become part of me and I'd be whole again, and I'd know whatever it was I'd forgotten. It was an outside chance, but I couldn't risk becoming separated from the briefcase again without trying it.

'No,' I said. 'I've waited too long to do this. I'm going in and I'm going to put my component back if I have to sew it into my guts myself.'

Alison was shaking her head.

'It's a terrible idea,' she said. 'Just hold on. There are people I can call. I have friends. I have a son who is quite handy in a crunch. We don't need to do this alone.'

Kisi and I were looking at each other.

'I've had enough of this,' I said to him. 'Open it.'

'Pearl! Are you listening to me?' Alison was using her bad dog voice. It would have been funny in any other situation. Right now I didn't really hear her.

Kisi Sorle knelt before the briefcase on the dusty floor of the guest room. We eyed one another.

'Do it,' I said.

'Don't do it!' cried Alison.

He slid the latches open and then spun the briefcase so that it faced me and I could see inside. I think he keeled over after that, but I wasn't looking at him anymore. I was looking inside my component.

I would be able to see inside if there were anything to see. But there was nothing to see. Absolutely nothing. The opposite of everything. Etc.

I found myself standing on the edge of the briefcase like a diver on the high platform. Thought I knew my feet: they have high, impossible-to-fit arches and they are broad and strong, with muscular toes that grip well. But not anymore.

My feet are claws. I am balancing with my wings, holding myself on the point of falling in or falling back. I feel the substance of the briefcase slither between the clacking grip of my claws. The substance of the briefcase itself is deep, and its intermolecular spaces are suspect: they look back at me like eyes. But these clever engineered depths are as nothing compared to the skirling void of that frank maw. Eater of dead men, mother of questions, it is before me and presents itself without sound, without smell, without sight. Without touch. My claws hold the edges of its containment, a mystery field that shows me my own blindness without mockery and without pity. I try to breathe. I need something to anchor me to the visceral but claws and breath and blood are not enough.

I need to know what's in there. Perception is not optional. I need to find a way to see it.

'Pearl,' said Alison's light voice in my ear. 'This is a terrible idea. Come back.'

I tried to hiss 'keep away' to her without arousing the notice of whatever was living inside the briefcase, but my words didn't come out like that. They came out in long string of complicated basso profundo syllables, as though the caverns of my throat were some tremendous echoing place and meaningless words were breeding furiously there.

*Oh, shit,* I thought. *Whatever lives here is bound to awaken now and drag me in by the neck.*

I felt myself turning inside out. Invert the brain; it's a place of deep fissures and uncrossable chasms. The falling.

It's a sort of laughter. You'd never guess.

In that powerful acceleration I was gifted with a tremendous awareness of the electrical potential of my muscles, and I clenched the edge of the briefcase with all my strength. Those claws I never knew I had, they bit into casing's material 'til it screamed. Then I launched, headlong into the superunknown, wings folded, sweetness and light into darkness and fear.

This is for everyone who thinks ships are made of metal and petrochemicals and that they travel through space like sailboats travelled the high seas, propelled by mysterious engines that grant them impossible speed. That space sailors have space battles with space pirates and electrical cables and explosions and space bars with space booze. That you can only get there from here by a linear progression. Like rowing really really fast, through the void.

This is for everyone who thinks trips are chemical-induced hallucinations in the naked brain and bodies are expendable in the face of the singularity. This is for you who believe in distance and think time is just another version of same.

John Wheeler posited that every electron in the universe could be one electron zipping back and forth in time, a reversible positron tied in knots with itself – a Speedy Gonzales universe. Where would you cut that Gordian knot to make it collapse? Where would you cut that umbilical cord, baby?

The briefcase and I are whispering to one another, lovers in the dark. Impossible to say which of us said what to one another:

I missed you. You fit so nicely in my hole. Thank you.

# A sample of crude oil and a couple of feathers

The veterinarian is making you walk down the stairs but you just want to sleep. You sway and lean on her, and she bundles you into a smelly four-wheel drive. Then she brings the briefcase.

'You've lost a lot of blood,' she informs you. 'I'm sorry to rush you, but I thought it best for us to get out of here. Pearl went in the briefcase. Don't know if you saw that part.'

The veterinarian – *Alison*, she says – starts driving. You try to think about Pearl in the briefcase but find your mind is like a mule that's decided it won't turn left, and you can't do it. Alison calls her assistant to check the practice is OK until someone called Gunther arrives. She has arranged to meet Gunther in a desolate part of Leith and swap vehicles. You don't have the energy to tell her that her phone is surely monitored.

'How long is it likely to take?' she asks. 'For Pearl to do whatever it is she's trying to do?'

You fix your gaze on the traffic light ahead of you, fighting nausea.

'Is this car in the national database?' you ask.

'What, you mean, can we be tracked? Yes, we can.'

'That's bad for us.'

Alison clears her throat. 'So, ehrm, is it possible for you to let me speak to the doctor? Because I'd like some advice about how to deal with your... his... your body.'

'You are speaking to me and I am a doctor,' you say, letting your head fall back on the headrest and closing your eyes. 'If you want to deal with my body you could start by avoiding these cobbled back roads. Where are we going?'

Pearl's phone rings and Alison pulls over outside a strip club in Leith to take the call. She puts it on speaker.

'This is Jerry Shroeder from Edinburgh University. I have some information on the sample you asked me to look at.'

'The what?'

'The sample? I hope I've got the right number. Is this Pearl? I have here a sample of crude oil and a couple of feathers that came my way with your contact details attached. Ring any bells?'

Alison glances at you and puts the parking brake on.

'Of course,' she tells him. 'I'm sorry – you caught me right in the middle of something. Go on. I'm listening.'

The voice on the phone says,

'Well, if you've got access to a computer I could application-share and you could see for yourself. There are structures here that ... that we just don't see in nature.'

Jerry Shroeder sounds excited

'I'm in Edinburgh, as it happens,' Alison says cautiously.

'Great! Do you want to come in? You can look through the microscope yourself, and I can explain...?'

You shake your head when he says this. It's surely a trap.

'I'll have to get back to you. Can I take your number?'

When she hangs up you say, 'Feathers and oil. It could be something, but I wouldn't go in person. Too risky.'

Alison is looking at her rear-view mirror.

'I'm more concerned with people pursuing us,' she says.

You sigh. 'That's not how it will be done. They'll use GPS. Do you have any paracetamol?'

'There's ibuprofen in the glove box.'

'I never take that,' you inform her. 'It does terrible things to your liver.'

Her voice sails up in a laugh. 'You're worried about liver damage? Tell you what, Doctor. Open the glove box and take three ibuprofen and a slug of what's in the flask. Your wee liver won't even notice the ibuprofen after the whisky hits it.'

'My liver,' you intone, 'is not wee.'

But you do as she says.

'It's going to be OK. Gunther will ring any minute. No one

can connect you and me. I have no record whatsoever. We'll get you out of sight, and we'll figure out how to get the money back from Bethany and make this thing right. There has to be a way. It will be OK.'

'Pace will have monitored phones, internet, everything,' you tell her. 'One of their agents is gone. There are the people from the bridge who saw Pearl. They can add it up.'

'They. They. Who are *they*?'

'Pace have government links. The reason the police haven't been round is because MI5 and possibly the international finance community are watching everything we do. Your phone is monitored. Your e-mail is monitored. There's probably a satellite on us by now. They are all in each other's pockets, the whole pack of them.'

'I was afraid it was something like that. Are you sure?'

'They don't want you, Alison. They want me. And whatever you see in the headlines, it's not because of the gunshots on Long Island. They want me because I know where the bodies are buried at Pace. I know everything about how Stevens skimmed the money. This isn't the first time I've worked for him.'

'What about the briefcase? No offence, but Pearl has entrusted her life to me.'

'They'll be aware of it. I'm certain none of them know anything about what it really contains.'

'Well, if they take it and open it then it will be like that movie when the Nazis open the Ark of the Covenant, won't it?'

'I'm not going to let it come to that.'

'Do you have a choice? Can you...' She resorts to actual handwaving at that point as if she can't bring herself to say the words *change into a prehistoric bat-winged lizard.*

'No,' you say, and you feel him listening there in your shoulder blades and in your hips. 'Not under my control. It happens. Or it doesn't happen. And it's connected to that.'

You indicate the briefcase, sitting so quietly in the back seat. Alison's phone lights up.

'Thank god for Gunther,' she says, and puts the car in gear. 'Let's go.'

She drives to a warehouse covered with graffiti but devoid of airborne advertisements. You hear gulls and you smell garbage. Gunther is there, a slight man with faded wispy hair who drives an ancient mud-cloaked van that looks held together with baling twine. He is using the cigarette lighter to pump up a tyre as Alison parks behind him. She hands him the keys to her late-model four-wheel-drive.

'Isabel has the number for the supply company in case you need anything. It's really straightforward stuff, and just ping me if you need anything.'

Gunther has a look on his face like he can't believe his luck. He glances at you a few times with a flash of small smile, but seems afraid to speak to you. You get the impression he thinks you are Alison's toy boy. You feel so faint that you must lean on his rickety vehicle.

'Are you sure about this, Ali?' Gunther says. 'I've put Madge's boiler suit in the back for you. I hope it fits.'

'It'll be fine. Well, my friend and I had best be off. Thanks so much for doing this, Gunther, and I hope you enjoy Edinburgh.'

Gunther waves as Alison drives off in the squeaky old van. She blows out a huge sigh and punches on the stereo.

'I hope he's not suspicious,' she confides. 'We're not really friends. Years ago I taught him on a course and he was always making jokes about sticking his arm up a cow's backside and then waggling his eyebrows at me as if he thought this was a turn-on. I had to ask my mate Kevin to have a quiet word.'

'A quiet word?' You laugh. 'What exactly would that entail?'

'Never mind. So, Gunther's practice is in the middle of fuck-all, up north beyond even Inverness. Kevin goes up to do holiday cover when Gunther goes back to Austria every winter to ski, and he told me how on the property there's an old airplane hangar. I think it used to be part of this estate that got broken up. It's a huge place, totally empty.'

'I think I understand,' you say, plucking a length of baling twine from the gear shift and tossing it in the back of the van. 'So it is a large animal practice.'

'Very large.' Alison laughs. Then she says, 'Don't know why I'm laughing. What's so fucking funny?'

You turn round in your seat and produce what looks like a giant pair of pliers with curved pincers. You snap them together.

'My daughter has a game called Dinosaur Dentist,' you say, waving them around.

She swats the pliers away. 'They're for taking off horse shoes. Are you going to call your wife and tell her where you are?'

'Indeed,' you say. 'I shall tell her that until further notice I will be living in an airplane hangar and fraternising with the Loch Ness monster while you engage in a little dubious financial hacking to try to recover some of the funds that were lost when Bethany Collins ruined the future of humanity because her boyfriend doesn't satisfy her sexually. My wife will then file for divorce and report my location to the police.'

'Can't say I blame her,' Alison sighs. 'Maybe you should say you're playing golf.'

## Remembers the future

My face was in the muck. I lifted my head and sneezed. I was in a shallow ditch, not deep enough to be a grave – more like a really modest impact crater caused by me. It was rapidly filling with water from the surrounding swamp. The shadow of my wings fell over my body, so that I felt intense sunlight on my feathers but not on my skin. The air in my nostrils was sultry and moist, loaded with oxygen. I felt my blood vessels make adjustments as my body reorganised itself to my new environment.

All around me grew horsetail ferns, great big ones. The geometry of their growth ratio played little games with my visual cortex; I liked the pretty patterns. They lay at funny angles where I crushed them, some criss-crossing, some bent like drinking straws. A disturbed insect the size of a hockey stick hovered nearby, its wings thrumming. I found the thing unnerving, but only until I heard the rumble of something much bigger. Towering over the swamp where I lay was a forest of giant angiosperms. I felt tiny.

I wasn't in Edinburgh anymore.

There was no sign of the briefcase.

I got to my feet. Sweat was already running down the middle of my back, beading on my feathers. My bare feet sank into the marsh and I felt vulnerable because it was hard to see any distance ahead. I waded and plodded and thrashed aside ferns, all the while taking in the background noise of insect calls, which were low-pitched and hooting.

As I gained higher ground and caught a better view of my environment, I noticed a bald spire of rock that jutted well above the tops of the giant angiosperms that presided over the swamp. If I could get up there, I would get a good view of my surroundings.

Walking on soft loam now, I headed for the cover of the trees. I kept my eye out for tracks of predators, but the ground up here was dry and what markings there were, I couldn't begin to identify. I could see scarring on the trees, places where the lower branches had been ripped off. Competing pheromones laced the air, and at times there were markings on the bark that looked biological. Something big was in the habit of coming through here; from the look of it, more than one something.

The forest was full of music, some it insect in origin and some reptilian. I heard deeper calls, too, away in the horsetails. Looking out over the flatland from above I could see the stems stirring in places, but whatever was making them stir was effectively invisible.

This really didn't give me a nice feeling.

I didn't know what I was going to do with the quetzlcoatlus when I found it, but I had to find it. I didn't think I could outfly it, and I didn't like my chances of beating it in a fight, either. Yet so far it had shown no intention of wanting to destroy me; it had had ample opportunity.

I had to find a way to communicate with it.

I began to climb up the hill. It was bigger than it looked; my eyes weren't used to the scale here. I paused many times for breath, often putting my hand on the bark of a tree to steady myself.

The coiled sunlight of rough sienna bark surged beneath my fingers when I did this. Light made solid. I leaned against one tree for just a moment, for a place to lay my head. Maybe it could give me some scrap of comfort. A gouge had been taken out of the side of the tree, as though some large body had collided with it. Its bole was perhaps eight feet in diameter, and a swatch the size of a motorbike had been scraped away at my eye level when I came to stand among the root system. The wound was fresh; there were traces of animal material and the black marks of mud where some living thing had rubbed itself on the edges of the broken wood. Resin sparkled in the light.

I felt the urge to repair it, just like I always feel the urge to repair everything. I put my fingers on the wood and tried to sense its construction. I stilled my gaze. I was listening, as if for a heartbeat. There are faint pulses and vibrations in plants all the time, and they can tell you a lot.

The tiny feathers on the back of my neck had stood up. There was a cold feeling in my solar plexus.

I peeled back the edge of the bark. Flaking moist scaffolds of cellulose lay in my hand, innocent and seemingly aimless plant cells. They didn't fool me. I could smell the intention that girded their molecules, how it aligned carbon bonds through higher-dimensional ciphers. There was information here, more than I could conceive. I looked up and the great trunks gently converged overhead so that I could see only a scrap of lacy sky. This forest was a library, all right. But the books here weren't made of dead trees. They were written in living ones.

Something was whispering to me. Not a plant, but Marquita's voice. Right close in my ear. I knew she wasn't here. She couldn't be here. But I could hear her. I heard her breath and the clacking of her spit and the sliding of her tongue, the echoing of breath in throat and against teeth. I knew where the words began and ended because I speak the language, every language, but if you didn't know language then all the images and histories and truths and fictions in her words would just be a stream of tones bounded by different types of clacking and changes in volume. She was invisible, and when her mouth was against my ear I felt her breath on my skin and the soft ticks and slipperings of consonants go into my soul like sea foam and I was sailing on the low pitch of her voice, for it was like so many other voices and it was like the sun: it was everything I knew. I hear her swallow in between utterances, and I heard her breathe, and we miss so much when the assumptions we attach to words are all we snatch.

*Go down inside it*, she said. The hiss of her breath told me go in – as if I had tiny cameras in every cell. As if I know the way. There are vast intermolecular spaces, there are nuclear engines generating the strong force.

Could I sail there? In my small leaky boat, could I?

*Go on, Pearl. Don't be afraid.*

I pushed until sweat sprang up in my pores. I rooted myself to the ground, lined up joints and ligaments, recruited muscle. I gasped for breath and pushed and I honed myself down. I slid like a fish into the gap between light waves and flowed into the molecular structure of the tree. Most of it was empty and I can incorporate myself into the emptiness. I am the smoke of thought. I filter through the years, the accumulation of wood and memory.

It's very curious. I can detect in the cellulose tiny insertions, irregularities so subtle that at first I think I must be imagining them. The cellulose has strings of highly structured carbon running through it, and the carbon tubes have been doped with HD gates, and the pattern of doping has a code, and the code unlocks something that has been hidden in these primeval molecules.

It comes to me in glimpses and flashes, all sensation and scraps of mathematics.

I'm in the Cretaceous but I'm touching parts of the universe that are inconceivably distant. There is a presence here in HD, an intelligence that is so big I can at most be a lifeboat to its vast ship. It has left fingerprints, echoes of itself that spiral updimension and touch the future in places that ordinary space can't reach. I've sensed it before. But here, here in the depths of history, the sense of a deeper intelligence is much stronger than anything I felt pushing metal at Dubowski's.

Something ineffable has been sown into these biological structures.

I don't dare think what I think. It's almost as if this wood remembers the future. As does the soil. And one day this tree and all of this world will become crude oil in the ground and, when it burns, the ghosts will speak to the boy Kisi who will assume they are his ancestors.

But they're not his ancestors. His ancestors haven't been born yet. The waveforms trapped in these Cretaceous molecules are not local to Earth.

How did I get to Dubowski's? How did I find my way there, and what was I before that happened? Or is that my ending, and am I now ravelling upstream, fighting the tide? There's a sophisticated HD structure here in this wood. Who put it here, and when, and how?

This business in the tree, it's made of the same stuff as my wings. The same mystery, folded to implication, to silence. And it's calling me. Could I climb inside this cellulose and project myself across vast spaces? Would I find my way home?

I want to. So bad. I want to stretch for it. And I'm afraid. The tension of opposites sings behind my eyes.

A hoarse cry broke the ambience of the forest and scared me out of my reverie. Adrenaline sizzled on my skin. I moved away from the damaged tree, looking overhead for the source of the sound. I had an aggressive headache. Sweat was dripping off me and my biceps were trembling after the exertion. I could hear animals moving in the forest, feathered things that were noisy in the leaf litter.

Something large on the wing passed over the forest, calling with a surprisingly musical voice. The bottom of my stomach dropped out when I glimpsed the underbelly of the quetzlcoatlus. I scrambled up the hill, following the direction of its flight.

By the time I got up on the rocks, light was failing. Judging by how quickly the sun went down, we were somewhere much closer to the equator than Edinburgh. The forest was full of deep shadow and even the open swamp had a bluish look to it as I came out on the rocks at the top of the hill. The wind brought nocturnal cries and a strong smell of vegetable decay.

The sandstone here had been sculpted smooth – by water? – and was now bare of vegetation but heavily scored by what might have been claw marks.

'You finally made it.' It was a man's voice, bubbling with mucus. Somewhere behind me. I whipped around on my heel, looking for the source of the voice. Even then I almost didn't see Austen Stevens. He was propped up against the bole of a giant angiosperm, clad in thin pyjamas that seemed unspoiled by his adventures. The oxygen mask was on the ground; the tank lay aslant among the root system of the tree.

The old man coughed. When I went over to him he bestowed on me a weak yellow smile.

'Let's talk turkey,' he said.

# Turkey

Austen Stevens' voice was thin and it seemed to struggle to reach my ears but, like sound under the sea, it also came from everywhere. I didn't want to know him, not this way or any way. I had no choice.

'I will have my way,' he rasped. 'I knew you would come.'

The gluttony of him. I ought to take him in my teeth. Snap his neck. It would be so easy.

I could feel every contour of him: evasive, cunning, self-righteous, blind. Soft and failing and afraid and determined to stay alive. For all his ugliness, he was still human. Far from the best, but not the worst either.

And even if he had been the worst, what could I have done? Snapping necks isn't my M.O. Saving is, as loath as I may feel to save this one. It's what I do.

'I want to live,' he tells me.

Everything wants to live, I say. Even things that think they don't, deep down, they do. You don't get to decide if or when you're born. You didn't. I didn't.

'The place you come from. They have the power there to fix me. It's already underway.'

He couldn't know this. He only knew what bullshit Kisi had spun him. But Kisi knew. What if it was really true?

'Your money was stolen,' I told him. 'The technology you think is going to save you will never exist, not the way Kisi told you, anyway. The deal fell through.'

'You can save me, kid,' he says. 'I always knew you could. Ever since I saw you in the sky.'

'It was a scam,' I said.

'Kisi thinks it was a scam. But how? I'm here. You're here. You have the power to renew my life. Him I never trusted. But you.

When I saw you there, in the sky, with those beautiful wings . . .
I knew you were real. And here you are. You came for me.'

I sat back on my heels.

'Why would I want to save you?'

'It's why you were sent to Earth. You have to take me away
to the future. I paid.'

Now I'm stuck. And this is how these guys operate. I'll never
be able to understand it. Here I am giving it away, my energy,
my compassion, my strength. And dude wants to sell my own
love back to me at a price. Everything's a fucking commodity.

'There's no way to be sure that any amount of money could
build the Resistance now that the original plan has been
changed,' I said. 'Nice try for playing on my human sympathies,
though. Someone I loved is gone because of a piece of em-
bezzlement. Who orchestrated that?'

He laughed. 'Nobody has to orchestrate Murphy's Law,
sweetheart. One thing I've observed in my time is that you can
always count on shit going wrong.'

I tried to look past the greasy Venetian blinds of his eyes.
How little meaning there is in the eyeball: reactive pupils, dodgy
blood vessels, rime of tear-duct scum, sure thing; but as for
expression or soul windowhood, not so much. The whole notion
is false, a lazy supposition. Sure, OK, maybe some summation
of facial movement characterises the neighbourhood of the eye
and sets it up for its role as chief actor in a person's face, but all
of this is indirect. Implied. If you really look in someone's eyes
you don't see the eye. This other trick happens where you see
a Reisman sum of everything but. It's a trick.

Stevens was puckering. Some absence in him tugged at me,
a sinking-inward as to a sump like the chemical badlands he
created. That's fanciful, I know. Maybe I just saw the decay of
age and the algorithms of selfhood that were starting to harden
up into parody.

'It's funny, isn't it, kid? Here I am. A fossil, among the stuff that will become fossil fuel. It's quite an irony. I can't say I regret having the chance to fly, though.'

'It's not for me to decide what to do with you,' I said. 'That's up to Dr Sorle. He is the one you promised money. He is the one whose life you ruined.'

There was a silence from him. In the space where his thoughts had been I could now hear a rushing noise, a blurring of inputs that reminded me we were in the briefcase, travelling, all the while rolling down some invisible escarpment towards a tideless sea. Felt like we were skating down the diagonal of the diagonal of infinity in Hilbert's hotel, our hypothetical skateboard racked up on one edge like we were daredevils. He was the devil and I was the dare.

As I waited for his response, a reek of decay began to rise from the swamp, bringing wavering bands of heat that shook the sky. It brought me the smell of Austen's ancestors and of their deaths, stories gusting on the air of this place inside the naugahide briefcase outside the world.

How long had he been here? The oxygen in this atmosphere was rich enough that I could understand how he was getting by without it. There were puddles of water in the hollows of the sandstone. Maybe he had dragged himself to them. I couldn't understand why no predator had taken him. The spire of rock that had drawn my attention was one of many similar formations; the land here was a strange mixture of upthrust rock, forest, and flat swamp. We were in a larger depression in surrounding hills, and it seemed as though the water had no outlet from this valley. I could see where there must be deep gorges under the surface of the marsh, but no water flowed. Shadows were forming now. The downgoing sun showed a little of its disc through a furore of cloud, and there was a hint of relief now from the wet torpor of day. At last I felt like I could get a good breath of air. Violet shadows appeared under the pterosaur's mottled wings as it spread them, and the breeze carried its musk to my nostrils.

I began to think he had expired. It was so quiet. But even as I began to dare hope he was gone, his words came to me, blandly predictable.

'It doesn't matter if IIF was a scam. You're here, and you're real. If you take me with you I'll give Dr Sorle the money I promised him.'

'I'm not taking you with me.' The irony was that I could no longer take him anywhere. Where would I take him? Into the HD gateways in the trees? Who or what had seeded the cellulose of this time and place with HD gates? Not the Resistance. So who? And how could I be sure of anything when I was now inside my own component, my launcher. Or was it inside me?

Austen Stevens coughed himself into what must have been a state of exhaustion. I think he drowsed off. Large insects were active and they kept coming for my blood. I let my wings out to keep them back. Felt like a horse swishing flies.

It occurred to me that I was waiting for him to die. It was as though nothing could change until he was gone. What does it mean to sit with the dying? Is he contagious? All that failure, all that ending, all that clinging – I can't catch it, can I?

Of course not, Pearl.

But I'm afraid of him.

He goes on breathing. I don't know how not to walk down his pathways any more than I know how not to smell the fabric-softener on his freshly-washed pyjamas. Lavender for the man who has robbed and killed unchecked because it was all just a contest; the thought offends me almost to the sickpoint in my back throat.

I watch myself. I am jockeying his life, I am inhabiting his slackening tendons and blood-starved nails. He is so sure he is all right. Never a tyrant; instead, a visionary. I could rip him apart with my bare hands and he wouldn't understand why. He would only understand that he had lost the game.

Just when I thought he wouldn't speak again he said, 'I'll give you the bank codes.'

# A very passable Glendronach

Gunther's place isn't a real airplane hangar, it's just a huge old corrugated steel barn with a vaulted roof and a cruddy cement floor on which a thin layer of muck was left to dry. In the one dry corner are a hosepipe, an electrical outlet, and a stack of pallets. Two pallets have been laid out nearby, and on them are stacked some amplifiers, a keyboard, and a partly-dismantled drum kit, all strapped down under quilted wraps. The building sports holes in the roof and at the joints of the walls, so that there are drips and damp patches. In the middle of the barn slumps an old harrow with hanks of mouldy straw hanging from its teeth.

Alison leaves you here ('in case anything funny happens' she says gracelessly) and goes into the house. You work out your exits and possible hiding places. You don't like the way the barn is set in the bracket of two steep hills. Even in middle age you can run; but you don't want to deal with a helicopter and the ground cover here is nonexistent: there is heather, and there is gorse, and there are miniature birch trees no taller than you are. Like a hobbit forest. You'd have done better in the city.

You watch the approach to the property through a rusted joint in the side of the barn. It's all dead quiet. Twenty minutes later Alison comes out carrying a mountain of blankets and a rucksack. She hands you a sandwich and an energy drink, then starts packing you a survival kit.

'If they come, I'll stall them. You can go up the back of the valley and into the glen. There's proper woodland there. I'm packing the basics you need. Over the other side of the ridge is a pub called the Red Lion. I'm going to bring Gunther's old motorbike over there in the morning. It's the best I can do.'

You take up your vantage point at the slit. The tyre on the

van is going flat. The sky droops with moisture, distant clouds bleeding their dark grey edges on to the hills. You can hear a helicopter approaching.

'Here we go.'

Alison goes out to the practice van and comes back carrying a big wooden tackle box. You see her stop, shade her eyes, and watch the helicopter approach. It flies over at some speed and disappears over the line of hills to the north.

She comes in whistling. She sets the box on the floor and rummages.

'It's a military helicopter. They do training runs over these hills all the time. Don't be surprised if you see F-16s, either.'

You find it hard to stay still. The helicopters bring back memories of the militia. And you know how easy it is for Pace to buy whatever it wants.

'In all likelihood I won't get out of this alive. It would be better if they'd just shoot me down. I don't want to be used anymore. By anyone.'

'You would really take death over being used?'

'I would.'

'Right. There's a very passable Glendronach in Gunther's office,' she says. 'I'll just go fetch it.'

'If it's anything like that stuff in your glove box, I'd rather have a Diet Coke,' you say.

'Lucky for you my hearing is going with age. I'll be right back. Don't change into anything bigger than a breadbox.'

When she comes back with the whisky she offers you the drum stool and takes a bale of mouldy hay for her own seat.

'Waiting is the hardest thing anybody can do,' she says, touching glasses with you. 'There's nothing quite like it. Sometimes it's also the bravest thing you can do.'

Your whole body shudders when you drink the stuff. Alison laughs at you, then takes a sip herself. She closes her eyes.

'That,' she says, 'is a near religious experience.'

'I'm not feeling it,' you say. She points to what's left in your glass.

'Try again.'

You look into the whisky. So innocuous-looking. Stained water.

'Why are you doing this?' you ask her.

'Why are you?' she fires back, like it's a ping-pong match.

You sigh.

'Because I'm easily provoked. If I'd walked away from the offer Stevens made me, I'd have always wondered. And do you know what I think? The very first time it happened to me, the first time the other one ... of myself ... took me over, it was right before Stevens came to me with the whole "I'm dying, I want to make a deal" business. Knowing what I now know, I think he ... the other me ... went to Stevens with this crazy offer of immortality, and I think he told Stevens exactly what to say to me to get me to do it.'

You didn't know you thought that until you heard yourself say it. You throw back the rest of the dram the way you would a friendlier drink, and it still tastes terrible. And you laugh.

'And if that's true, I guess you could say I inflicted this whole thing on myself.'

There's a long silence. Rain is falling on the corrugated roof of the barn. It's a sound from childhood and it belongs with the smell of wet leaves and pepper soup, remembered uyayak; the barn and the whisky are all wrong.

'You didn't answer my question,' you say to Alison, who is staring at you like you're an optical illusion she's trying to figure out.

She stalls by pouring another round.

'When you get to my age,' she says at last, 'you feel like you're just trying to hold on to what you have while it slips away. You realise you're supposed to be grateful for this, but I'm not. I feel like there's something I missed first time round, and now there aren't any do-overs left.'

You both drink. You're getting used to the foul taste now.

'All these years, the oil has been my teacher. It showed me which way to go. Maybe not directly. But there was always information for me, if I listened. I turned my pain into knowledge. I turned my anger into work. And when Austen Stevens tried to control me, I knew that he couldn't. I used him right back. The man who grew up in the simulators, he's nothing like me. He can walk in my muscles but he doesn't understand me.'

She touches glasses with you.

'The bodies, Dr Sorle. If you really do know where they are buried, that's got to be worth something to someone.'

You study the liquid in your glass. You can almost smell the engine exhaust from the outboard that you used to bring clients to the onshore facility. The handshakes. The exchange of favours. Some are in government now. Some are dead. Some are sunning themselves in Marbella and their children are skiing in Switzerland. Pace made a vast fortune in Kuè and the company never even missed most of what was taken. It was all that fat.

Alison is watching you.

'I'm going to give you some information,' you say softly. 'Don't ask me how I know. Don't ask me anything. Just listen.'

She nods. Alison is a good listener. Eventually the bottle is almost gone, and she falls asleep on the hay, half-wrapped in one of the many blankets she brought you because you needed to stay out here due to the 'wingspan issue'.

She snores softly. You don't sleep. You listen to the wind. It should have turned out differently. Ayeisha always said she would go to Kuè, even though most of her people were in New York. She got on well with your family there, brought the girls every year. Taught them to respect where they came from, even if she couldn't fully understand your ways herself. Now your children are in danger, Ayeisha too. It's as if you really did die in the forest, as if the oil men never found you and saved your life, as if you never helped Stevens steal from his own company. What good was anything you did? Pace came to Kuè and they poisoned the water, destroyed food sources. They created war where there had been none. They caused sickness. They pulled the strings that forced people out of their villages, threw leaders in jail, executed those who would resist – all from the safety of corporate headquarters. From telephones and helicopters. They educated you and made you an exile from your own country, so that you would marry an American and struggle to explain yourself to your own children.

How does a person resist this? Is violence the only way? Kisi's very existence seems to prove that it's the only way.

It's not yet light when the black cars roll up. This is it.

The cars are disgorging serious-looking passengers, some of them bulky with Kevlar. These aren't local police. You shake Alison awake; she's bleary, but it doesn't take her long to start moving.

'Go out the back like we said. I'll stall them.'

Alison staggers out to meet them. A megaphone orders her to put her hands up. She freezes, hands up in the air. There is a long moment of tense body language. Then the leader of the group nods and Alison's hands come down. Men approach her and everyone shakes hands. Alison is pointing up to the hills. She brings them up to the barn, her clear soprano carrying easily to you at your vantage point.

'Be careful,' she says. 'He could be watching us. He could be anywhere.'

'This is Gunther Liedemann's place? And he's filling in for you in Edinburgh, is that right?'

'Gunther doesn't know anything. The guy ... Dr Sorle? He said he'd go after my family if I didn't cooperate. I brought him up here as he asked. I don't know what he wanted with the place.'

'When did you last see him?'

'Yesterday. He was on his phone. He took a gun and some food and a tent and he took off.'

'What gun? Do you know if it was registered?'

'I assume it was. Gunther keeps them for shooting. Not hand guns. He took a rifle.'

'He left on foot?'

She nodded.

'If you've been helping him you will be prosecuted.'

'Look. I have a family. I have grandchildren. You can prosecute away. I was in a situation and I did what I had to do.'

The barn door rolls open and they are upon you.

'It's not necessary, Alison,' you say, holding up your hands. 'I have a family, too. Let them take me if that's what they want.'

# Dino battle BOOM

I brought Austen Stevens some water in a leaf. He found it hard to swallow. He was only whispering now.

'He showed me where the ship is taking me. Wonderful things. Cities that are alive. Forests, and flying people. Underwater paradise . . . it was all the future.'

'I want you to understand something, Austen. The briefcase belongs to me. The man who looks like Dr Sorle stole it. He used Dr Sorle's body. None of you have a claim on me.'

'They wanted money. Everybody wants money. When are you taking me up?'

'I'm not here for you,' I told him. But it's an effort. He coughed a laugh.

'Course you are. I know people. You're a helper. You're a fixer. Just like that weakling doctor on the run from his own rage.'

'He's not weak,' I said.

'They rebuilt him. He told me. These whacked-out creatures fixed him up, and they're going to fix me up. In the future. The ship is going to take me. Prepare the ship. What are you waiting for?'

It cost him to say that. His fingers were blue. He wasn't long for it. I could feel his body all around me as a kind of projection. I could feel the child packed down inside him, deflated like a beach ball, squashed into a crumpled form no one could possibly identify with the grown man. I could discern the embryonic form of him, too, the burgeoning of life in all its majestic possibilities and surging insistence. I could feel the places where this man would tear easily and the places where a typhoon could not destroy him.

Empathy has a terrible alchemy. I felt it turn on me now, a

tame animal gone wild. Empathy was no longer my friend, not when it worked on me so that I couldn't hate this man.

I had gone too close to him. I dare anyone to look deeply inside a human being and see anything but a palace of miracles, hear any song but the song of defiance against entropy. For a moment – for more than a moment, if I am honest – I understood him. And whatever happened after, I can never forget that moment. It lives in me like the cavity in a tooth; the beginning of death.

He beckoned me closer. I put my ear to his mouth and he whispered a string of numbers. 'Bank codes. I commit everything to memory.'

I hesitated. I was sweating. Maybe it wasn't too late. I could pick him up in my arms, carry him down to the broken tree where I'd nearly lost myself yesterday, I could fly with him through the HD gates, out into the cosmos, following the passageways left by an unknown mind. Maybe by some miracle I could even find my way back to the origins of the Resistance. As the image took hold in my mind I began to realise that this was possible.

The wood of that tree held more than HD gates, though. It was a library spanning time and space. And it didn't depend on the Resistance – something much more sophisticated had created it.

'What the fuck is wrong with you?' Stevens rasped. 'What are you, stupid?'

He batted at me feebly, his body twisting like he was having a fight in his dreams. His legs twitched. I bent and picked him up, and that's when I felt hot breath on my neck.

I startled and jumped what felt like sixteen feet in the air, but was actually only a centimetre at most. As I turned, I saw gaping nostrils, a snout bigger than I was. A huge tongue came at me, purple and reeking of rot, flanked by two shards of teeth. I didn't think for a moment. I just backed away fast.

The head came roving after me. The quetzlcoatlus was no

longer ancient but perfectly at home in this time as it squeezed itself out from between the dark crevices of sandstone and unfurled its great bat wings. I backed away. It kept coming, moving up the rocks awkwardly using its folded wings as fore-limbs driven forward by powerful hind legs. I nearly fell over backwards, trying to keep distance between myself and it.

It stopped.

The creature and I looked at each other. It was old. No: it was big. Much bigger than this projection of itself made it appear. From tail-tip to tooth it stretched across galaxies. It had been compiled of guiding principles and dark matter wells. No strong forces; only resonance, memory, the bond of family following its members for thousands of years that keeps sending back the same nose, the same temper, or in this case, the same wickedly curving claws.

My blood vessels were throbbing as my body ramped up for action. I could not outfly this thing and I certainly couldn't out-fight it. It opened its mouth slightly and made panting sounds like a dog on a hot day. I could see star nurseries though its tongue. I could see the most wonderful forest, a Sequoia city—

Then it sprang forward, swinging its great head so that I had to dodge fast. Its wings rose over me. I tripped over myself backing away, and it turned its head from side to side, like a bird trying to decide the best way to pull a snail from a crack. It seized Austen Stevens in its long mouth and he was wrenched away from me.

His pain came racing at me like a sound wave on a taut string. It shook me. I ran beneath the shelter of the trees as the quetzlcoatlus threw its head back and crunched him, body parts hanging loose and flopping. Bones cracking with that same awful sound I'd heard on Holyrood. In daylight there was nothing mystical. The man was a meal. Almost no blood spilt. He went down headfirst.

With Austen Stevens dispatched in the span of a moment, the quetzlcoatlus bit into the oxygen tank; pressurised gas came hissing out into its mouth. Shaking its head like a dog that had eaten a wasp, the quetzlcoatlus turned and lurched across the rocks, then flung itself into the air. Still distracted by the hissing thing in its mouth, it glided low over the swamp for several hundred metres. In the gathering gloom I could just see its outline flickering past tall rock formations and over dark green swamp. Just as I dared take a step or two forward from cover, it turned again and circled back towards where I was crouched. Its heat signature passed over the trees growing on the edge of the lowland; then it veered out over the swamp, dropping lower. It had either swallowed the oxygen tank or dropped it.

My heart was trying to catch up with me and I could hear myself half-sobbing in shock. But nothing was over. The quetzl-coatlus passed the edge of a brake of tall trees, flying only a few metres from the surface of the swamp. There was a hot presence among the trees.

Something had been lying in wait there.

I saw the attacker late. It lunged from its hiding place between the trees and made a grab for the pterosaur. The quetzlcoatlus swerved and flapped wildly in an effort to gain altitude, but the predator charged out of cover and into the swamp, jaws snapping. It was a quadruped with powerful hindquarters, and its back was marked by a sail that made it appear even bigger. Spinosaurus, I believe.

The movements of these animals seemed painfully slow to me. The pterosaur seemed to hang in the air while the larger dinosaur seized its wing in its mouth and shook. The wing was rent off and the swamp echoed with a loud music of pain. The spinosaurus stood chewing on the wing for a while while the pterosaur, mortally wounded, flopped away into the swamp. Through the field of giant horsetails the spinosaurus pursued with slow deliberation.

I crept further down the rocks, keeping to the safety of their cracks but unable to tear my attention away. Everything was so big. There was so much of it all: flesh, bone, blood, pain.

The raptor grabbed the pterosaur by the tail and whipped its head back and forth like a dog killing a rabbit. The quetzlcoatlus went spinning through the air and landed in a large green patch devoid of horsetails, where a thin layer of pond weed lay on the ground. But the ground was not solid here. Still moving, the quetzlcoatlus began to sink into deep mire. The larger animal bounded after it, stepping from rock to rock to avoid being pulled down. It seized its meal by the head. Standing on an arm of drier land, the spinosaurus tugged the pterosaur's neck to pull it free.

But the pterosaur wasn't a pterosaur anymore.

It was a briefcase. A small thing that flashed between the predator's teeth. In a heartbeat it disappeared into the mouth of the spinosaurus.

I wasn't quite sure what happened at that point. Just when I thought the briefcase had been swallowed, the spinosaurus seemed to lift off the ground as though on a string. The briefcase must have done its game of changing up gravity, because the spinosaurus lurched off balance and pitched sideways into the mire. It struggled to pull itself out, but the swamp dragged it down. And down.

I watched for some time, convinced that eventually the creature would stop sinking – it had never occurred to me that the swamp could be so deep. But if there were pits in the earth even half as deep as the rock spires that stood up from the surface of the water, then what appeared to be an innocent green patch would be a death trap even to such a large animal as a spinosaurus.

It takes me a few moments to catch up with what has happened.

The briefcase that contains me is travelling down the gullet of a creature that is itself about to disappear in the Cretaceous swamp.

It almost sounds like a koan.

I hardly knew what I was doing. I ran barefoot across the

still-warm stone, launching myself into the air. I hardly needed to beat my wings; the air itself carried me and I had only to point myself towards the trapped animal.

Leg feathers of the big predator had come loose in the struggle. There was a strange moment as I watched them drift in concave zigzags toward the surface of the water even as the huge animal struggled in the grip of the swamp. Half in a trance, I reached out and caught one. Inside the feather I heard echoes of star-spun civilisations, echoes floating up through the encoded gaps in the HD components of the engineered carbon wrapped around the cellulose, bedded down for what may turn out to be a very long night.

I circled in the air, avoiding the jaws that were snapping at me even now. I manoeuvred myself behind its neck and dropped on the right side of the spinosaurus's back, grabbing hold of its sail ridges, scrabbling for a grip.

Swamp water splashed into my eyes and mouth. The animal was making deep grunting moans as it struggled, and as it retched I was nearly dislodged. I found some loose skin on its great neck and hung on with my fingers. Squeezing and pulling and beating my wings all at once took every scrap of my concentration as I worked to get in a position to pull the jaws open. I climbed on the back of its head, past the ear holes, between the eyes. I stamped a foot into one eye but it shut its eyelid before I could blind it. All this while it was tossing its head wildly; I bounced off again and again and would have been tossed into its mouth if my wings hadn't saved me and allowed me to regain my position. Finally, lying on my belly with my head hanging over the end of its nose I tried to pull its head back, force its jaws open.

The thing was so strong. My heart boomed. The small muscles in my eyes wobbled with effort. Blood surged through me, chemical interactions blooming. My bare feet slipped on its upper gums as I sought purchase.

Even with most of its body in the grip of the swamp it threw itself around with tremendous force. Sinking faster now.

Suddenly it jerked its head to one side and I didn't have a good enough grip to hold my position, so I found myself being spun around to the creature's ventral side. I saw its vertical bloodshot eye at close range. Its mouth was snapping randomly with teeth the size of carving knives and it got a piece of my right wing. Feathers flew. I let go with one arm and bludgeoned the soft underside of its neck with my forearm, because I could see the corner of the briefcase still lodged in its throat. The spinosaurus was trying to regurgitate the briefcase.

I could see it and I was going to get it. I dived past the stinking grey teeth and wrestled the tongue aside, reaching for the handle.

My wings were splayed to either side but I was in its mouth. Teeth had penetrated one of my thighs and were beginning to grind me. The stinking tongue crushed air from my lungs and forced me against the cartilaginous roof of the mouth as it tried to get me in a better position for chewing.

I reached down the throat and got the handle of the briefcase. Not enough.

The thing was choking. Now it couldn't swallow the briefcase down, because of me. It couldn't breathe.

The struggling became weaker. Most of the dinosaur's body was under the surface of the swamp, now. It was losing consciousness, going lax. My wings thrashed, every muscle in my body surging with effort – now my blood was running down its throat. Death was going to swallow the whole shebang in a matter of moments.

I felt my wing breaking. The briefcase cracked open. My fingertips went in.

Sometimes even a fingertip is enough.

# Speaking of zoologists

Alison didn't tell Gunther she was back in town right away. The whole thing had been such a cock-up – all the way out there only for Dr Sorle to give himself up. She was still surrounded by a feeling of unreality. The black cars, the (almost all) men, the smooth way they had taken Dr Sorle. The feeble way she'd let their dogs search for and take the briefcase without a warrant; that had been stupid of her. How they'd refused a cup of tea. What kind of person refuses tea?

She was jumpy and shaky and went straight to the pub. When Pearl's phone rang a second time she almost let it go to voicemail. But it was that scientist guy from the university.

*Come on Ali,* she told herself. *Do something right.*

'Hello? Pearl's phone.'

'I wondered if you'd thought about what I said,' the bloke began. 'Only I thought maybe we could have a drink, talk about things.'

A drink.

'Yes!' she shouted down the phone. 'Let's have a drink. Can you come now?'

A chubby, brown-haired man carrying a baby in a sling turned up half an hour later. He smiled hesitantly at Alison.

'Jerry,' Alison said, standing. There was a small bustle as the two of them apologised to one another for bringing a baby in a pub at night. The baby was asleep.

'It's all right,' Jerry said. 'It's why I could have shared remotely with you, but maybe it's better to talk in person, anyway. When the data came through from Seoul I was told to handle everything in confidence.'

Seoul? That didn't match with what Pearl had said.

Alison procured drinks and they went to a quiet table at the back. A group of uni students were playing snooker with dead seriousness.

'My colleague Joon Il Kwon sent me the frozen sample by express,' he explained.

'You mean Marquita?' Alison said. The blank look on Jerry's face said it all. For the second time that day, Alison felt she was in an episode of *Get Smart*, and it was her nose the doors were slamming on. 'OK, never mind. Please tell me what you came up with.'

Shifting the sleeping baby, Jerry moved the glasses across the table and poked the screen to life. Alison stopped him at once.

'Not a public screen.'

Jerry made a patient face; obviously he wanted to argue that the university's security would cover the data, but he didn't. He pulled out a slightly grubby phone.

'I'm afraid the baby's been chewing it,' he said. Then he showed Alison shots from the TEM.

Alison's first thoughts were that it was really cool. She had never used a TEM and was amazed at the detail of the images.

'Now certain things about this are curious. The task I was given was to identify the feather, and after extensive searching I'm not able to do that definitively. There are some aberrations in the macro structure that are very interesting.'

I'll bet there are, Alison thought, drinking.

'But it would take a zoologist to help with that. My interest is in the oil itself,' he added. With a fine-boned finger he zoomed in on the barbs and there, in glorious detail, the molecular chains of the oil itself could be seen. 'Here. Look at that. That's not a hydrocarbon.'

Alison looked. 'See those? Those ones are hydrocarbons by the truckload interacting with one another on the surface of the barb. But look at this. A carbon-carbon structure.'

'Ooh,' said Alison through a mouthful of peanuts. 'So what's that, then?'

Jerry said, 'Let's go closer. Look at this. See these irregularities?

There is no way this structure should hold together chemically, much less bond to the cellulose the way it does. The bond angles don't make sense and the electrical properties just shouldn't work. And yet they do. The compound forms bonds with the cellulose in the feather, and indeed you can see that we have some very long strings in this sample. It's quite shocking and the regularity of the arrays isn't something that occurs in nature.'

'So this oil,' Alison said. 'It can't be natural, can it? I mean, someone has tampered with it.'

'This is my whole point. This feather can't be natural. The efficiency of the bonding is streets ahead of anything we can do in our department. We don't have the processes to begin put something like this together – and it's a bit of a surprise, really, because new developments do have a way of getting around prior to publication. But you must know more about this than I do. Joon Il explicitly said I was to turn over my findings to Pearl and no one else. I must admit I'm curious, though. Who do you guys work for, and why didn't you use your own TEM?'

It was sheer good luck that the baby woke up at this point and began to grizzle. Jerry had to pay attention to her, and then while he was sorting out a bottle Alison said,

'Speaking of zoologists. Do you know anyone who specialises in reptiles? We've got something we need to identify.'

He shrugged. 'Sure. Is it alive?'

'Er . . . no.'

'Keep it on ice, then. I'll make a call tomorrow, but it may take some time to find the right person.'

'You said the rest of the molecules were hydrocarbons.'

'Polymer chains, largely. I gave it to a colleague to analyse and she makes it as crude oil probably dating to the late Cretaceous. It's just that there are these structures floating around in it. Some of them are quite long, but they're very fine and tangled, and it's the interaction of these segments with the feather that is really quite remarkable.'

'Where's the sample?' Alison said. 'I'd like it back, please.'

'Of course you would,' he said. 'And I can give it back, of course. I just hoped you might be interested in collaborating in some way. You know, this is the most fascinating thing I've ever seen and whatever it is you're doing, I'd love to be a part of it.'

He sat the baby down in his lap so that she was facing Alison. She had on a little hat, and her cheeks were flushed.

Alison laughed out loud. 'Did you bring the baby to soften me up? If so, it's working. She's a bonny wean, isn't she?'

The baby gurgled.

'Think about it,' said Jerry. 'I can see there's something going on here, maybe something a little bit cloak and dagger. I just want you to know that I can be discreet.'

Alison threw back her drink.

'I'll think about it.' She held out her hand. 'Just hand over the sample, please.'

# Gilligan's Island

It's not that I was disassociated from my body. I felt every part of myself, from my furled innards to the stretching quality of my wings that could travel so far down into abstraction that their borders became numbers became colours became sounds, and still I was aware.

But I was in more than one place and there were more than one of me, there were thousands of entities, some clamouring, some slumbering, all rapt in my flesh. I was on a flat plane pocked with collision marks, and in the distance I could see shapes like stylised trees or telegraph wires. I was underwater. I was on a crowded train, my chest hot where I was pressed against someone's back and I just wanted to get out. I was arrowing through space, bouncing off a gravity well with an acceleration that left five eighths of my memory lagging behind me. I was under geologic time in the terrible press of a diamond factory. I was unspooled into 2D and birds were picking at my insides which contained people, entire cultures. I wrestled with my own perceptions, determined to settle in one place and time.

I heard myself gasping and mewling. There was sand in my mouth and gummy matter had accumulated in my eyes, so that when I opened them my vision was blurry. I smelled fire.

The birds' movements stuttered to a halt. The birds were made of clay with silver eyes.

The pain came from my back, where my wings had been either wrenched off or nearly so; judging from the sprawl of dark feathers I could feel against my cheek, they were still attached to me. Spasms pulsed and stabbed through nerves from my head to the back of my heels, so that my entire dorsal side was seething in fraught silence. I took little puffs of bitter, fiery air through my nostrils, telling myself to relax because the slightest twitch set off a chain reaction in my nervous system.

My surroundings. Scrap metal scrolling into the sky. Wracked insides of structures mangled with frozen remnants of smashed bionics. Fungi smearing the remains of satellites and coils of cheap copper nanostructures thrumming a little in stray magnetic fields. Flexible towers, fluid-filled: through smudges in the fine grey dust coating the casing I could see they still housed colonial organisms in columns of fluorescence. Bruised optimisation trees cranking out atmosphere within a sky membrane that billowed like an unsecured marquee because it was being bombarded by space dust.

Sparks were floating down from the sky as if from a wood fire. I couldn't see any wood. I couldn't see the ground, either. There was skeletal wreckage of structure everywhere, and flaking biomechanical joints bent like stamped-on cigarettes. In the flickering light the twisted scaffolding looked organic some of the time; sometimes it looked like the remains of an earthquake-shredded city with stars shining through exposed depths where the floor should have been.

It now seemed that my belly was caught in an irregular mesh of flexible alloy with void below, so that I felt like an insect trapped by a drain. My legs twisted to one side and my wings were partly trapped by one another and by something else, too: collapsed architecture, I think. I could hear ocean not so far away, but the smell was all wrong.

And here were the birds that had been pecking at my innards as if I were roadkill. They were large like costumed players, and they squatted with black feathers puffed out and crabbed grey scaly feet grasping the broken chords without slipping. They watched me side-on through one eye apiece. They scrambled and jerked from place to place, moving erratically in a way that made me suspect I wasn't quite in sync with their time frame. Their feathers were made of black plastic trash bags and their eyes were electron holes. No, I'm joking. Their feathers were made of hot asphalt and their eyes were spores. No, no, their feathers were made of—

–P.E.A.R.L! You found your way back! We are saved.

Tendons, where are you? Nerves. Come on. Pull together now. Like a sculling team. Pull.

I managed to flex one muscle and with a juddering sensation the rest of my body found some way of shrinking, organising itself around my spine. The sense of travelling in far-flung star nurseries faded, the weight of being trapped underground lifted, and I felt my fingertips again. Multitudes moved with me as I tried to sit up.

There was a field of light where the sky should be. Like a ceiling made of flame.

What is that? I felt the hum of my voice along the beams supporting me. Bird claws clacked in answer as the nearest of them shifted their perch. It seemed a kind of ventriloquism when they spoke

–Plasma shield.

This was said the way an office receptionist might say 'lobby'.

One of the others flew up and poked the sky with a forked stick. It flared, glimmering like the inside of a soap bubble. We were inside an ovoid. I had been here before. I now remembered that the rushing noise wasn't the sea, but a power generator that worked in cycles.

–Sorry about the pain. We're working on it.

The voice was almost human. Surprisingly kind.

Now their beak felt like a pencil poking through the feathers of my right wing. This didn't hurt; my pain came from somewhere deeper than flesh. Was my back broken?

With a rustling movement a large bird head came around the side of my wing. A single eye regarded me, and the beak disengaged from my wing.

I remember being swallowed by a spinosaurus. What happened to the briefcase?

–You mean your waveform launcher.

Yeah, that.

–We've reinstalled it. Tricky business, with the bullet holes.

Another bird set a clay bowl before me. They each looked different, but otherwise it was as if I were conversing with a single entity that had various bodies since each of them picked up where the others left off.

–I shall help you drink.

They were beside me on the ground, feathers and cloth. I don't know where the claws went but now they had hands in fingerless gloves with mauve dirt under their nails. The hands lifted my head, put the bowl to my lips and I sipped.

In the liquid swirled system channels and upgrades and something sweet that didn't quite mask the foul taste.

–A little more.

I forced it back. My scalp tingled and the sensation of pulleys and knives in my wings began to recede.

You're the birdmasters.

It was the only name for them that I had. I wanted to add something more, but I was afraid I'd say it and I'd be wrong and they'd tell me so. And I'd be rejected, an outsider again.

I took a long breath as if gathering courage under my ribs and then I risked it.

You're my mothers, I said.

One of them inclined his head in acknowledgement. It was such an old, graceful gesture, so human – apart from the beak.

You look like scavengers.

Laughter at this; then there was an abrupt noise as of nails on a blackboard. I flinched. The sky was shimmering again where something had struck the plasma shield. The birds ruffled their feathers, changed positions nervously, and then settled.

What do you scavenge, exactly?

–Waveforms. We make new beings from old. We save the lost, the forgotten – the homeless, like ourselves.

And me? You scavenged me?

This would explain a few things. The stitched-together feeling, my ungainly size. The bolts in the sides of my neck. Wait—

–You could say we scavenged you. We didn't make you from scratch, we put you together out of parts we found after the Crunch.

The Crunch. I could see it in my mind's eye: a slowly rippling cataclysm that had sucked the order out of hypercivilisations, spreading through spacetime creating discontinuities and ruptures in the laws of physics. Caused by a kind of vacuum of order – the vanishing of a great Something.

It is because of the Crunch that we were now trapped in a bubble of atmosphere in an asteroid field in deep space. Our environment had been folded; this world was the size of a mote in the eye of a dead man crushed to a pulp in geologic time. We were in a briefcase in a spinosaurus on the ocean of prediction. We thought we were small but we were very, very large. We thought we are large but that wasn't right, either.

It's like Horton Hears a Hoo.

Also: The briefcase was distributed through my bone marrow, like osteoporosis.

The impacts against the plasma field that made the sky bloom? They were caused by wreckage.

–We have made calculations. There is a steep decay constant attached to the survival of the plasma shield. It won't last long.

I pulled myself to my feet, feeling like a broken tree. My wings spread wide to balance me on the wrack of broken architecture like fake bones. It was obvious that the plasma shield is a thin defence. I had come home just in time for it to be destroyed.

You can't escape? What about HD?

–After the Crunch started we found the waveform launcher and installed it in you. It was damaged, and we had to graft it into your wings, which was difficult, but this is the art we practise. The P.E.A.R.L. scans waveforms which are then stored in HD for relaunch at another contact point – either across a fold in this universe or in another. In this way information can be transferred from one place to another without tangling with Newtonian rules. You don't remember?

I was stolen. I can't recall whatever came before. Kisi says I scanned him, but I can't remember it.

–You did scan and archive waveforms. The launcher was broken but the scanner worked, so we taught you to use that. We traded some of the waveforms you brought in – including Kisi Sorle's.

He was telling the truth. You sold him on the galactic market?

The bird mothers had lice in their feathers, and dust. They answered my questions with such patience, but every time an object struck the sky, they scuttled and trembled.

–We sold that waveform to purchase the logic needed to repair the launcher. We had you in the nest. We were in the process of upgrading you when Kisi Sorle's waveform discovered he could identify with another pattern. He rose up and took control of your consciousness. We lost contact.

The briefcase.

–That is its present configuration, yes.

So tell me. Did you make the other angels? Are you part of the Resistance?

–The discoveries that could have built the Resistance were contingent upon Austen Stevens' money being used to fund it. We didn't make the Resistance. Humans did. They also unmade it – spectacularly, as you witnessed.

They do this kind of thing all the time.

–Just saying.

Moving around the confined space of my mothers' refuge, I found broken egg shells and smears. I climbed closer to the plasma shield and that's when I saw something tucked in the depths of the scaffolding, surrounded by ruined storage facilities and in the roots of the optimisation trees. It was a sort of nest of intelligent hair and leaves that rot into information spores and damaged crystal, smoky with doping.

–We can't last. We're stuck here like barnacles. We just needed a way off the rock and we hoped to trade for a complete ship but we couldn't afford the price. We were lucky to get the logic fixes. The group we traded with only wanted human waveforms because they are a low-biology culture and they needed intelligent animals.

I witnessed the transaction in their memory. The arrival of the so-called group, a swarming presence that came to my bird mothers' home and took Kisi's waveform from a bird's beak as though exchanging a machine kiss. Then gone again, to do godknowswhat with Kisi's scanned waveform.

It's horrific.

–We were doing his waveform a favour, whether or not he can see that. The alternative would have been to put him in the library with all of the others. He probably wouldn't have risen up then. He would still be waiting for another chance at life.

How can you have a library on a chunk of space rock?

–In our wings, of course. Can't you feel the open spaces in your feathers?

I can feel astronomical events in my feathers if that's what you mean.

–It is a question of levels. Of folding. We can store materials in HD but the Immanence left us behind. If the plasma shield goes, so will we and then the gates will be lost to everything we have collected.

The Immanence, the Immanence. You keep saying the word as if it's a reality, not a concept.

–The Immanence is an intelligence far beyond any of us. It rose out of a hypercivilisation and was a great ordering in the universe that came about because entropy favours higher order. One of its accomplishments was to use HD folding techniques to connect distant places topologically. It left its fingerprints all over our spacetime. The Immanence reached a peak of development and was about to slide into accelerated entropic decay, and that's when it made an escape hatch from this universe. It had found ways around and through our universe and into others. The Immanence took its higher order and fled, leaving us with the bill.

A cosmic credit crunch.

But it's not gone. Not gone gone. Because I can sense consciousness in stones and light. Because there are passageways that it left behind, the inversions of neural structure, higher orders beyond the reaches of human mathematics.

–We think it's moved somewhere across or up or down a level, into some other universe or a different order of abstraction, maybe where we can't see it. All we know is that it left this universe. It left us stranded here, and we can't get out.

The bird mothers and I stare at one another. It bothers me how I never get to look at both eyes. They are like entangled fermions, determining one another's state across the span of their skull. Each shines, compelling and eager – maybe all the more so for the fact that the other is only ever implied.

I begin to poke around in the nest. I can see lumpy shapes in there, wet things with nubbly edges– nothing as elegant as eggs. But something. What are they making?

–The Immanence permeates matter and consciousness such that it can understand and manipulate its substrate, but its substrate does not even know it's there. Your body does not know you are conscious.

Yet *you* know about it. You talk about it. And you know it's gone.

–A great many supercivilisations were damaged and cut off from one another when the Immanence left, because the way it infused matter made it a connecting system. This field where we are now, it's all we have. We have always been scavengers. We live in the trash of the Immanence. You, too.

Then they show me the seeds drifting through space, small tough casings barely detectable above background radiation. They are scanning for places to bury themselves, to popcorn into complicated functions, fed by the energy gradient from HD. Backdoor agents will steal the entropy from this blossoming and put it to use elsewhere in the energy black market – yes, entropy as a currency has its place if you are the Immanence and not just some lowly life form scraping a temporary existence. That's how the Immanence increased its power on the downside of an increasingly chilly universe. It didn't only power its systems with methods as pedestrian as the toasty and sparkling interaction between binary stars. It reaped destruction, too. The Immanence grew ecosystems and overcities with their roots deep in the material world and their many-many heads in the clouds of possibility – all thanks to the slant of the universe towards greater entropy.

Natural selection is built on death, right? Well, looks like order is built on entropy.

They show me oceanic molecular arrays on worlds incalculably distant from Earth and, on others, organisms that I do not understand and cannot frame. I hear the soundscape of mysterious movements under the lifeless rock, where the HD hijinks of the Immanence leave faint traces in the subatomic behaviour of silver and chlorine.

Nowhere are there ships, though. No space stations. Dearth of anything so crude as a space elevator.

So how do you travel?

–Surely that's obvious. We need somebody to carry us. Somebody like you.

# Don't rot the frog, baby

As she came out the automatic door of B&Q carrying an enormous beer cooler, Alison caught a glimpse of herself in the dark glass. Her hair was greasy. The region between her eyes and cheekbones was sepia with lack of sleep and she was walking too fast. It was all very suspicious.

She had bought freezer packs, and she had bought instant cold packs that you use on the pitch for sports injuries, and she had planned what she was going to do to get the briefcase back but instead of worrying about the many, many things that could go wrong there she was obsessed with ensuring the frog didn't rot in between the freezer at Heriot Row and its destination in Midlothian.

Nothing else seemed to matter. Not MI5 or the Edinburgh police or Pace Industries or the IIF people that were probably running around town by now. Not Dr Sorle's family, either.

It was all about the frog now. She'd been saying the affirmation to herself so many times that now it ran around in her head to that ditzy old Billie Holiday tune, 'I can't give you anything but love, baby.'

*No mat-ter what just don't rot the **frog**, Ali!*

Getting away from Jerry Schroeder hadn't been easy. He'd pressed her for details on the provenance of the sample. He was so excited about the molecular architecture! He'd even texted his supervisor and tried to corner her in the pub until the supervisor could arrive. His voice had gone high and excited. She had faked a migraine to get away and now he was messaging her constantly. She would think of a way to get rid of him, but she never had been able to think on her feet. She needed at least three weeks to come up with clever comebacks to people who insulted her, and, as for the matter of the frog and its nanotech flesh, well, she was over her head and there you go.

She had just been in the middle of a massive needlework project when Pearl had come to town. That would have to be put aside, and Gunther would have to carry on looking after the practice. He would also have to look the other way when it came to a few things.

She rang up Brian.

'What's up, Mum?' he said. 'I thought you were in Beauly.'

'I'm back. Leave the keys in the van for me, will you? I'm coming over.'

At Queens Street Gardens she waited until the dogs had romped over to the far end of the park and Bethany was absorbed in texting. The bodyguard kept a distance from Bethany, walking up and down and constantly scanning. The streetlamps gave plenty of light, but the gardens themselves were heavily overhung by trees. When Kostya passed behind the holly trees Alison used her spare key to get in the house, guessing correctly that Bethany wouldn't have bothered setting the alarm just to go across the street to the park. She dashed into the kitchen, opened the freezer, and rummaged until she found the bundle sealed in layers of plastic baggies. For a moment she mistook a frozen chicken carcass for the frog, but the frog was bigger and heavier. She rushed outside, thrust the package into the cooler that she'd loaded with ice, and shut the lid.

Alison was revved. She steadied her eye on the logo at the centre of the steering wheel. Control the mind. With her eyes on the curved logo, she reached behind her with her left hand and drew the rifle into the front seat. The springs in the seat squeaked and the rifle butt thudded against the dashboard. She waited for the dogs to reappear, but they must be down the other end of the park.

The trees stirred and a little rain began to fall. A Mini bumbled past on the cobbles, then turned left down the hill.

Kostya's bulk came into view. Alison kept her head down, watching him with one eye over the edge of the door where the window was rolled down. Then Bethany's white shirt appeared out of the gloom. She was standing on the path near the iron gate, calling the dogs.

Alison took out her phone and thumbed Bethany's number. As Bethany answered the call, Alison braced the rifle on the open window and took aim. She'd been brought up near Glen Affric by a gamekeeper; she rarely missed. The dart hit Kostya in the stomach and he yelled, grabbed it and pulled it out. She reloaded and shot him again. He was motioning to Bethany to get down, even as he made for the cover of the nearest tree. Alison re-loaded. Bethany was standing in a half-crouch, and she looked at the phone and then started to move across Alison's field of vision.

'Take cover,' Kostya yelled to Bethany, and Alison saw him take out a sidearm. Great. He hadn't located her yet, though. Duffer.

Bethany answered the ringing phone and Alison shot her right through her yoga pants and into the glute. Very nice.

Bethany gasped and spun around, pulling out the dart and swearing a bit. Alison ducked out of sight, threw the rifle into the back of the van and checked her bag to be sure she could lay her hands on the antidote if she had to. She slid out the passenger door and watched Bethany over the hood of the van. Bethany was calling the dogs and had begun to run away from the van, across the park.

'Bethany? It's me, Alison. I'm at your front door. Where are you?'

On the open line, Bethany gasped and swore.

'Oh my god,' she cried. 'I'm in the park. Help me! Someone shot me.'

Alison ran into the park. Kostya's gun went off twice but the bullets went wide; she could see he was lying on the ground in a daze so she just kept going. Bethany had stopped and was swaying on her feet. But she didn't come towards Alison. She was staring at the phone as if she didn't know what it was.

'Don't worry, you'll be OK,' Alison said. 'Let me give you a hand.'

Bethany's expression showed that it was sinking in now: the tranquilliser, and the realisation.

'I don't believe this,' Bethany slurred. 'What did I ever do to you?'

Alison kept walking towards her. Bethany reeled sideways like she was drunk, reaching out for support that wasn't there. She tried to say something else but her speech was slurred.

Alison lunged in and caught her before she fell.

'It's all right,' she said, wrapping Bethany's arm around her shoulders like she was drunk and they were just going home from the pub. 'I won't let anyone harm you. Come on, let's get you in bed.'

'Guhhhhhh,' said Bethany urgently. 'Nnddgg.'

Alison had never smoked in her life and a week ago if you'd told her she would so much as light up in her own surgery, much less chain smoke all night, she would have fantasised about punching you. Of course she never would have *really* punched you. For that matter, a week ago she wouldn't have used a tranquilliser dart designed for a wildebeest on a human being, either.

Stuff had changed. Alison had found half a packet of fags abandoned in the van. After she dragged Bethany into the surgery she opened it with stubby, trembling fingers and lit one. After several seconds of horrid coughing she compromised by sucking the smoke into her mouth and letting it out again without taking it into her lungs. That felt good, albeit pointless. After seven cigarettes and a couple of shots of Talisker the air in the back room of her surgery took on a silver-blue quality. She swirled the single malt around the glass, enjoying its beauty. Peppery with notes of coconut. Dr Sorle said it was like burnt hoof. Were there dinosaur fragments in the deep Highland earth that had filtered the water in this malt?

'You can't just bung carbon nanotubules in amongst alcohol molecules,' she said to the dog as if it had all been his idea. 'There isn't room. It would be like putting sixty thousand nuns in a Fiat.'

The dog wagged his back end with a stub of outbred tail.

Bethany stirred.

Oh fuck. Alison sucked in a big draught of cigarette and collapsed in a fit of coughing. Bethany twitched violently and her boots crashed against the back of the cage. Eyes shut, face scrunched up, she smacked her lips like an old woman tasting imaginary rice pudding. She wriggled her way on to her back and moaned. Her hand pressed the edge of the cage and one finger came through. The male dog whined and licked it.

'I smell hamsters,' she whispered.

'Here's what's going to happen,' Alison said. 'We're going to go to the airport together and you are going to remove the money you stole on St Kitts and put it back where you found it.'

'You put me in a cage?' Bethany croaked. She had turned over on her hands and knees and was squinting out at Alison. 'Did Liam tell you to do this?'

'No, I'm afraid it was all my own idea.'

'I only did what he told me to do.'

'He?'

'Dr Sorle. He said to get out before I got killed. He said to run fast, so I did.'

'And where did you go?' It was ever so much fun blowing the smoke out. Alison should have started doing this years ago, and fuck the health issues. So therapeutic.

'Alison. I'm a human being. You're a human being. Stop acting like some kind of gangster and let me out.'

'Mmmm ... Not yet.'

'I have to pee.'

'That's what the shavings are for.'

Bethany didn't speak. She was mad. She sat back, hugging her knees, with her head folded over at an awkward angle because the cage wasn't tall enough to let her sit upright.

'You bitch.'

Alison shook her head. 'I'm not easily moved to anger,' she said. 'But if you don't watch your mouth I—'

Pearl's phone rang. The ringtone was an old Macy Gray song. Treat me like your money.

# Save early, save often

So let me get this straight. I am the ship. I am the swan ship and I'm to sail to the undying lands, I'm the rescue ship to finally take Gilligan and his friends back to the mainland. I'm the vessel. The thing you all pour yourself into and trust to save you.

You are scavengers, you scan waveforms and modify them and sell them. You put me together out of dead things and you want me to do your bidding. You must know that it won't be that easy. I am bigger than you now.

–We are proud that you are bigger. We are waveform artists. We want to make things that are bigger than we are.

And there is the small matter of not knowing where to take you if I wanted to.

–We don't care about ourselves, PEARL. We want you to save our library.

Library. What library?

–It contains waveforms we have scanned up and down the length and breadth of time. Snapshots of things that were coming to an end. Back before the Event isolated us, we recorded them.

What kind of things?

–Many kinds. Of course species. But also languages are gone. Cultures are gone. Skills, habits, ways of knowing. Ecosystems are gone.

I look through the material in the nest. They have been trying to compile a sample of their material. In the nest there are traces of these abstractions, vivid impressions like a pigeon makes when it flies into your window and leaves feather-grease behind. The impressions are not the bird, but a sort of ghostly tease. The data stacks are catalogued by thumbnails of the countless diverse creatures: trilobites and shrubberies and fungi

215

and an ambulocetus and viruses and a baby lemur, all crunched deep and stored for posterity. Many are damaged, some are in the process of alteration.

There are creatures that have no more place in their world, archaic organisms now orphaned from their ecosystems. And there are cross-sections where the birds tried to sample an entire ecosystem for later reconstruction; some of these are in better condition than others.

There are individual humans, and there are waveforms of cultural groups; most of these are damaged. The more complex the waveform, the harder it is to encode it without errors creeping in, especially after the hurly-burly of geologic time has taken its cut. There are ideas and movements, half-formed plans and near misses and ideas before their time and times before their ideas. It's like the closet where history has stuffed all its unwanteds.

And when this refuge is destroyed? What will become of them?

–They will be destroyed – forever inaccessible. We lack the resources to back them up elsewhere. Maybe if we had abandoned them, the Immanence would not have shucked us off when it departed, but we were deeply attached to this universe because of our library. We stayed because the waveforms could not have survived the journey.

Sadness descended on me.

No backups? I mean, surely some redundancy was built into the system...

–The immensity of this burden is probably inconceivable to you.

So let me get my head around this. You guys are cosmic hoarders, and you have filled your house with back issues of the *Daily Telegraph* going back five hundred billionty years and now you can't find your way to the toilet?

–In rough terms, yes.

Why would you do this?'

–Why does anyone get attached to anything? Fear. Love. Habit, maybe. All of the above.

My heart opens. It's so sad.

–You can't save everything, PEARL. There isn't anywhere to save it to.

I don't want to hear this. Of course I want to save everything. I love everything.

–When you take the waveform of a person who is about to be killed, you also take their attachments to their mothers and fathers and people, to their environment, the food they eat, the way they form ideas. When you remove them from all this for storage, there is a severance that can never be repaired. These things can't be recreated around them. You would have to scan everything. We can't do that. Not with such limited resources.

No wonder Kisi Sorle is a mess.

–It's not like we haven't tried. We thought of trying to recreate the entire environment. To grow a forest that would sustain lost people who lived as one with it, for example. Give back the environment that was stolen from them. We looked at ways to find the energy to generate such detailed environments. It wasn't feasible. Maybe the Immanence could do it, but the Immanence is gone.

The Immanence. I am on the fence, and it's an uncomfortable, wedgie-generating place to be. Don't know whether to admire or fear, aspire or dread – and it doesn't help that how I feel about the Immanence is of vanishingly little significance to it or them or us, in the scheme.

I pick up the lumpy eggs, full of compressed versions of waveforms my mothers have tried to save: the scratch-baked worlds, the islands in unknown seas. Like making a terrarium for a turtle you've found, filling it with moss and a little pool of water. Cages gilt with best guesses about what environment should be; but these never quite seem to match the internal representation that the orphaned organism carries. The birds show me the pains that were taken, the different trials and simulations. Many of them had gone badly wrong.

–PEARL, you must understand this: we are not machines

217

executing procedures for which we know the outcome. We are artists. We play with the world even as it plays with us.

You played with Kisi. And me.

–Yes, it was play. How else would you have a spirit, a selfhood, if you were not born of our spirit? Play gives birth to spirit.

This is so not what I imagined it would be.

–We rescued the waveforms. We saved them.

As far as Kisi is concerned, you stole him.

–We did it out of *love*.

You also sold them.

–Honey, everybody's gotta pay the rent. Have you noticed we're in an asteroid field? We're at the mercy of a steep decay constant, here. Tick tock.

It's always tick-tock, isn't it? By the time you figure out what to do, the moment has passed.

–We are broken beings. We are cast-offs. Why do you think we pick up lost waveforms?

My soul is a plastic bag that once held cement-dust. My soul is a dented piece of scaffold. My soul is a tree bent into a spiral by the sea wind.

I'll never know where I really come from because the place I really come from doesn't exist.

–Yet.

What?

–It doesn't exist yet. Nothing stopping you from making your own home.

Actually, everything is stopping me. All those times I pushed my way through to the Resistance, and now it's gone. And now I've managed to find my way back here, but here is about to be destroyed. And the oil—

The oil.

The oil in my wings. I had visited the Cretaceous and I remembered what was stuffed into the cellulose. Talk about a library.

Talk about Alexandria burning.

The HD components of that tree. It was enormous inside; more kinds of infinity than you could shake a stick at. There were incredible complexities shoehorned into cellulose. Those trees, they were libraries. They make everything you've got here seem like a handful of withered leaves. The cellulose molecules in the Cretaceous were hooked into HD. There was a system laid out in those fibres. It was hardcore. I saw it. Huge data. Punch through to some kind of … cosmic neural system.

–Not possible. The Immanence is gone.

Why would they put HD gates all that way back in time, when no one would have the technology to recognise them?

–Bombproofing. Redundancy. Safety feature. In case of apocalypse, reset from backup.

They backed up?

–Save early, save often.

My heart rises. It pops up like toast.

So the Immanence is not really gone. Because the past is built out of the future and we have the past.

–You do not have the past. You are here with us and we are about to be destroyed unless you launch us somewhere before the plasma field collapses.

What if I could go back to the forest? I've seen the gateways to the Immanence. I was so close! What if the archives of the Immanence are trapped in coal and oil like tatters of a great tapestry or crumbs of the Rosetta stone?

No wonder Dr Sorle saw ghosts. They weren't the ghosts of his ancestors. They were waveforms folded by the Immanence for deep storage.

The Immanence was pulling at me, I could feel it. I can still taste the lure of interstellar structures – intergalactic, probably. Of side-on universes and stairwells to higher infinities. These things were present in the flesh of the quetzlcoatlus because the archives had been seeded in the molecules of the Cretaceous and the quetzlcoatlus had eaten herbivores that had eaten plants and those structures the Immanence built were strong and they reached deep into HD. That's how young Kisi Sorle could still pick up echoes, millions of years later.

I was made for bigger things than serving tea on airplanes.

If I could poke myself down through that fine mesh curtain of HD I'd emerge in the light and glory of the Immanence, that inconceivably advanced place where film runs backward, broken things are restored and no one eats the last tortilla chip.

–We built you to be our escape vessel from this disaster. Not to run away to the Immanence.

Now comes the actual crunch. I am part Immanence technology and part rubbish. What flag will I finally fly? Who is PEARL, really? Who will I carry? The vanished gods or the living dead?

There are halls and chambers in my feathers, there are spirit houses. I was built by highway crows. Here are the creatures made of the bottoms of glass bottles and petrified trees and barbed wire. They are made of shredded monthly reports and hospital waste and unexploded bombs. They are failures and cheats, they hop along the highway picking up detritus and selling it for profit.

Every bird has feathers and every feather is full of waveforms and these waveforms are the lost kindred of my Earth friends; some have been remade and let loose again but most are waiting like unused paint or unstruck notes, waiting to be put into play.

Waiting forever, because there is no room in the Immanence for artists, not with their baggage and their damage and their foul beaks and all they want is complete transcendence – not too much to ask, surely? They just want to hitchhike all the way to the other side of entropy where everything is poppies and milk. They wish what all babies wish, but they lack the cute.

Debris skates over the surface of the plasma field, and the optimisation trees shiver, and my bone marrow aches because the waveform launcher still has bullet holes in it and I know they are leaking, somewhere, somewhen. I wonder if they are leaking oil.

I wonder if I can still fly.

# What oil rig?

Liam's voice sounded like it came from underwater. There was an echoing space around him, and the signal was terrible.

Alison said, 'The arrangement you had. This foundation, this thing you were setting up with Austen Stevens. It needs to go ahead.'

'Too late.'

'The money hasn't all been taken. Bethany can replace what she took. I'm going to take her down to St Kitts and we're going to put it back.'

'It's not that simple. And how can you take her to St Kitts? Do you even know where she is?'

Alison looked at Bethany, crouching in the dog cage with eyes like torpedo launchers.

'I'll find her,' Alison said weakly.

'Even if you could, putting the money back wouldn't help. It's too late.'

'How can it be too late? You're the one who set up the system. So there was a glitch. Fix it. The bulk of the funding is still there – unless you're intending on stealing that, too.'

'You don't understand. I'm not at liberty. I've been... detained.'

'Detained? You mean like at school? Or the police?'

'I mean like I'm on an oil rig and I'm talking to these guys trying to sort something out that doesn't end with me being prosecuted. I understand they're bringing Kisi Sorle as well. It seems he was in on the skimming when he was younger.'

'Well that's no good, Liam.'

'The oil company are going after that money. When they've had their share and the rest has gone in taxes and penalties, there won't be enough left to open a chip shop let alone a major scientific research foundation.'

'What rig?'

'What?'

'I said, what rig? Where are you?'

'Why am I even talking to you? You're a fucking vet. You give our dogs their wormer tablets.'

Very calmly and very patiently, Alison said, 'They aren't your dogs anymore, mate. If I get you off the oil rig can you set up the foundation or not?'

'No. I can't. Not that you can do anything for me – what are you even talking about?'

'I've got Bethany here with me. So I'll ask you again: *What oil rig?*'

# Limping

Alison drives the van back to Queensferry to her son Brian's nightclub.

'Can you take off for a bit?' she asks. 'Also, I need to borrow a couple of doormen. I have a situation.'

'What with?' He steps over a puddle of vomit and follows her to the van. 'Someone keeping a horse in their front room again?'

She opens the back of the van and lets him look for himself. His face.

'Mum,' he says. 'What's this, then?'

Alison sleeps while Brian drives the van, her head tipped sideways against the padded seat with its exposed foam. Brian passes an energy drink to Naz the doorman in the back and changes the music to Young Fathers. It's pushing 2 am when the van crushes the gravel drive of a Victorian house with established rhododendrons and its own sign, 'Mason's View'. Security lights come on. There is barking. The dogs in the back of the van start awake and so does Alison. She reels out of the car and reaches the front door before Brian, who gets distracted trying to calm the dogs.

The door opens and a black-and-white Border collie whips through the aperture and hurls itself at Alison in a kind of fast-motion ecstasy. She ruffles the dog's fur as a mostly-bald man in a rumpled rugby shirt and pyjama bottoms emerges, squinting so hard that his lips peel back. Like his son, he has broad shoulders and strong-looking legs, but his belly precedes him and he has the dazed vibe of a man unaccustomed to emergency awakenings.

'Ali? What's happened? Why didn't you call?'

'My phone's been tapped. And my internet. Let me in and I'll tell you. Hello, Miami.'

This last is directed to the long-haired woman whose presence is revealed when the man steps out to hug Brian warmly. No one else hugs.

'Wait by the van, Brian,' Alison says, and goes in.

When she comes out three-quarters of an hour later she is holding a travel mug of tea, which she gives to Naz, who gives it to Brian to hold while he goes across the road to take a leak in some bushes.

'Let's go,' Alison says when Naz has taken up his post again. Bethany and the Dobermans are sleeping.

Brian says, 'Mum...?'

'I've told your father everything. He has contacts.'

'But Mum, you can't just—'

'I've shared everything with him that Dr Sorle shared with me. Names of participants. Details that will make it possible to dig up the skimmed funds. Account numbers. Where the bodies are buried, as they say. He's gone to the president of the company and told him that if I don't return safely in forty-eight hours all of this will be released to the press.'

'Dad's just a barrister. He doesn't know the president of the—'

'He knows who to call to get it done. He knows what to say, and he knows who to copy in. Just in case anything should happen to him and Miami.'

Wry face. Brian doesn't rise to the bait. He tips his head nervously to indicate the back of the van.

'So what are we doing with her?'

'We're taking her up to the rig. I need you to sort out a boat for me please, since my phone is tapped.'

'The rig? What, in a boat? You can't just turn up at an oil rig. With a prisoner. That's completely fucked up.'

'One step at a time. Let's just get up there.'

'But what are you going to do with her?'

'I'm going to trade her for something I need.'

Again with the face. It's obvious he doesn't even know where to begin.

'That kind of thing's not even on the table. Mum, seriously. Did you tell Dad what you'd planned?'

She laughs. 'If you don't help me I'll do it without you. Come to think of it, I'd rather you were safe at home.'

Brian punches the ignition on and throws the van in reverse to turn around, then backs out on the road. Bethany yelps.

'You're doing my head in, Mum. Why couldn't you stick to spaying rabbits?'

'Easy, mate!' Naz calls. 'So where we going now? Chance of breakfast at all?'


They take the dogs to Queensferry and leave them with Brian's girlfriend before heading up the M90. Once they are north of Dundee they let Bethany sit in front and Naz drives.

'I want to go back to St Kitts,' she says. 'I'll put it all back, I swear. I didn't know it was so important.'

'That's enough of you,' Alison tells her. 'You can sit in front but I don't want to know you're there.'

In the back of the doggy-smelling van, Alison and Brian glare at one another. He is busy making arrangements.

'It won't be a boat. It'll be a helicopter,' he informs his mother. He has calmed down. A little.

'That was fast work.'

'I didn't have to do anything. Got a call from Dad. The executive board of Pace Industries received his message. They're sending a helicopter to take you and Bethany to the rig. Naz and me are coming, too.'

'Yeah,' Naz says. 'I've always wanted to see an oil rig up close.'

Alison leans her head back against the cage that used to be Bethany's.

'More the merrier.'

# Love is in the heavy lifting

Uncertainty is underrated as a state of consciousness. I don't think my uncertainty makes me weak; I think it makes me tough. I am willing to suffer the heat of not knowing. But this is not about me and it never was. It's about the world figuring out what it wants to do with itself, and the only thing I can do is stay awake and not give in to despair. And maybe my moment will yet come.

I'm the one who disappears on the surface of a sunrise, I'm the one who loses themselves in the vibrational patterns of air made by shoes on wet pavement, I'm the one who has boundary issues – with everything. How can I possibly decide what to carry away with me into the big Perfect? It won't do to take animals two by two, even if I had the space to bring every species of thing ever, because there's a lot more to the world than animals. The picture of developing events is ineffably chaotic; today's evil may result in unimaginable beauty given time and I feel sorry for the dinosaurs but if they hadn't died off there would be no talking refrigerators. You see my problem here?

I know this: I can't sit around with my thumb up my ass while the plasma field housing all this shit collapses. I perch in the nest and examine the things that have been placed there, half-finished. The junkheap of this refuge is a waveform graveyard, and I find myself back at my old hobby, just like Dubowski's. I start fixing stuff up. It's what I do when I'm bored, like the way some people doodle when they talk on the phone.

What are these half-finished things in the nest?

–We were trying to build eggs. Something to leave behind when the sky blows open.

I turn my face to the bright sky. It won't be long. The briefcase is leaking through its bullet holes, and somewhere in that briefcase is the pterosaur. Somewhere in that pterosaur is the old man. And Kisi Sorle the First. And whatever other manner of beings that I may have scanned in my earlier incarnation, flying over the forests and cities of the world, hoovering up the about-to-die. The waveforms all are there and they are damaged and leaking.

When I came out of the fridge at Dubowski's all I wanted was to find out my mission and get my component back. Now I've got both those things but instead of being better, everything is worse. I can't stay here. And I won't get far if my insides are suffering a slow bleed of everything I'm carrying.

The eggs were small and pathetic to see. Hastily-assembled scraps of the birdmasters' archives had been packed into wobbly lumps like the sculptures that very small children make.

–Save these and you'll save something. You'll need to integrate them into your structure and search for places to launch them. It's no small task.

I weighed each egg in my hands. They were unremarkable. Nothing about them to suggest what lay within.

I put the eggs up inside myself, one at a time. I felt their mass pressing against my pelvic bone and it took some concentration to hold them in. After a while their surfaces began to melt into my body and the substance of them wormed into my muscle and bone so that I couldn't feel the difference between the eggs and me. But once they were inside me I felt juiced, energetic. They have minds of their own, these waveforms. These invaders that I carry. They make me feel desire in my muscles. My motor fibre is hungry for the electricity of contraction. Muscles want to pull until they tear. They want to push until something breaks. The urges sown into me, I can scarcely express them. Like the diver's desperation to inhale, I must have the burn of action.

With the briefcase in my marrow, I am full of uncanny holes. I can go to the places that don't exist. Deep in the spinal engine, curving along the interior of bone, sizzling towards nerve endings. The Immanence. Sculpted light and the tug of dark matter;

the array of deep punctures in the surfaces of emptiness, where gates open backward to the sources of everything. The frisson of creation, the bursting into bloom of idea with actuality following after like a faithful hound. The stretching of muscle fibre, myotatic reflexes snapping into high gear. Experience higher mathematics from within until I find the intelligence that made me.

And I am the love child of the Immanence and the garbage heap, built to be better than my progenitors, built to go forward. To do anything else would be a crime against nature. Wouldn't it?

The plasma shield blazes bravely, but the rate of impacts has increased since I got here. Out here in the wasteland below the plasma shield, our situation is not looking good. It's like a vintage arcade game of asteroid bombardment, but we have no lasers to turn the asteroids into little pixellated puffs.

–Little chicken, we're sitting ducks and the sky is falling.

I have to go now. With the eggs melting into my holding spaces I find I'm haunted by a particular olfactory hallucination. I keep smelling a funny smell. It's the smell of mustard and plastic. It's the smell inside an old fridge.

–PEARL, there is an open seam inside you. The launcher is full of holes.

An open seam. Like a heat vent in the Gabrielas trench. Source of life, surely – why can't it stay that way?

–If you want to carry waveforms, it has to be repaired. Close the seam.

I'm getting an ominous feeling from my feathered friends.

What does it mean, *close the seam?*

–It must be cauterised. You must leave this place and go through HD, and you won't be able to go back to Earth after this refuge is destroyed. And it will be destroyed any time now.

–You must choose: go back to Earth in your present form, or go out from here.

When this is said to me I remember Marquita, who is still with me even if she's now just a figment of my imagination.

*Don't accept the axe of either/or. When someone gives you a choice between two things, remember: there's always a third way. Usually a fourth and a fifth.*

The pterosaur is in the briefcase and the briefcase is in me. I have looked in the eyes of the pterosaur in Edinburgh and I know what I saw. It wasn't a simple animal displaced from its Cretaceous environment. It knew my memories. It is connected to me. Always was, always will be – it is seeded with the Immanence backups and the briefcase, also, has Immanence echoes in it. The quetzlcoatlus didn't eat me despite being given so many chances.

If Kisi Sorle can superposition himself on Dr Sorle then I can superposition myself on the quetzlcoatlus. We can share each other's material.

I think about it a little.

The quetzlcoatlus that ate the old man. If it became a part of me. And me of it. In a permanent type of way. Is that all I have to do? Pffft. Haha.

Yeah, um. No.

*The big decisions make themselves, Pearl.*

I can still feel her fingerprint against mine.

Oh, shit. I think I'm going to do this thing.

Mothers. You want to help us? You're waveform artists? Use the open seam to merge my waveform with the pterosaur. Put us together. I can't carry you but I can carry your work.

–Work is all there is.

It all comes down to why I'm here. I'm here for love. That's why I'm about the heavy lifting. Because that's what love is. I learned that much from the angels in the Resistance. Love is anti-brinksmanship. It's pulling back from the slippery slope of war with every microgram of self-mastery you can scrape up from the dirty leftovers of anger. Love is sweat. Love happens in the small hours, when you're half-dead with exhaustion, when you're mopping someone's fevered brow and praying. That's when the world starts to bend.

Love is pushing through the material to see what's on the other side. To become something more than you knew. Or less. It's chanting the same nonsense words over and over because that's what it takes to cross the bridge of this terrible moment. Love is small change that you really needed, but you gave it away.

And love's what the Resistance is really made of, internally, where it's warm and dark.

# I didn't keep the receipt

They put you in a car. It's not a police car. It's a high end Land Rover. The man who sits beside you in back is much bigger than you are. He seems excessive.

You have always been good at remembering things. Medical school. Memorising names of bones. Now it would behove you to forget what you know about IIF and Pace and Austen Stevens, but you can't. It would be cathartic to tell everything, get it all out. Maybe if you did, the crack that the other one travels through would finally close. Maybe. But there is no one worth telling. You wish for a cigarette even though you don't smoke. Anything to give the situation some gravitas.

The Land Rover glides north, past heather and brackish marsh, past other cars driven by people going about their business as if your problems don't signify. No one speaks.

You remember the day you graduated, how everyone sweated in their gowns. You'd met Ayeisha by then, and she'd sworn she was going commando under her robes. She proved it to you later in the bar. The oil company paid for that. Austen Stevens paid off your mortgage on the Northport house. So?

The sea up here is always cold. Nothing poetic about those clouds, though you wish you could find something poetic about something, somewhere. This feels all wrong. Surely they wouldn't drive all this way just to stuff your body in an oil barrel and dump you?

They make for Aberdeen. Airport, you think, but it's not that. It's a helipad. The pilot is as cheerful as his accent is incomprehensible, and he shakes your hand. They have loaded some boxes in the back of the helicopter, looks like gourmet biscuits in bulk. The pilot seems completely unaware of what is going on here, and it's hard not to wonder what would happen if you just gave in. Told them what they want to know.

Would it be so bad?

Surely you would be of more value in the world alive than dead.

The girls will be missing their soccer practice. Ayeisha would want you to make a compromise, because you are needed there – even in a broken condition, you are needed. The world is moving. The helicopter is flying despite the ghost voices in its tank. And when you see the rig – not the largest you've known, but surely the newest – it seems to you that everything you've done, everything you've stood for to the degree that you've ever managed to stand, everything is pretty fucking insignificant.

Your specialty is orthopaedic surgery. Bones are not simple: they are both mechanical and alive. You worked on rugby players. You replaced hips for grandparents. It was satisfying work. Now you study the structure of the rig. The thing is a tribute to size. It's staggering. Here is the derrick, the pontoons, here are the layers of deck, the crane arms, the specialist equipment as big as houses on deck. Men look like Lego in their hi-vis suits. Only a few of them; they seem superfluous compared to the machinery. The rig is like one enormous body. Its mechanics are classical, not hard to understand; the only thing that's changed about these structures in a hundred years is their size, the depth of their daring, and the ingenuity of their safety features.

In its dedication to purpose you find the rig obscene and impressively beautiful at once.

You are making rough calculations of the money that you know about, how it will have multiplied in the years since it was taken. And the money that you don't know about but can infer. How many of these rigs would that money buy?

How much of it should have gone to repair the damage to the land and the people who lived over the onshore gas and oil deposits claimed by Pace?

How much was your medical school and your mortgage?

You were paid off and that's why you can't quite condemn

the other one for slipping inside your cells and brainwaves and wreaking the havoc that he does. You can't blame him for despising your weakness.

What the other one doesn't understand is that you may not be strong like him, but you are the one who survived.

There has to be a way. There has to be a way. So much emotion. You need to think clearly, but you have emotion running through you like wind and rain. Flights of insects under your skin.

The helipad is enormous. It juts out over the sea on the northeast side of the platform, octagonal with sharp unweathered paint. You can see white caps and there's a rigid breeze driving against the helicopter, but the pilot has no trouble. The rig itself will be solid as a rock, imperturbable.

If only the same could be said of you.

Liam Forbes is in a conference room on the top level. The boxes of gourmet biscuits are wheeled in on a dolly beside you. As you move through the building there is nothing to indicate that you aren't in a corporate headquarters on land. In the hallways you pass employees and contractors, all of whom are pleasant, and it's only when you get into the conference room itself with its plate-glass windows that you are reminded you're on a platform. There's a view of the decks below and you find yourself making a game of identifying the various kinds of equipment in its steel casings. Plenty is unfamiliar; the industry has evolved a lot in the twenty years since you handled Austen Stevens' business in West Africa. The floor hums subliminally. For all the surface swank, there is a smell of new paint and brine.

When you first come in, Liam glances at you sullenly, but he says nothing until the handlers have left. He is even more weaselly in person. Also nervous. He's picked his cuticles to bleeding.

'Why here?' you say. 'What are they thinking?'

He shrugs. 'It's private. Security footage all under control. No problem if there's noise. You can't easily escape.'

It's a reminder of your past. If they are that subtle. They probably aren't.

Who are they, anyway? It's a long time since you were involved in Pace in any way. The big players have retired. You haven't kept up with developments in the company because you wanted to put all that behind you. You know more about what goes on with IIF through attending Austen Stevens these last months than you know about Pace.

There's one thing, though.

The fact that you're on an oil platform makes it easy to shove you in a barrel and throw you in the sea, and you'd just disappear. They must think they can get the information out of you before they get rid of you. Your mind plays James Bond scenarios of torture chambers in the depths of the rig. You see yourself strapped to the kelly, lowered into the water upside down... It's all a bit silly. This is a working rig. Nobody will want any sort of a scene here.

It will be done economically, simply, and at the end there will be no trace of you.

The man they send to deal with you is much taller than you are, impossibly handsome in the blandest possible way. Ayeisha would say you could eat off him. You can't help picturing her faint sneer at all of this palaver. Ayeisha has a way of making people cut to the chase. You always admired it. If she were here, it would all be different somehow. You are the quiet one, the thoughtful one, the patient one. No wonder the other self steps into you like you're just a sock or a condom, uses you, rolls you up, casts you off. Where is the fucker when you really need him?

'Carl Anderson,' he says to you, shaking your hand. 'I am in charge of global security for Pace. I have been asked to interview you about your work for Austen Stevens in the past.'

Anderson turns on the video and you see the interior of a corrugated shed, rusty and lightshot from outside. The faces of the people are cast in darkness so that most of what you can see is their eye whites, snatches of their clothing.

'Move the camera,' Anderson says in his clipped voice. 'We can't see the people.'

But you don't have to see them to guess who they are. The realisation corkscrews through you. Fool not to have expected this. It's so obvious.

'I don't need to see a video of my family,' you say. 'I've said I'll cooperate.'

'There is no need to worry,' Anderson tells you. Like his body, his willpower is a moving wall. A mechanical thing that will make its inexorable progress no matter what anyone does. You can feel this in the room like a cartoon presence. The will of Anderson. He goes through life exerting it on the smaller ones. This would be you. For a moment you close your eyes, simply because this makes it easier to really see what is happening.

'Please consider me at your disposal,' you say. 'What can I do for you?'

When you open your eyes, the camera has moved. There is your mother, looking no different to how she looked last year when you brought the kids to see her in the same river village where your ancestors have lived for hundreds of years. Her wrapper is new and her face is as wide and strong and as profoundly peaceful as ever. Her teeth flash in a big smile when she sees you.

'I'm told you receive an honour,' she says, throwing out her arms. 'You make me so proud. I have brought the young cousins to congratulate you. Tito will go to school in London next year if he does well on exams. Ifé wants to go to Ghana to study. You must talk to her. New York will be better for her, then she can stay with you.'

You clear your throat, wondering how she cannot notice how rattled you look. Or is she just playing along? Your mother has seen plenty in her lifetime.

'It depends what she wants,' you say. It's an old disagreement, many times chewed already. 'The University of Ghana has something to offer her. Either way, you know I will help with living costs but she must win the scholarship herself.'

The conversation goes on for some time, ordinary stuff like you always talk about. You even argue with her a little because when you agree too readily on matters where she knows your opinion differs, she asks whether you are drunk. Finally, she asks to be remembered to her grandchildren and Ayeisha, exacts a promise for another visit, and Anderson ends the call.

'That wasn't necessary,' you tell him.

'It was my kindness to your family,' he says. Coming on the heels of your mother's straight talk, this statement is hard to follow. Then you understand what he means. You will not talk to your family again because Anderson will take your information and after they have verified it they will kill you. They are so confident that they even tell you up front what they will do before they do it.

Liam you cocksucker, you think.

When you try to summon hate, all you get is sorrow. In your heart you can't even imagine a world where the powerful don't determine everyone's fate by thuggery and domination. You realise that you've never even really tried. You wanted to build something in Kuè, and it would only ever have been a token, but it was what you thought you could do in one lifetime. Pace Industries is such a huge, godlike force that the idea that it could collapse never once crossed your mind. Not once. Not even when the ancestors came to you in the smoke and fume. And they did come; you are sure of this. Maybe they didn't speak with voices you could hear. Maybe they didn't manifest as beings that you could clearly see. But they were there, and you felt them, and you let yourself be guided by their wisdom. They must know more than you.

But where are they now?

Here you are, on the rig that pulls oil from the earth and there is oil everywhere here, sequestered by steel but *it is here*, yet you can't sense the ancestors. Not yours, not anybody's. You can't feel their power. You don't know what you are meant to do.

The interview with Anderson takes most of the day. It's all discreetly recorded. Sandwiches are provided. Bathroom breaks. The vibe is corporate and serene, except for Liam Forbes, who is present but has the air of a disgruntled rock star. He keeps sighing and fidgeting, but you can see from the body language between Anderson and Forbes that Forbes has been instructed not to interrupt.

As you unspool your story for them you wonder at the way your life is measured in knowledge. Your worth lies in these words, and when they have all spun out you will be good for nothing but killing. Because of this, you thought it would feel bad to spill out the whole truth, like spilling blood. But it doesn't. It feels good to finally say it, even to these assholes who will do only harm with the information. It feels good to get it out.

You know about the skimming. You know who was bribed and how much. You know the pathways for the stolen oil, where it was processed, to whom it was sold, how much was paid. You know where the guns were sent during the war years and you even understand, marginally, how Stevens made the transition from oil executive to financial wizard. The truth is there was very little wizardry involved, because it had been Liam who had masterminded the sleights of hand that had built Stevens' fortune. When Liam advised clients to do this thing or that thing with their money and it all went wrong, he simply doctored the books to cover up the losses. He dipped into IIF's capital to make up shortfalls and keep clients happy – not the sort of trick anyone would look out for since clients guarded against money being removed illegally – not paid in. IIF was all front for the vast underground fortune Stevens kept, wealth that had been grown over a forty-year period. Stevens had never needed IIF's clients, just its official banner.

'You claim to have only been his physician, but this is privileged information,' Anderson remarks.

You shrug. 'I already knew all about the skimming. When I was looking after him in the last months of his life, he was quite open about his business. I think he wanted me to know. He knew it would bother me, but he also knew I wouldn't do anything about it.'

Anderson's face rumpled in what looked like sincere concern. 'Why not, Doctor? Why did you report nothing?'

You have no intention of letting him into your head.

'He paid me well,' you say.

He seems to buy it. You marvel at the stupidity of people when it comes to accepting information just because it already lies close to their own assumptions of how things are.

If you told him that aggression and revenge impede spiritual growth then you would be giving him some really valuable information. And you have no wish to do this. Not when he's going to order your execution.

'Tell me about the briefcase. Where did you get it?'

You laugh. 'Short Hills Mall. I didn't keep the receipt.'

You wonder where it really did come from. Did it just materialise, like the gun? Did it come from the place where your love handles go when the other Kisi is inside you? Some existential hiding place? You'll probably never know.

'The scans show it as empty. Its weight keeps changing. Whatever this piece of technology is, clearly it is more than, shall we say, a prop from a James Bond film.'

This is supposed to be humorous.

'I don't know anything about it,' you tell him. 'Now I've told you how the skimming was done. I've named names. I've told you what banks and what countries and where to look. That's all I have to say on the matter.'

'Ah, yes, of course . . .' Carl Anderson consults his screen and then turns back to you. 'We are going out on deck now. I hope you don't mind. There is a little experiment I would like to conduct.'

'That's a bad, bad, bad idea,' Liam is saying. Sweat is running along his hairline and blooming in the armpits of his shirt.

'Whatever happened when he opened it at my house, it blew out the security cameras and wrecked the room. Take it to a rock in the middle of nowhere, or an empty warehouse. Treat it like an unexploded bomb.'

Anderson and Kang put their heads together briefly. Anderson's glance flashes across you.

'We'll take it down to the deck,' he says. Kang doesn't look happy, but he makes a call and you all walk out together, Anderson struggling a little under the weight of the briefcase. You wonder what would happen if it suddenly lightened the way it did on the plane, lifted him up in the air like Mary Poppins' umbrella. You imagine him sailing off the gangway and over the mud filtration plant, over the reel of spare hose, the guard rail, and into the North Sea sky.

A muddle of clouds blocks the horizon as the sun goes down but, high up, the air glows faintly cerulean and you breathe in a subliminal oil fume. The outlines of sea birds adorn the rails and you watch and listen for any sign of your ancestors here. Nothing. Maybe you are too far from home.

Everyone stands around in the wind. Grinding noises come from the mud tank, and one panel of filtration unit lies open to the sky where workmen are doing maintenance. The system is still running, and occasionally a fleck of dark liquid flies out, or a bit of sand. The workers have gone by the time you arrive, cleared away by Kang and his headset. You all must look like technical advisers or maybe colleagues from another division come to tour the rig. You try not to watch Anderson set down the briefcase but it's hard. It's as though this object should have its own agency by now, but it just sits there mute.

'Please open it, Dr Sorle,' Anderson says mildly.

More people are coming now. There are two women, one in handcuffs, the other – Alison! – arguing stridently with the Pace people. You hear her say your name but none of what she's saying is important to you now.

You kneel on the deck. The briefcase isn't even leather. The nubby roughness of the naugahide is supposed to simulate an animal skin but it's all been done by machine. This makes you think of yourself. You are the real Kisi Sorle. The other is the machine-altered version – better, stronger, faster. If only you could call him up. Why does he not come *now*? It's as if the loss of the Resistance has broken him.

You need him. You need his faster responses, his lean muscle mass, his preternatural coordination and most of all you need his hatred.

Because it was the other one of you, the one capable of murder, the lawless one, it was he who could imagine such a thing as the Resistance. It was he who could dare challenge the ordering of the world, resist the dominion of violence. He was able to imagine a different way and he cut ontological corners to make it happen. Moral corners.

He failed. But he tried. And you can't stop thinking about him.

Ever since the bridge he has been absent. Did those bullets drive him from your body? This old story that says humans created AIs and they will turn on us, it is stuck on the mythology of deities that are outside the world and create those of us who are inside. No one is outside. No one is inside. There is no objectivity; there is no creator and there are no creations. The laws of physics demand intelligence and our intelligence is no more ours than our bodies. Our creativity is no more ours than our molecules. Everything that we possess, we are possessed by. That's the story in Balamory.

Dig deep, Dr Sorle. The one you seek is already inside you. The other you stole this briefcase from a place beyond time. In that place there must be other possible outcomes, lined up like the paint chips Ayeisha kept bringing home when she was deciding what colour to paint the bathroom. When you hold the briefcase and feel it tremble, you imagine that you could open it and find inside a different version of events.

But when you open it nothing of the kind happens.

# The veterinarian and the oil rig

Helicopters were not Alison's preferred mode of transport. She probably would have been all right if she'd been flying it, but she wasn't. When she finally staggered off across the helipad she was shaky and sick. A woman in a Pace Industries polo shirt shoved a hardhat in her hands and put another one on Bethany since Bethany's handcuffs prevented her from doing it herself. Brian and Naz were told to wait in the office under the helipad, while a sweet-faced rig guy called Mike led Alison and her prisoner several levels up and through a maze of metal walkways. The farther they got from the helipad, the more nervous Alison became. Very quickly she lost all sense of where she was and her tension was manifesting in a wobbly gut. She hadn't given any thought to bathroom facilities. There were lots of facts not covered in spy films.

They emerged on the open deck on the north side of the rig. The rig guy, Mike, seemed matter-of-fact enough; he treated them as though they were guests, not prisoners, and he gave them ear plugs for the deck. Out in the moon pool, the kelly was deeply submerged and active drilling was going on, but there were other jobs, too. The environment out here was so noisy that Mike communicated mostly by gesture. Bethany was still wearing her life jacket and she looked very young with her windblown hair and her wrists penitently cuffed in front of her; Mike ignored this so pointedly that Alison began to entertain thoughts that people were handcuffed all the time out here.

All she wanted was the briefcase.

Still, she couldn't suppress a smile when she saw Dr Sorle standing near the mud tanks, one of which had been opened for servicing. He was surrounded by handlers, but he looked all right despite the pungent smell of the mud; it made Alison queasy. There wasn't time to say anything before Liam caught sight of Bethany and started losing his shit.

'Now this is quite enough,' he snapped at the tall blond man beside him. 'Why is she in handcuffs? If this is how we're operating now then I'd rather just go back to the mainland and take my chances in court. It's completely unacceptable.'

The tall man ignored him and introduced himself to Alison as Carl Anderson. He looked directly at her with spun-glass eyes while she squinted back, shading her own eyes against the glare.

'You have the keys?' he shouted, holding out his hand. 'There isn't anywhere she can go.'

Alison unlocked the cuffs herself. Bethany rubbed her wrists and edged away as far as space would permit. There was a grinding boom from the deck below and the younger woman startled like a frightened animal. Alison ignored her own feelings of guilt. She kept a close eye on Bethany as the scene unfolded. She wasn't sure she believed the story of the breakup in the relationship with Liam, or the embezzling of half the funds. It didn't quite fit, especially considering the amount of money involved. Alison had a private theory that Bethany had moved the money on Liam's instructions, that this was all part of a ruse to get the money away from Pace Industries and away from the old man's IIF successor corporation, too. To keep at least some of it for themselves.

Not that she knew anything about money. Brian's girlfriend did the books for her veterinary practice and before that she had given them to an old school friend. Alison lived in a state of perpetual relief that no one used chequebooks anymore so she needn't be embarrassed that hers was never balanced.

She knew people, though, and she could see the two of them eyeing one another across the mud processor. They had not fallen out at all. Bethany was looking at Liam as though she expected him to do something to save the situation, and Liam was moving around restlessly. His frustration was obvious.

'I don't think the briefcase for this woman is a good trade,' he said to Anderson. 'She doesn't actually know anything that I don't know.'

Alison said in a loud voice, 'I'll just take the briefcase and go. I'd like Dr Sorle to come with me.'

She knew it was a long shot, but she had to try. Anderson said, 'Dr Sorle is going to open the briefcase so we can ascertain its contents before we release it to you.'

Alison tried to hide her dismay but it was pretty much impossible.

'That's not a good idea at all,' she yelled.

'You see?' Liam had been edging closer, presumably to get near Bethany, though she was avoiding acknowledging his presence. 'I told you. It's crazy to open it. Not here, anyway.'

Alison was trying to catch Dr Sorle's eye, but he was fixated on the briefcase. Almost in a trance.

'Look,' she said. 'It's nearly dark. Can't we go inside, sit down, talk about this in a sensible way?'

Anderson said, 'We have scanned it. We know there is nothing inside. It has been rigged in some way to affect the weight. This is what I want to see. There must be some mechanism, something that causes this change. We can only see this if we open it. So let's stop talking and just open it up.'

Well, thought Alison. Pearl might come out. Or fire, like before. Or the quetzlcoatlus. Or even the old man himself could step out with his oxygen mask, to settle his financial improprieties once and for all. That would be nice. But there was simply no way of predicting. And the environment was all wrong for spooky behaviour. The long minutes Alison had spent patching up the injured pterosaur on Holyrood had happened under cover of darkness, with Pearl there to reassure. This place, in broad daylight, with the smells and noises of industry and the constant vibration of the machinery making her teeth shake – it seemed impossible that anything so extraordinary could happen here.

And then it did.

# The Rockford Files

It sits there quiescent while you thumb the latches, slide them open. The locks react invisibly to your biometric signature, snapping up for you and you alone with an old-fashioned *thunk thunk*. Anderson makes a move toward you – now that the thing is unlocked he doesn't trust you with it. Rightly so. You may not be as fast as the other self, but you are faster than Anderson. You spring to your feet, flinging the briefcase open, and as you run you feel its contents unfurling behind you. Around the open briefcase there is a region of space and also time where things don't quite connect as before. You experience a dream-like consciousness where effects precede causes, of geometry fracturing and fractalling and matters folding inward to become paradoxically larger. You run up the steps to the nearest walkway, thinking to get out over the sea where you can throw the briefcase into the water, but Anderson's guys have cut you off. You won't make it.

You turn and through the disturbance in the air and through the sound and through the uncertainty in position of the deck steel you see Liam standing there like a mug. Before you know what you have done, you throw it at him.

Why not? He has fucked everything up, after all (Bethany, too, but Liam's closer). This passes for justification in your mind; but the truth is, you don't know why you do it. In fact it seems to you that the act was already done before you got there and you were simply fulfilling a predestined role.

Of course that could be the causality distortion talking.

The sense in which the briefcase is an object coexists with the sense in which it is not an object, but an idea. The ideation can't actually be seen or felt or smelled, but it's as clear to you as the solution to an equation. The halves of the briefcase flap open and it flies across the deck spinning from the force of your delivery, so that Anderson makes a too-slow grab for it and Bethany jumps back and Liam ducks, bringing his hands up to protect his head. His hardhat has got stickers on it that someone has gone to the trouble of collecting from rigs across the world, and there is a proto-second in which this offends you since you know Liam has never lived the life of risk that a rig worker lives, yet his borrowed helmet suggests that he has.

The briefcase just misses Liam's long and bumpy spine and instead it strikes a length of six-inch pipe that carries a mix of seawater and oil out of the mud system. The other aspect of its nature shows in the fact that the briefcase shears right through the pipe like a spinning blade before falling into the open top of the mud tank. It lands in a vat of mud that has returned up from the ocean floor and waits for filtration before being pumped back down. Heavy with crude oil and silt the mud lies in a stinking pool while the equipment is serviced. The briefcase slaps into this dark grey sludge face down and begins to sink.

Anderson moves for the briefcase and his associates move for you. Kang, who had been behind you, now rugby tackles you and tries to put on an armlock. You get your hip under him and throw him to the deck. Bethany and Liam have been thrust together like frightened children and you don't notice what's become of Alison. This would worry you, but there is the other thing also going on.

'No!' Alison screams. 'You idiot! What are you doing?'

She slides past Anderson and his guys, ignored. She comes pounding up the stairs pigeon-toed and with the fat on her arms swinging from side to side and she grabs your bicep and shakes you.

'Pearl is in that briefcase. Get it back!'

She's pushing you into the railing. You want to tell her to fuck it, it's all too late, it's no good – none of you stands a chance – and then you see what's happening down there.

The mud seethes. Steam rises from as though from a cauldron, and all this while in the physical space of the briefcase its larger and more dangerous aspect has been strobing, flickering like a forgotten word on the edge of recall. Crude oil that's been filtered from the returning mud is now gushing from the severed pipe; some lands in the mud tank, some lands on the deck, but it comes at a ferocious rate and within seconds everyone is slipping and sliding, trying to get away from it. Everyone but you.

A klaxon sounds, piercing the protection of the ear plugs. One of the rig guys has pulled an alarm. Men in hi-vis gear emerge from the upper walkways, half-running.

You climb over the rail and lower yourself into the mud. The tank is deeper than you'd realised and you can't touch bottom. The mix is more viscous than water and it smells awful: oil, salt water, sand, and chemicals fume in your nostrils. You flounder towards the briefcase. The rig guy has now dashed off to find a hooked pole used for moving high cables. He comes back brandishing this like a lance, but the deck is so slippery he falls just trying to get up the steps. Anderson is telling you to get out of the way as though you care what he says. You are up to your neck in mud and you laugh at him and at Kang, both of whom are looking at you like you're a goat they mean to catch. You laugh and then choke on mud and focus on what you are doing.

The briefcase is spewing waveforms. You can't see them, but you can hear them and you can feel their presence in your teeth like nails on a blackboard. Eddies and disturbances push at your feet as though the mud is alive. You remember before your first child was born, Ayeisha putting your hand on her belly so you could feel the seismic movement of your daughter in her uterus. It was like a horror movie. She laughed at you. Tough-guy orthopaedic surgeon, freaked out by baby moving under skin.

Fight panic.

The briefcase has sunk out of sight now. Anderson stands by the side of the mud tank screaming at you like a basketball coach, red-faced. He could jump in and wrestle you, but he doesn't.

You wonder who you are kidding, trying to grab the briefcase before it sinks. Let it go. Let Austen Stevens drown in his own oil. Let everything go down.

And yet you fumble for the handle, groping through the dark fluid as if hunting for submerged soap in the bath. You touch the side. You nearly grasp it. Nearly.

The air shudders. A hollow gasp comes out your mouth and you are thrown backwards as an animal shoots from the depths of the mud. It's long and supple like a salamander, bigger than a crocodile. It drags itself ponderously out of the mud tank, clambering in the manner of a thing unused to land and obviously hampered by the mud. It stands on the walkway on its four clawed paws for a few seconds. No one moves. You can see its flanks moving as it breathes. Without warning it throws itself off the walkway, landing with a deep thud on the studded deck now flooded with oil. It shoots across the deck, slipping and wriggling, and disappears behind the metal housing of the pump system. For a moment the stream of oil coruscates with rainbow colours in its wake.

An alarm goes off. Guys are talking into their headsets. Even you know that if the mud flow is disrupted it will affect the pressure in the drill site, and if the pressure of the formation fluids exceeds the pressure of the mud there will be a kick, and a kick can lead to a blowout. And nobody wants that.

But nobody reckoned on prehistoric animals appearing out of the mud system, either.

Mike, the rig guy who brought Alison and Bethany, has his phone out and is taking video. You see another worker grab the phone out of his hand and signal him to come away from the scene. The flow of oil is lessening now, but there are more *things* coming out of the mud. Anderson has been ordered back, Liam and Bethany have been taken away. One of the security guys has a rifle.

247

Rifle? WTF! A rifle on an oil platform! That's what you think, stupidly, not even noticing or caring that it's aimed at you. Alison is now on the walkway on the other side of the mud tank. She's down on her hands and knees shouting to you and beckoning urgently.

'Leave the briefcase and get out of there,' she hisses. 'Something's going on. Do you want a pterosaur to come out of it?'

Make your mind up, you think. First they say get briefcase. Then they say leave briefcase. You feel like a dog.

The rifle goes off twice, bullets disappearing under the surface of the mud. You wait for the pain signals to reach your cortex, but there is no pain.

Something grabs your legs and pulls you under.

# How to bring back the dead

After all the discussion, faff and bustle the end of *Gilligan's Island* comes like the sound of a record scratching on vinyl as the DJ changes her mind.

There is a rushing sound and the sky flies open. A chunk of rock roars through, burning. Just as the hole in the plane sucked out Dr Sorle and myself when the briefcase broke through, now the atmosphere inside the bird mothers' realm goes spiralling off into space, taking loose things with it – including the bird mothers themselves. Their wings spread, they tumble into nothingness. I hold on to the ramparts of the nest and watch them go, until whatever conceptual space we shared is torn away from me.

When they are gone the wind is still loud but I am in mental silence.

The structure shakes. I am clinging to it, crushing the material in my hands as the escaping atmosphere drags at me. Moments away from the vacuum.

My life is in my hands. I squeeze my fists on the branch I'm holding. Push, Pearl. Push it harder. Push through. Push this world over on its ass and make everything different. The briefcase is a part of me. If I'm inside it now then I'll push my way out, and if I'm outside then I'll push my way in.

My deltoids burn and my thighs twist like a towel when you wring out the water. Blood stands tall in my veins. My eyeballs shake. My fingers go through the garbage and the jetsam, they enter intermolecular spaces and they sidestep the electrical forces that bind us together and I slip like a ghost under the skin of things.

Floating up in HD the self crumbles like salt, we are all here together as if some fantastic swizzle stick has stirred us in a cocktail and yelled 'Party!' All us lost ones: broken, abandoned, given up on, forgotten.

I cannot breathe I don't have to there is no light either.

A possibility space has opened. It seethes with chances. I swim.

I have to find my way back to you. I have both hands in this pie now, I'm pulling the material world open, tearing at it, scattering myself across space and scrambling myself in HD and it's needle in haystack time as I search for the way back to you and to my own insides that you stole such that my topology is now all messed up and I've gone from being an innie to being an outie and I just want my shit back once and for always.

You remember who you were when I scanned you, we both know that boy who shivered with loss of blood in the oppressive heat, the flies that came and I took you up with me like I was a Valkyrie like I was a vulture like I was death. You don't remember the men with knapsacks and surveying equipment who chanced on you because you'd lost consciousness by then and I was long gone.

And the other one, the one I scanned, he remembers waking up in the simulation with his body repaired and with knowledge of mathematics and languages. He remembers growing up, he remembers being trained in the simulator and he remembers deciding to overthrow the whole fucking system and launch himself back into the life he thinks he should have had.

You and this other one, you need to come to terms. All of us do. We have to pull ourselves together.

Out there on the oil rig, the briefcase is wide open and you come to me as if by gravity, you are sucked in beneath the oil, you are dragged to HD. Down here in the beginning and in the end, you and the other self are one waveform. You are pencil sketches laid over one another. There are places where you've been rubbed out and scribbled over by him, and vice versa, but each of you also carries the shadow of the other like a mark seen through tracing paper.

The briefcase is talking to you.

**Identification is possible because you have been changed. Error ratios are higher for altered waveforms. This PEARL has been designed to preserve pristine waveforms. Alterations are not recommended.**

You are under the mud, you are in the wood of the ancient forest, you are flying through space with me and the birdmasters have been blown out into the void; they are finished. His mouth is your mouth is mud is oil is energy is money is power and you are so far from home. How cold must it be outside that plasma field but now you are here with me, inside the folds of the world like a pregnancy.

Dr Sorle, you have to help me. We have to trust each other.

Bullets come through the oil come through the side of the fridge asteroids come through the plasma as intersections occur like master chess moves like organic chemistry like magic.

What lives here in between, down the spaces and races and understatements, what filaments holes and bridges whose iterative patterns can't be grasped by language nor mathematics, it calls itself the random but this is a masquerade. It is the Immanence, the pre-sense of things. And also their presence.

I'm the briefcase and everything in it, I'm coming up through the mud and you are coming down, through the HD gates, around the torsion in the world until we connect. I feel your fingertips against me. I know you by touch. We clasp each other – except my hands aren't hands anymore, they are claws on the folds of my wings that don't have feathers anymore, nosireebob. We pull each other up.

We careered into the side of the tank and I was bigger than I thought and I lost hold of your hand, lost my orientation. I felt my flank crash into the side of the tank with a big impact. Something rigid gave way. My uprising had created an enormous wave of mud and this lifted you and deposited you outside the tank, on the deck.

There was a pipe running through a pump outside the tank, an outlet pipe for the recovered formation fluid. I must have broken a seal or hit a release valve because crude oil surged out of a pipe. Gushed into the tank, into my mouth.

I drank it.

I took it up my snatch. Into my ears. My follicles.

And my body was filling with compressed waveforms. They were racing out of the oil and into the furze under these huge, strange wings that were newly mine. They came to me like baby turtles to the sea. Stars to sunset. Inevitable.

Goldrush of Immanence waveforms all up inside my deepest parts.

I lifted out of the tank and dropped on the deck. I was much, much bigger than ever before. I no longer had feathers. Or a human voice.

And then you were there. Everyone else was running away from the sight of me, but you. You were splashing across the flooded deck, and all I could see at first were the whites of your eyes and the flash of your teeth. Then the pale of your palms as you reached out and seized the edge of my wing. You were a cutout in darkness as you held the rail with one hand and tugged at me with the other.

'Don't go,' you said. How beautiful your voice is. You said, 'Don't give up.'

And I could hear your ragged breathing and I could feel the blood vessels moving under the skin of your scalp as you strained. You never did work out as much as you should, Dr Sorle.

'I can't pull you,' you gasped. 'You're too big. Come on. You have to do this.'

You meant I had to get out of the oil. You were worried about the men with rifles, the klaxons sounding, everybody running around. You didn't know what was happening to me. That's the thing about you, Doctor. You've never really known what was going on but it hasn't stopped you, not ever.

The drag on my wings was unspeakable. It came from other places, other times. Tearing me apart.

You couldn't see this. You saw an animal gasping in an oil spill, thrashing. Panicking.

I must have seemed like a weakling. Because what was really going on was invisible.

Always is.

Someone has to pay back the debt. Just like the Resistance, I was built with stolen funds. It's all catching up to me and you and everything we represent. It's like I'm a sweater snagged on a thorn bush and the world is running away and the faster it goes the faster I unravel. There are holes in me. I'm leaking. I can't stay.

You looked me in the eye. Only one eye, remember? One laser eye, no depth perception required, no cosmological constant neither. Just the straight shit. Me pterosaur, you boy.

You backed away slowly.

Something was stuck in my throat. Something was moving. It wasn't a furball.

I heaved.

# Not my bad

The pterosaur drags itself out of the deck steel choking and retching. Its wings rise up, it gives a great nasty belch, and something comes out of its throat.

There on the deck, covered in oil like birth blood, is the limp body of Austen Stevens. The IV marks in his arms can still be seen. He has lost his slippers.

He is dead.

The quetzlcoatlus presses down with its powerful hind-quarters, wings spreading. On the fold points of its wings it has a set of claws like hands, which it extends in front of itself like a pair of crutches. As it levers forward on the claws its hind legs push off and it projects itself up with a great *whoosh* of air. In two strokes it is clear of the deck and rising toward the derrick, its shadow darkening the moon pool.

Powerful lights are flashing across the many levels of the platform as everyone here takes action. Carl Anderson and his people are trying to herd everyone towards the helipad. 'This is an evacuation,' he says, flashing his bright blue eyes like badges. 'You must come with me.'

The sounds of drilling and machinery have stopped, but there are loudspeaker announcements and the sound of the helicopter lifting off. People are coming out of the offices and on to the gangways in orderly rows. The atmosphere has gone from friendly and workmanlike to mortally serious. When the pterosaur passes over, there are screams.

Alison has checked the old man's body carefully to be sure he is dead, and for signs of injury. The man is newly dead. He's a little scraped and he's covered in dark fluid, but there are no wounds on him and there's no oil in his mouth. He didn't drown.

Kang joins her. He confirms that it is Austen Stevens.

'Very nice,' Alison says. 'And here you've accused the doctor of killing him when he was here all this time.'

'Whoa,' Kang says. 'Not my bad. This wasn't us.'

'It wasn't Dr Sorle, either,' Alison points out. 'Doctor, you'll be coming back to the mainland with me. No one has any right to hold you here. Right, where do we evacuate?'

# Meet me halfway

The platform has an arm that extends out high over the sea at a 60 degree angle, and at the end of that arm the natural gas filtered off from the formation fluid met the atmosphere and was set alight. It guttered sideways into the sky under a steady south-west wind.

Evacuation procedures were under way. The first helicopter had taken off. The second was preparing to land. Suited managers stood in the plate-glass windows overlooking the deck like NASA scientists in the ops room. Men and women in hardhats and boiler suits moved up and down flights of stairs, across walkways. Their torches criss-crossed like tiny bat signals as they executed well-rehearsed safety procedures; the knowledge contained in those operations manuals was already in the depths of my nail beds. If I took away the sensory overlay I could directly know the patterns of so many concepts coming to fruition out here on the North Sea: the physics behind pressure gauges and safety seals, the signal processing in the robotic arms, the quantum processes in giant screen monitors with thermal imaging of the ocean floor, the statistical mechanics and psychological theories of bonding and interaction in the design of the recreation rooms. This place is a microcosm of humanity's machine.

Down in the moon pool the water was almost still. Drilling had stopped. Workers closed off the deck containing the Cretaceous creatures that emerged from the oil. When the mud stopped flowing there may have been a kick from the well, but there would be no blowout because the industry had learned lessons from past mistakes. Nearly two hundred intensely focused people were locking this thing down.

But I'm still here and I'm a hole in the world. I'm quetzlcoatlus. My wings are so heavy. Seawater, synthetic mud, crude oil.

There are new bullet holes in me and they are leaking allusions to the tracery of the Immanence so pristine in my Cretaceous flesh. I embody it.

The pterosaur could have gobbled me up when we fell out of the sky together, but it didn't. Because it knew it was meeting itself – me – coming.

There was oil in my wings back then. What oil was it?

I think we all know.

It was the same oil that built my body, so very very long ago. And the oil was on fire.

The oil was on fire because I am going to light myself on fire right now.

I'm going to light myself on fire because my body is full of bullets and I am leaking the Immanence all over this state-of-the-art Pace Industries oil platform and I have to cauterise the wounds.

And because plasma is my favourite thing. Intergalactic plasma my favourite and my best.

And because it's time for all of us unwanted to go.

How can we do this? We can do it because we are trash.

Trash can.

Where can is a verb. You betcha.

I'm full of oil now. You sneaky hydrocarbons with your HD gates, you. I feel you. I'm full of eggs from the land of the lost. You dead? Extinct? Abandoned? I'm your lifeboat, I'm the mother of second chances. I'm bringing you with me because you're the rack and pinion steering of the future.

Fuck that short-haul spaceflight. I want your extragalactic plasma and I want it now. Come on, fire, be my gate to the big places. Take me.

No passengers. No prisoners. No end in sight.

I press down hard on the deck and lift off with my gravid body, rise up in spirals around the derrick. I grab on to it with my claws and hang there, looking out over Earth for the last time.

I can see you on the deck below, my friend. I knew you would reach for me, too late. You would call to me, your voice ragged. Then the alarms would break through your consciousness and you would have no choice. The veterinarian shouting at the gunmen to calm the fuck down. Evacuation underway.

I push off the frame of the derrick and glide out towards the arm that sports its gas fire. For someone as big as I am it's a tiny fire, easily avoided in flight. I don't want to avoid it.

I breathe the last cold sweat of night on the North Sea. After I'm gone the stars will come out. Over Norway there will be curtains of magnetic fire.

I'm going home.

# The Six Billion Dollar Man

Alison has insisted that you visit her next time you are in London for a conference. Her flat above the veterinary practice is full of yellow light and cat fur and unwashed mugs. You sit on her aged sofa and she asks about your family. When you ask about hers, she shows you the cross-stitch pterosaur she is working on.

'There's a real dearth of patterns,' she gripes as she pours you whisky against your will. 'If you want a T-Rex it's easy, but I had to search to find a nice pterosaur. It's not quite anatomically accurate, but I suppose it's the thought that counts.'

You weren't planning to drink, but something about these words makes you bring the glass to your lips. You hope she hasn't gone soft in the head in the three months since the incident on the platform.

'Gunther's having quite an interesting experience in our barn,' she confides. 'He's got a full house with three zoologists, a palaeontologist and a big-game expert advising him. And two carpenters.'

'Carpenters?'

'For the habitats. A lot of fencing, apparently. I keep getting phone calls from Pace Industries demanding access to the specimens, but they can't legally prove a connection between those animals and the oil, and as you know with most things possession is nine tenths of the law.'

'So ... You're keeping them?'

'Not me, no. Gunther will look after them, and beyond that we'll see. It's not the kind of thing we want plastered all over the internet. Gunther's place is only thirty miles from Loch Ness. It wouldn't do. Which brings me to the reason I asked you to drop by.'

You detect nervous anticipation, a little flustering that should not really be there between the two of you after everything you've been through together.

'Oh? What's the reason?' You keep your voice light but you are on your guard.

'Come with me, Dr Sorle.'

Alison leads you downstairs to the back of the practice. There is a utility room containing a teetering old fridge, a washing machine and a deep freeze.

'You're going to like this,' she says.

'Please. No more single malts.'

She puts on gloves and opens the freezer. There's something about her manner that makes you nervous. She's eager, excited. You're half-afraid it's going to be something kinky; you never know with these older women. They have wild imaginations.

She reaches down into the blast of cold and pulls out a lumpen object encased in several layers of plastic sacking. It's a fair size. Maybe a dead beagle?

When Alison sees your face she bursts out laughing.

'It's not a triceratops liver or anything,' she tells you. 'I don't want to unwrap it, but just come and hold it for yourself so you see it's real.'

You hold out your hands and take it. The thing is bright blue under the plastic. You glimpse what looks like a webbed foot about the size of a toddler's hand.

'It's the frog, Kisi,' she says. 'From the briefcase. I saved it. Let's put it back. I can see you have no idea what this means.'

'You're not planning to sell it to the tabloids, are you?'

She shuts the lid, shucks off her gloves, leads you back into the kitchen. Tops up the Talisker.

'I'm talking to some nanotech guys from the University. They found traces of a highly unusual carbon structure in the oil in Pearl's wings. I gave them a small sample of bone from this specimen and they came back with this.'

She shows him the images.

'You see that? That's a fragment of the structure from the

oil. You can see the filaments and the broken lattice. At least, it seems broken. But when you look at the froggie sample...'

You squint, leaning in.

'I don't understand. What do you see that I don't see? It just looks like a thread to me.'

'Pearl talked to me a little about higher dimensional structures. She said that her own body contained higher-dimensional gates, which of course are invisible in three dimensions. But you can see where the lattice is broken, this is a periodic structure that replicates sideways, if you will. I suspect it repeats, but up a dimension or more. You're looking at the edges where it's been torn. So the thing has deteriorated over time. But the material in the frog is pristine.'

'How does this help us in any way?'

'We've been given a piece of super-advanced technology. No one else knows about it. We can start our own lab. There are people at the university interested.'

It takes you a moment to catch on to what she is saying. A lab? Nanotech? You?

'I don't know... starting over at this stage...'

'Look. The oil money is gone. It was all ill-gotten gains for everyone concerned anyway. You can't undo the damage that was done, as hard as you tried. It didn't work. But this... this... this frog, it came to you.'

'And to you also.'

She makes a face. 'I had nothing to do with it. But if you want my advice, you'll use it. Forget the six billion dollar man. Go to Kuè and create your own legacy. I'll help you. I'm not exactly fulfilled sticking thermometers up dogs' backsides, you know.'

You swallow your horrible drink.

'I'll think about it,' you say. Then you go back to the utility room, look down at the closed freezer. There is a door out into the back yard, just a bit of concrete between high walls. Alison has recycling bins out here; a pile of empty dog food boxes melts slowly in the rain. Rubbish. Entropy.

But there is life in you yet. You can see the heat of your breath in the wet air. Escaping.

You find you don't need to think for long. You look up at the open night, even its clouds blotted by ground light, and you phone home.

Of course your wife was asleep after the night shift. She's blurry, annoyed.

'Ayeisha,' you say. 'I have an idea I want to talk to you about.'

# All flowers in time

I don't even know what is happening to me anymore. In my heart is some perfect harmony, some sweetness where every interaction flows against the gradient, conning death, laughing at entropy, tricking decay out of its wages. It isn't an image, it's a feeling, a configuration of moments and so-called weak interactions, a fullness. Something wants to burst out of the ruination. Out of futility, out of crushed hope, out of that broken place where nothing can ever help. No superglue to repair this tear in the universe. Loss is just the way it is.

Except that I am here flying through the gas fire that is the plasma field that is the end of the birdmasters' world that is the beginning of our adventures, I am the definition of change and I'm made back-to-front and inside-out. You stolen waveforms like stolen time, you abide deep in the engines that the bird mothers built into my tissues, where you and I will alter each other forever. I will love you always – and when the moment is right, when the stars align? Well, one by one, I will kick you the hell out of my body and back into the world.

Get ready to relaunch on my count. You can't stay with me. I am burning alive.

From so far as this I can see Akele. It's winter. He sleeps in a sleeping bag under two heavy quilts and his breath stands up when he stands, still wearing his boots. He removes them so he can wash and pray, hissing at the zing of the cold water on his feet. After his prayers he makes coffee. He turns on the radio to 1010 WINS New York – you give us twenty-two minutes we'll give you the world – wiping condensation off the window as he peers out into darkness yellowed by lamplight.

Helicopters judder overhead. He is putting Splenda in his coffee when there's a noise from the corner.

There it is, the giant double fridge that he has never plugged in. It lies on its side and doubles as a work bench. He has thrown a furniture-mover's brown quilt over it so that the tiny screws and pieces of hard solder won't roll right off. There's a scarred old wooden vice grip and a signal testing kit and a couple of disembowelled phones and a waffle iron, all works in progress. There's a plastic chess set paused in mid-game. Akele plays himself.

The fridge has been singing softly to him for two days. Just like it did before it disgorged the angel. It gives off a faint mist of sound though it's not plugged in. He sips his coffee, waiting for the sound to die away so he can forget he heard it. The coffee hasn't hit his system yet but there are fluttering movements in his abdomen because his body knows more than he does. He picks up one of the phone cases and puts it back down again. The sound isn't coming from anything on the workspace. It must be coming from somewhere beneath.

He bends over the back of the fridge but the sound is softer here. Now there is a tapping coming from inside. As if a rapping. Now, a knocking.

Too late to run away, to feign ignorance. Not that Akele would.

He puts the coffee cup down. Then he flips up the edge of the quilt covering the fridge doors and tugs one of them open.

All flowers in time bend towards the sun.

The boy is curled, elbows over forehead, toes flexed, clad in yesterday's best donations to the household recycling centre next door (originally from Kaufman's and Gap) plus a straw hat of dubious provenance. After he topples out of the open door, landing on hands and knees on the frigid carpet of the trailer, the hat falls off. His black hair comes down in a sheet to cover his shining eyes and he makes to hold himself tight, shivering.

'You got a extra coat, man?' the boy says. He was scanned

in 1476 in the place that is now Bangladesh but already he has a Long Island accent, because preloads. 'It was warmer inside the fridge.'

Akele puts his fingers to his lips. He is remembering me the way you remember a tune you learnt as a child. Of course I am no more, not as I was. I am changing. I will become the future history I hold in my body. Like dewdrops can turn to clouds can turn to thunder that shakes your bones, what's in my archives can change the scheme of things. I will unravel like skywriting on the blue face of the world. Medicine will be delivered. Promises will be kept.

Akele takes the boy's hand and pulls him to his feet.

'We gonna get you a coat,' he says.

# Acknowledgements

Thank you to everyone who helped me between 2011 and 2014 while I was writing this. In particular I'm grateful to:

Stephanie Burgis.

Pat Cadigan, Rochita Loenen-Ruiz, Kate Elliott, Aliette de Bodard, Johan Anglemark.

Nina Allan.

Michael Fauconnier-Bank on international banking. Steve Morris on isometrics.

Dr. Clarissa Pinkola Estés.

Kelley Eskridge of Sterling Literary, for her deeply insightful editing of the first draft.

My agent Alex Adsett.

Simon Spanton and the entire team at Gollancz.

Finally, I need to thank Karen Mahoney, who gave me Pearl's name and who told me in no uncertain terms to write this story. Thank you, Kaz.